A GOOD MOURNING

BRIAN DeLANEY

A Good Mourning

ISBNs:
979-8-9852578-0-9 (print)
979-8-9852578-1-6 (eBook)

DEDICATION

I dedicate this book to my dear wife, Cynthia. Without her support, encouragement, belief and love, there wouldn't be one. Thank you for giving me the gift of time so I could write. I loved you yesterday, I love you today and I'll love you forever.

CHAPTER

- 1 -

"**I** want an Irish Funeral," stated Winnie Ahearne, a comment to her grandson into the cooling air as if a thought not meant to escape her lips snuck its way out. The last of the early evening sunlight shimmered through the maple tree on the driveway side of the house, illuminating her face and making her look younger than her seventy-seven years.

"You're not sick, are you?" asked Axel. "Is there something you're keeping from me?"

"Oh heavens," she snapped at him before softening her tone. "I don't mean now. I mean when the time comes. We're all going to die someday. I want to be prepared."

"Thank God," he responded. The relief escaped him like the last bit of air from a balloon before it fell to earth. "Don't scare me like that!"

Ignoring his request, she continued. "Lots of whiskey and stories told. I want laughter, not tears. You'll do this for me, won't you, Axel? God knows, your brother wouldn't know the difference between good Irish whiskey and Kentucky bourbon. 'Cept he'd drink 'em both."

Winnie looked down at her feet and asked, "Have you spoken to Leif lately?"

"Not in a while. You?"

"He hasn't called or written. Heck, I haven't even gotten so much as a text. The last time we spoke, he asked me for money." Winnie looked up. "I told him not until he paid you back."

"I bet that didn't go over well."

She shook her head. "There's a fine line between helping and enabling. I'd rather pour gasoline on my foot and set it afire before I enable him again." The old woman paused, and the two sat in silence in the cool evening air before she added, "I do miss him. You know, the way you were as kids. I don't understand how two boys growing under the same roof can be so different." The silence returned briefly until Winnie sat up straight and looked at Axel. Her head cocked to the side with one eye closed, one eye gazing at him. It reminded him of Popeye the sailor.

"Well, fool me once, shame on you. Fool me twice…Who are we kidding. Ya can't fool me twice. Let's get back to work."

Winnie was a planner. Years as the sole proprietor of the Falls Inn restaurant taught her that without a plan, chaos ensued. She planned her funeral like it was a grocery store shopping list.

"Winnie, you may be up there in age, but you're not gone yet. Let's not talk about death, OK?" her grandson pleaded.

"Look here, you wake up every day until one day you don't. Before it happens, I plan on having the last word." She raised a hand to silence any objections. "And reserve the right to have my say while I'm still able."

Axel did not argue the last point. His grandmother brandished her gift of gab like a badge of honor. Living under her roof had its advantages, relishing her stories and gobbling them up like a child with a handful of candy. Today was different. He had noticed the serious tone in her voice when she made him promise to come home straight away from work. *Pleaded* with him.

But he had not followed her wishes, keeping his weekly appointment to visit the residents at the local assisted living facility. If she would have told him they would be planning her funeral, he might have stayed longer or come up with another excuse to get out for the evening.

"I've lived in this house here in Benton Falls my entire life, and I plan to spend my final day here." She waved a tiny thumb behind her shoulder. Like a drill sergeant, she barked, "Put the coffin in the parlor by the bay window. Leave the curtains open. It'll give that nosy neighbor of mine a fit, having to see me one last time."

The corners of Axel's mouth rose. Even a serious discussion with Winnie had its comical moments.

"Now," she offered, "Let's have us a taste of good whiskey as we finish the plan, shall we?"

"Do you think it's a good idea? In your fragile condition?"

"Pshaw," she exclaimed. "Son, I'm old and thirsty. I don't think a touch of the Irish will kill me any quicker. Although some days it'd be a blessing." She rubbed the knuckles on her left hand with her right thumb as if kneading bread, her arthritis making its presence known.

Axel shook his head as he went into the kitchen. He opened the cupboard where she kept a bottle of whiskey. When the boys were young, she referred to the liquor as "her medicine." He chuckled at the recollection as he walked through the house.

"Did you find it?" Winnie called from the porch.

"Here we are," he responded as he placed the bottle and two small glasses onto the wicker table in between their chairs.

Axel poured two fingers into each glass before she rasped, "Three fingers for me. Don't be stingy to a thirsty old woman." He winced at the 'old' part but did as instructed, then handed her the glass before lifting his own. "To a life well lived," he toasted.

"And a death worthy of Irish Kings," she responded before taking a sip. "Ah, that's the remedy," she said with relish. Axel loved her spirit and courage, guaranteed to be on display right to the end. In silence, he asked God for a long and worthwhile life as she'd had. *Without the arthritis, if you please.*

"What are you working on now?" asked Winnie, smacking her lips.

"Your funeral plans, I thought."

She dropped her head and looked at him over the rims of her glasses.

"Oh, you mean work. You know, accounting stuff like bankruptcies, balancing books, debits and credits. Nothing exciting. Thank God tax season is over," he explained.

"But you're very good at it." Winnie said, the pride in her voice apparent.

Axel worked for an accounting firm and was *exceptionally good* with numbers. They were clean, crisp, and infinite. And although some tried to make them disappear or turn a blind eye, one thing was clear. Numbers never lied.

Winnie wiggled in her rocker as the cool evening air surrounded them. Axel noticed a tinge of auburn by her right ear, recalling the red hair of her youth, now all but covered over by the snowy white of her old age. He hated to see her ageing before his eyes. She was always on the go, working at the restaurant she once owned, raising the two boys. Tending her garden, visiting the sick and infirm and even traveling. Like the battery sponsoring rabbit, she would not stop. But with age came slowing down, and pain. A lesser man would have questioned his faith in God at this injustice, but Axel's was unshakable.

He broke the silence. "Would you like to go inside and watch TV?"

"No, but I'm not going dancing either. Quit stalling. We have a job to finish."

They discussed her funeral as if planning a wedding. Each detail dictated by her and written in a notebook by him. "Cullen's Funeral Parlor is the place. Patrick's family has been burying Ahearne relatives since I can remember. And Father Groghan to officiate the service. Can you make sure…" She stopped to take another sip before continuing, "Make sure you tip the altar boys."

Axel smiled at this. She was always putting the needs of others first. Selfless to a fault. "I will," he said as he cupped her hand in his, careful of her arthritis. "I promise."

"You're a good boy." She paused before changing the subject as if the next thought had just occurred to her, "Are you aware of why they call it a parlor?"

"No, I never thought about it."

"In the olden days, before funeral parlors, folks used to have wakes in their homes. Prop the casket in the front room or parlor and let the visitin' commence. Then, people needed another room in the house to gather without being reminded of their dead relatives. And that's why we have what they call… the living room."

Axel laughed, giving her a wary eye. "Are you making this up?"

"Would I lie to you? A weakened old lady planning her own funeral? Shame on you."

"It wouldn't be the first time. You've told me plenty of tall tales."

"And all of them true. Well, most of them. I don't want to go to my maker with a white lie on my lips." She looked away before adding, "Soon this old bird will no longer be a burden."

He was about to protest but thought better of it. Instead, he let her continue.

"One good thing will come of it. When my time comes, it'll be grand to hug my boy again." For a moment, the gleam of youth came back, all her pain forgotten. "He was a wonderful son and I miss him every day."

Winnie had taken over the parenting duties after a hit-and-run auto accident claimed Axel's parents. The other driver was never found. She insisted on the boys calling her "Winnie."

"None of that Grandma crap out of your mouths," she'd scold.

"And my mother?" he asked. Winnie was not as keen on her as she was on his father.

"She was something else. A blonde Scandinavian beauty with a powerful spirit. Too strong, if you ask me. To saddle you and your brother with Norse first names to go along with a fine Irish last name was such a shame."

Axel was very aware of this sore spot. "But they loved each other, right?" he prodded. "And us as well?"

"They did, lad," she answered. "With all their hearts. I would have rather he'd married one of his own, but I can't begrudge a woman for knowing her own mind." Winnie paused, looking towards the street. Axel set his gaze towards the oak tree to the right of the house, its large branch hung across the front lawn like an outstretched arm. She sipped her whiskey to clear her throat before continuing. "Let's not talk any further about the past. It's your future we need to discuss. I've got a job of my own to finish."

Axel scrunched his nose, forcing the top of his glasses to rise above his eyebrows. He was not in the mood for what came next, but it did not stop her from asking.

"When are you going to find a good woman?" She said, wagging a bony finger. "I'll never see a great grandchild from the lot of you, will I? Your brother is gallivanting all over God's green earth, so it's up to you to keep the Ahearne name alive. Isn't there anyone special?"

"Not at the moment. I'm busy with work and the church—"

She cut him off with a wave of a hand, "You should never be too busy to raise a family. Before I'm gone, go out and find a nice Irish lass and fill your home with love and babies. What is the saying? Blessed are the fruitful, go forth and multiply?"

"You're making things up again. Not the best idea for a woman on her way to talk to God. Besides, if I had lots of babies, the correct phrase would be 'Blessed are the poor.'"

Winnie shifted her frame in the chair and again the wince of pain did not escape the notice of her grandson. "Stop wasting time with this old lady. Go out and live your best life, my boy."

"I thought I was," he said, a hint of disappointment transparent in his tone.

"Son," she said, leaning in towards her grandson, "Life is to be lived, not hoarded like a squirrel collecting nuts. Enjoy it while you're able. I don't mean to go all helter-skelter like Leif.

Outside of the church, you have no friends. And no girlfriend. It's like you're invisible. And you'll not find the right match there with all those old people."

"I can't argue with you," he said. He loved spending time in church. The only place he felt comfortable. At peace. "We've been attending St. Simons since I can remember," he began. "I enjoy taking part in my church community. It's where I belong." As an afterthought he added, "I still haven't forgiven you for making us quit our altar boy duties."

Winnie fidgeted in her chair, discomfort crossing her face. "As I told you then, you outgrew the role."

"Leif was pleased," countered Axel. "I wish I could have served another year or two."

"Nonsense, you were both taller than the priest. It looked awkward. I stand by my decision," she snapped. Winnie turned away from Axel as if scanning for what birds were invading her lawn. Axel took this as a sign the topic was closed.

"So, this job you need to finish is about finding me a girlfriend?"

"All I'm trying to say is you need to get married and have children. A purpose. I've protected you my entire life and as of late, you've cared for me. Find a nice girl to take care of you once I go. Spend the savings you've got stashed away on her."

Axel frowned. "You always told me to save my money for a rainy day. Now you want me to squander it?"

"Rainy day saving is a good principle in theory. But let me ask you this? What if the rain never comes?"

Silence enveloped them like the darkness creeping onto the porch. Axel got up and flicked on the switch, illuminating the shadows as they danced across the front yard.

"There, that's better. Let's talk more about your after-party," he said, a subtle attempt to deflect from marriage, kids, and rainy days. He was twenty seven. Plenty of time for those responsibilities later.

"I want you to tell delightful stories. I've begun writing a few in a notebook." She tapped the side of her head as she recalled one, "Remember the day Leif climbed the old dead tree in the back yard? As I recall, you also wanted to climb, but I talked you out of it. A good one to tell."

Axel had a different recollection. "I didn't want to climb because it was a dead tree and dangerous. I knew the difference between smart and forewarned. You know Leif's going to be mad. He's always hated that story."

With a sly grin, she said, "Tis the point." Axel softly laughed. Even while discussing the inevitability of her own death, Winnie took pleasure in finding someone to poke.

"And don't forget the punchline." She was a skilled storyteller. "A joke is merely a dreadful story without a good punchline."

How could he forget a line like that? His grandmother was not only witty, but she also had a great sense of word play and subtext. "You're smart not to climb the tree," he remembered her warning. "Do you know what happens to a Leif in a tree?" She would pause for effect before answering. "They always fall."

"I won't forget," he promised her. "But who should I tell? People at the wake?"

"No silly," she said, adjusting her glasses. "You'll do my eulogy." The foregone conclusion shocked Axel. "Winnie, No! I'll fall apart. No one wants to see a blubbering idiot on the altar?"

She wore the stern gaze of a woman who got what she wanted in this world. Despite his protests, Axel determined she would also get her way once she left it.

"You are the only one I trust. Not some priest who knows very little about me. You've done an admirable job with other eulogies, why not mine? Boy, to overcome your fears, you first have to face them."

Axel could not argue with her logic. He had delivered a few eulogies and had prepared as if giving the State of the Union address. He was happy his fellow parishioners could count on him to deliver a last word for those who could no longer speak.

"If I can't have the last word in person, I'd want no one but you to deliver it for me." She gave him a wink, "And to make sure, I'll write it."

"All right, Winnie, whatever you want," he laughed, lifting his hands in surrender. "But if I turn into a mass of quivering jelly, don't say I didn't warn you."

"Blessed are the speakers of truth," she said. "You'll do fine."

"Is there anything else on the agenda, your highness?"

"As a matter of fact," she said, a twinkle in those hazel eyes spelling mischief. "There are three items."

"Do tell," he said.

"Number one, it's time for me to say goodbye to this old house. Been good to my younger self, but not this old lady."

"Wait, you can't sell. This is our home!"

"Relax, I'm not going to sell. I'm giving the house to you."

Axel was speechless.

"But I am moving. I've already applied to live at the Benton Falls Assisted Living and Memory Care Center."

The FALM, as it was known, was nice enough. Axel visited enough residents there to decide its value, but Winnie loved this old house. She had lived here her entire life and now she was leaving? Axel may have been quick to discover numbers never changed, but slow to realize the only constant in life *was* change.

"What? When did this happen?" he said, the shock causing his voice to rise an octave.

"I've been talking to that sweet Julia, over there. If I'm going to move, I might as well go to a place where I have friends. No stairs, no cooking, and most of all, surrounded by people my age, so you can get on with your life. I raised you boys here. It's your turn to fill this house with laughter and love. End of story. But promise me..." Winnie took another sip of whiskey before continuing. "If I am incapacitated for any reason, unconscious with no chance of returning, pull the damn plug."

"What? C'mon, stop joking." Her penchant for gallows humor might have been her way of putting him at ease, but Axel was not in a joking mood once it came to her death. "No one is putting anyone out of their misery. You need to keep this in God's hands."

"God does not want his children to suffer," she whispered, leaning in conspiratorially. "But if you change your mind, go right over to St. Paul's parish, where you'll confess your sins and get absolution from Father Champlin. Then all will be well."

St Paul's was the Catholic Church in the next town, overseen by a priest where anyone's secrets would be safe. The priest, it so happened, was deaf.

"And remember, blessed are the merciful, for they shall be shown mercy."

"Now you get it right?" Axel said, shaking his head.

Guilt was a terrible weapon, and Winnie brandished it like the sword of a warrior.

"Buck up. I've got a long standing dinner date with your grandad and father. You know how I hate to be late."

Axel laughed at his grandmothers' joke. "OK, what is the last thing you wanted?" he asked, changing the morbid subject.

Winnie drained her glass, looking at the bottom, mulling over her next words.

"See what I've done here? I tell you good news, then bad news, to set you up for what I really want."

"You led with moving out and then a request for me to kill you, and this is what you call setting me up?" Axel said, his head shaking in bewilderment.

Winnie leaned in again, the wagging finger for added emphasis, "Even though you're the younger, you need to watch out for your brother. He's in for a fall. You know the scripture, be the keeper of your brother."

Axel was going to respond but decided it pointlessness.

"When Leif falls?" she asked. "Because he will. And when he does, you must catch him."

"Winnie, he won't fall- "

"Shush." She cut him off with a wave of her glass, signifying a refill. "He *will* fall. And you *must* catch him," she repeated.

But in the end, he would not.

Hours after Winnie announced her plans to move into the FALM, a hooded figure entered the building, tiptoeing along the corridor where the residents were too infirm or disease riddled to care for themselves. The employees nicknamed the wing 'The Passing Lane,' where management placed people to die away from the healthy population.

Squeezing past the heavy door and into the room of Mr. Joseph Franz, the intruder went to the bedside where the resident lay motionless. In a low sing song manner, as if soothing a child to sleep, whispered, "It's time."

The patient had been battling a nasty case of lung cancer for some time now. Hope for recovery was the only thing left for his family and that in short supply. Talk about bad luck, Franz wasn't even a smoker. Nothing remained but the pain and his shriveled husk.

Funny thing about those quartered in an assisted living facility. Most pushed thoughts of their death away, believing they had more time than they did. The things we tell ourselves, the visitor thought before shaking it away. Time to focus on the task at this late hour.

Mr. Franz was losing the battle and with it came the loss of his voice, so why let the man linger? He stared up at his visitor with a sereneness reserved for the calmest of souls. The visitor interpreted the calmness not as resignation, but of acceptance. It said, "I promise I won't struggle."

Finding a pillow in the closet, the softness comfortable in warm hands, the visitor stood bedside once again. *Why let him linger, indeed.* As the pillow hung above the old man's closed eyes, the intruder prayed to make sure God knew Franz was coming. "O Lord, welcome Joseph to everlasting life in your presence. Go with God. Amen." The rationalization that the short prayer coupled with the sign of the cross against his forehead should be enough for the repose of his soul. "Blessed are the merciful, for they shall be shown mercy." These were the last earthly words Joseph Franz would hear as the merciful visitor placed the pillow over the old man's face.

True to his word, Mr. Franz kept his promise. There was no struggle.

CHAPTER

- 2 -

Benton Falls, like the train engine in the children's story, was a little town that could. It began with a mill built by Thomas J. Benton in the early 1800s, situated near the water falls north of the town. A strong river current provided power to run the mill and a mode of transportation to send goods to downstream markets. The Falls became a source of recreation for bathers, fishermen and kayakers.

In the early years, the small town grew on the backs of manufacturing and Benton University employment. Growth in the last few decades was spurred by healthcare, tourism, and a small influx of entrepreneur startups.

The present patriarch of the town was the last in the line of Benton's. Under Harley Benton's leadership, the town prospered. As did Harley. His many ventures created jobs for the town's residents while driving the stream of profits flowing into his own coffers. What would not flow past Harley's death was the bloodline from ancestor Thomas, which if alive, would no doubt be troubled. Harley, a bachelor who shunned the idea of taking a wife, was content to live the way he chose without oversight. To Harley, a wife would have been tantamount to an anchor, weighing him down. And then there would have been the added expense with which to contend.

There were plenty of women in the last Benton's life, all hoping to become the First Lady of Benton Manor and collecting the perks of the title. He wined and dined each, allowing them to think they were next in line to be the one. He took them on trips, bought them trinkets, romanced, then bedded them. Once bored, he unceremoniously dumped them. No, one woman would not do to satisfy his lustful cravings. Money could not buy happiness, but it would make it easier for him to get what he desired from those wearing rose-colored glasses.

Harley relished the role of the playboy. Imagining himself as the equivalent of Bruce Wayne without the hassle of having to save everyone from their fears or worse, themselves. He had neither the time nor the inclination to do either. He lived in the old Benton Manor house, away from the prying eyes of the town. The Manor, a place where they would look up with longing, as he looked down in contempt. This advantage gave him the ability they would never have. To view everything.

The rich man had a plan, and for years it worked to perfection. But there were two hitches of which Harley Benton did not count. The first was a special woman who told him *no*. It was the one time he had ever considered marriage. The second was age and its ravages to his body. In the beginning stages of decay, there was always money to throw around to eager young women. But then his health took a turn for the worse. Now, at age eighty, the only people to care for him were a butler, the cook, and a stodgy old nurse who came to the mansion yet took none of his abuse. She had an iron will and used it extensively on the man who always made the rules. He fired her to make himself feel better, regaining control of the reins once more.

In his eighties and wheelchair bound, immobility imprisoned him in his own castle. This did not please the former man about town. He once had vigor and received everything his heart desired. Almost everything. But age had ruined Harley's plan.

"Age is the damned destroyer of dreams," he said as he sat out on the balcony listening to the noon church bells ringing in town. "And there's nothing I can do about it." A hacking cough wracked the old man. When the fit was over, he spat a huge wad of phlegm and watched as it dribbled leisurely from the rail onto the drive below.

Two things drove a man like Harley Benton. Getting what he wanted and power. He had successfully wielded the second, still did. Power was a drug to the old man, and his addiction never let up controlling the many aspects in town like a puppeteer. But a specific want from his past went unacquired, gnawing at him like an unreachable itch. Had ever since the first *no*. But now he saw an opening. A way to silence the gnawing.

Harley Benton gazed out over the town, *his town*, whose people he lorded over and began plotting an alternative plan. One even age could not touch.

The door flew open and everyone in the bar turned their heads as Leif Ahearne made a grand entrance. "Now the party can start!" he yelled, walking through the crowd, shaking hands with people he was familiar with, introducing himself to those he was not.

"Brother!" he shouted as he approached the bar and gave Axel a big bear hug. "It's about time we got you out into the real world!" And to the bartender, "Scotch neat. No, make it a double." Axel noticed the subtle eye shift towards himself, telling the bartender to put the drink on his tab. Classic Leif.

Unamused, Axel spoke through teeth clenched in anger. "Why are you late? I've got things to do."

Leif gave him the most charming smile. "Sorry, had a last minute meeting with my editor. A few issues needed attention." Axel regarded his brother's answer with suspicion, quite aware of those issues. He smelled one on his breath. It would not surprise him if the issue of gambling were involved as well.

The two men were total opposites. Axel proved to be pious, law-abiding, thrifty, and cautious. Leif, an avowed atheist, had no respect for authority and was reckless to a fault. He had travelled extensively and paid his way by bar tending or doing odd jobs, took no responsibility for his actions, never apologized, and always seemed broke. For Leif, one could afford to be carefree as long as others paid the tab. Axel heard his brother's voice in his head, spouting his selfish catchphrase, *We're all going to die, but not me and not today.*

"Well, I'm here now," Leif said, before leaning in to whisper, "My book is getting published, I'm getting a fat advance and I get paid travelling to promote it. Ain't life grand!"

Leif had written a self-help book entitled, *Climb Your Own Tree- Finding Your Role in Life.* Axel found it incredulous his lost brother wrote a book on finding oneself. It baffled him people would buy, let alone read it. In Leif's defense, his publisher assured him it would sell a lot of copies. Some things made no sense. Like the rift in their relationship. Axel wasn't sure when it happened, perhaps before Axel turned ten? It was as if a light switch had been flipped. Instead of the happy and adventurous brother he'd known, Leif had grown sullen and withdrawn. He became overly bossy of Axel who came to resent Leif's heavy handed ways. Resentment turned into frustration as Axel saw his brother change for the worse.

Leif scratched his chin and bowed his head sheepishly at his brother. "Uh, and I may need a little bridge loan until I get my advance. Help me out?"

"We'll discuss it later," Axel said, the bitterness in his voice surprising him. As the more Christian of the two brothers, he should know better. The guilt made him soften his tone. "We need to talk about Winnie."

"Why, what's wrong with the old bird now?" His tone had a ring of exasperation, as if he were speaking of an ex-wife and not the woman who raised him.

"She's moving into the FALM. Says she wants to spend the rest of her days playing cards and sharing gossip."

Leif's expression changed in seconds from exasperation to keen interest. "What'll you think she'll get for the house, huh? Gotta be worth a couple hundred grand at least."

Axel bristled at the question. His brother not only felt entitled to an inheritance, but by the look in his eyes had already spent it.

"Hate to break it to you, but she's not selling."

"Renting then? Smart. It's paid for and the housing market should increase with time. As long as she gets tenants who won't trash the place."

Axel sighed. He knew this was the troublesome part. "No. She's not renting it. She's gifting it to me. Wants me to get married and fill it with kids."

Leif's face scrunched in as the realization of lost revenue sunk in. "What the hell? How do you get the house? I lived there, too. I'm blood!" Axel noticed his brother's face redden with anger. Not a good sign. "What did you do to con her?" Leif spat, the volume rising with each syllable. "What did you do to turn her against me?" His finger pointing close to Axel's nose.

Calmly, Axel took his own index finger and pressed it against Leif's digit until it was at least six inches away. "I did nothing of the kind," he said. "She planned this all by herself. She even planned her own funeral. All I am doing is going along with her wishes." This seemed to take the wind out of his brothers' sail as dejection replaced the anger.

"Are you planning on selling?" he asked. Axel guessed his brother still sought a payday, even if it was down the road.

"No, Leif. I'm going to live there like she asked."

"How's she gonna pay for the home?" Leif was always looking for an angle to accept money, but also another to steer clear of expenses.

"Relax," Axel said in a reassuring tone. "She has money set aside. She doesn't need us to pay for her care. But if the time comes where she may need some, I'll handle it." He bit the inside of his lip before the words came out. *No one expects you to help at all.*

"Phew. What a relief." Leif picked up his scotch and downed the double with one gulp, rattling it on the bar for another. There was an uncomfortable pause before he turned the conversation away from lost inheritance and possible expenses.

"Hey, you know what?" Leif asked with a wink. "I've out-lived Bruce Lee."

Axel put a hand against his forehead. "You've got to be kidding me! You're still playing that stupid game?" Since childhood, Leif had played the game of 'Who I've outlived.' Find someone famous who had passed at his age and brag. At twelve it was the child actress from a spooky movie series. At fifteen, the girl with the diary from the Holocaust they had read about in school. Eighteen brought the young man celebrated world-wide because he spoke out before being consumed by the Aids virus. There were too many rock stars to count when he turned twenty seven. The fact he pursued this silly game at twenty-nine highlighted his ongoing immaturity.

Axel frowned, "Don't forget the singer who died from Anorexia."

"Right, thanks!" He responded; Axel's sarcasm lost on him.

Axel sucked in a deep breath and asked, "Have you gone to see Winnie yet?" then added as an afterthought, "How long are you in town?"

"One, I thought I'd surprise her. So, don't tell her we met first. Second, not sure. Once the book is ready for publication, I was thinking about putting down roots here. They want me to write a follow-up book." Leif gazed off in the distance. Axel interpreted it as calculating the advance and residuals his brother hoped would pour in to his own pocket.

Axel closed his eyes, disgusted. How did two brothers a mere two years apart turn out so differently? He sighed, deciding to turn the proverbial cheek. It would serve no purpose to lecture his older brother about rainy day funds or how to manage one's money in a roomful of drinkers looking for a freebie.

"Go visit her tomorrow," he breathed. "You can tell her all about your book."

"Yeah, sure I will," said Leif as he extended his hand, wiggling his fingers as if a child saying, 'Gimme.' "How about the loan you promised me? I'll pay you back after I get the book advance."

Axel grunted at the lies. Leif, his relationship with Winnie also strained, had no plans to visit her and had never paid him back. Ever. Axel felt the urge to yell at his insincere and disrespectful brother, but held his tongue. Recalling an old saying, *You cannot control what others do, only how you react to them.* He closed his eyes and took a deep breath. *Even if it is your slouch of a brother.*

"Well?" Leif asked, shattering Axel's thoughts into tiny fragments. He looked at Leif's outstretched hands, fingers wiggling with impatience. Axel finished his drink, then begrudgingly reached into his pocket and pulled out a wad of cash.

Winnie had taught the boys many lessons. How to be courteous. To live a charitable life. And especially how reflection was good for their souls. The best place to accomplish this? The church.

"I hate Sundays," Axel recalled Leif exclaiming one Sunday before Mass.

"Why is that youngster?" Winnie had asked. She also believed young men should form opinions early on. Then defend those opinions.

Leif hesitated before answering. "I don't want to be an altar boy anymore. Church is boring."

"Church and Sumdays are *not* boring," Axel said, mispronouncing the word.

Winnie had focused in on Axel's mistake. "Sumdays. How appropriate. You boys need to take sum of your actions and what you must do in the future to become better men. And you love being an altar boy. It's character building."

"It's still boring." Leif sulked.

"Reflection always is. But also good for your soul." Winnie gave her final word on the subject.

These days, reflection proved exceptionally good for Axel's soul. He continued to take sum of opportunities to be better, like giving eulogies or volunteering at the community food bank. Today it was joining the group known as the Visiting Angels. Driving to St. Simons, he would pick up Becky Root, Helen Bolden, and Gil Pooler before driving them all to the nursing home known not by its long sounding name, Falls Assisted Living and Memory Care, but the easier acronym, FALM.

Gil insisted he had come up with the shorter version, but the other three chided him on his boast.

"Really?" said Helen. "I remember it having that name since we were children. But maybe you came up with that before I was born?" Helen was two years older than Gil and he knew it.

Becky joked, "I bet you also came up with the acronym for Benton Falls University? Their advertising slogan is 'Go FU!'"

"Not funny," said Gil. "In fact, it's vulgar."

"Or the Benton Falls Memorial Hospital, 'F-ME!'" giggled Helen.

"Ladies! Keep it clean," Gil said, admonishing the women. "After all, we're in a church group."

Axel saw the blush on his friend's face. But even he wanted in on the teasing. "BFF." he added.

"Best Friends Forever?" asked Gil. "I'd like to think so."

"Benton Falls Florist," said Axel. "It's the only clean play on words I could think of."

Both girls cackled at Axel's attempt at clean levity.

Axel, noticing the hurt on Gil's face, tried to make amends, "C'mon buddy, we were only joking."

Helen piped in, "Yea, just a little teasing. But don't make a claim if you can't back it up."

"Cause we're vicious VAB's," said Becky, finishing Helen's statement.

Gil fell right into it. "VAB's?" he asked.

"Visiting Angel Bitches!" screamed Becky with delight.

Everyone int the car with the exception of Gil roared with laughter.

"You're all being bullies and I hate bullies," Gil said. Angry at being the butt of their jokes and at Axel for joining in, he sulked all the way to the FALM.

The Visiting Angels were formed by the resident priest, Father Tom Groghan. A team to visit former parishioners and others too infirm and no longer able to attend Mass. This was in response to the time it took from his already busy schedule of priestly duties. He solved this problem by recruiting members of the parish and giving them their wings, so to speak. "It is your duty as good Christians," he pressured. The guilt worked. The priest still visited the home and hospital himself, but now it did not consume all his time. His claim of "Many hands make light work," was true—with the Visiting Angel's hands, his workload was lighter.

Upon arrival, each parishioner would call on a resident either too infirm to leave the home or one who had not had a visitor in a while. Most of them in the Passing Lane. After a brief visit, each Angel would move to the next resident so the elderly had multiple visitors.

Axel's first visit this day was with Mrs. Hunter, who had lost her husband several years before. She was in the throes of dementia, and Axel listened patiently to the same story about him over and over again. Mrs. Hunter also repeatedly asked how Axel's grandmother was, having been friends since childhood. She also asked about Axel's wife. "They're both fine and in good health," he would respond, not wanting to repeat the facts; Winnie would soon be her neighbor and his 'wife' non-existent.

There was crotchety old Mr. Brown who complained about everyone and everything as though the only way to achieve happiness was to make sure he and everyone around him was miserable. When it was time to move on, Axel hid his relief.

Mrs. Kalling wondered where her children were—all infrequent visitors who lived out of state. Mrs. Walsh spoke of her bridge club as if she had a game later on, Axel unsure if any were still alive, let alone playing cards. The round robin proceeded until the last visit of the day.

Mr. Strong was anything but. He lay in a coma and the consensus was his time was close at hand. Axel sat in a wooden chair bedside, watching the man, unable to die or wake, his life signs not very vital. A far cry from the sturdy mechanic who owned the gas station off Main and Front Street in town. Axel recalled hearing the bell whenever Winnie's car ran over the rubber hose running from the station to the pumps, prompting Mr. Strong to stop what he was working on to pump gas for her. You did not get service like that anymore.

The one sided conversation never centered on the weather or politics. Or even the news. Axel found those topics to be mundane or too depressing. With the alert residents, Axel would let them lead the conversation. Mr. Strong could not lead, allowing Axel to do something different. Axel was compelled to make the visits worthwhile, whether or not Mr. Strong understood. He crafted stories to entertain the man. It also helped Axel practice for eulogies.

It was in the middle of the story of Sumdays, when the old man did something he had not on any previous visit.

He opened his eyes.

Surprised, Axel sat back in the chair. His next inclination was to call the nurse, but before he had the chance to stand, Mr. Strong reached over to grab his hand, squeezing it to the point of causing pain. The old man was alert and smiling. Mr. Strong mouthed the distinct, yet unmistakable words, "Thank you."

"Excuse me?" said a startled Axel, backing up and knocking over the chair.

"Axel," Mr. Strong began slowly, his voice garbled, as if he chewed gravel. "Thank you for visiting." The old man took a deep breath, which rattled in his chest. "The stories have been a godsend."

Strong tried to sit up and Axel, regaining his composure, helped him. The old man shook his head as if to remove any cobwebs caused by the months of sleep. "I heard every word. I've been aware of everything since I fell into this damn coma. Can you comprehend what it's like being trapped in your own mind? Unable to move or communicate? It was as if I was in purgatory." The old man paused and lowered his head in contemplation. When he lifted it again, Axel witnessed the pain in his eyes. "I'm glad to be out of the dark."

"Mr. Strong, "Axel stammered, still trying to comprehend the situation. "It's a miracle you came out of the coma! Can I get anything for you?"

"Yes, please." The old man waved a slender hand at Axel. "Sit and finish the story."

Axel complied, and as he finished, he noticed the old man's eyes were closed. "Mr. Strong?" he asked, fearing the man had fallen once again into a deep sleep.

Strong opened one eye and smiled. "That was a doozy. Promise you'll come back with more stories. I really enjoy them. Your Winnie is quite a character."

"She is, and I promise," said Axel. "But first, we should let someone know," he said as he pressed the nurse's call button. While waiting, Strong peppered Axel about everything he could. "What day is it?" "What's the weather like today?" Evidently no topic was mundane to a former coma patient. Axel was pleased to answer them all.

The nurse came through the door and leaned against it, dumbfounded. This morning the comatose man, with no chance at recovery, was sitting up and smiling at her.

"Nurse?" Axel said, stirring her from her surprise. "Can you call his family?"

After she left, Axel stood to leave. Before he reached the door, Mr. Strong yelled out, "Axel? Don't forget your promise."

"I won't." Axel said, nodding at the old man, and opened the door. It may not have been a holy day, but if this was not a Sumday, Axel did not know what one was.

CHAPTER
- 3 -

Harriet Spellman sat at her desk staring at her phone. She hated death days. They were a double-edged sword. On one hand, death took the breath out of the building as if getting hit in the solar plexus. The only laughter came from those two insensitive curmudgeons she labeled the "Gossip Goons." Edwin Hearst and Ralph Kaline were so callous they placed bets on the next resident to go. Men were such children. It was why she never married. She could not stand the thought of childish behavior.

The other edge came at the end of the day when the residents returned to their normal activities and the exit pushed into the past like an uncomfortable secret. A payoff being the concession for being in this horrid business. First came the death, then came the reward. Each resident contract included a line item ensuring the resident's funeral expenses would be covered with a donation coming from a portion of their life insurance money. Although not mandatory, the box was almost always checked. Harriet made certain each resident was aware of the line item; her bonus tied into each signed plan. No new resident wanted to burden their surviving relatives with final expenses, and she played on the sentiment to perfection.

Each Exit Day, Harriet performed a ritual she was none too fond of. It began with setting in motion a series of tasks culminating in calling the owner. The dread would creep in, causing an ache in her stomach each time she called the man. And when she finished the conversation, the urge to cleanse herself was strong and unquenchable. In her contract she had insisted and received a private bathroom off her office. She swallowed hard, glanced at the bathroom door, then picked up the phone and dialed.

"We had another exit last night," she said when he answered. A death was referred to as an 'exit' because the word "died" was not an effective term for one who was administrator for the Falls Assisted Living and Memory Care Facility: a community for those in their retirement years to live, meet with old friends, enjoy activities, and lighten the load from their children. A safe and enjoyable place to live out their golden years. This word had no place anywhere near her marketing vocabulary.

"I've been expecting your call," said the man. Harriet noticed an edge of impatience in his voice.

"Uh, Mr. Franz exited in his sleep last night—"

He cut her off. "Yes, yes," he said hastily. "Don't you think I know everything that goes on in my various enterprises?" He then added, "Especially this one."

Harriet did not appreciate the implication he had eyes and ears in her building, nor did she enjoy working for the man, but he paid her handsomely for the pleasure of serving him. Where else in Benton Falls would she find a job this lucrative?

Her hope he would 'exit' himself faded a long time ago. Most likely, the old man would outlive her. The thought filled her with sullen resignation.

"It was the eighth this month," she commented, thinking even though he was aware, she would get kudos for being on top of the business. She did not.

"Then it's been a good month," came his response. "For some of us."

She was about to respond but thought better of it. How do you respond to a statement like that? Most homes wanted to keep their residents alive. Not the FALM. An alive resident paid through Medicare, retirement, and relatives. Once dead, they paid by contract. The silence was awkward and untenable. Like at these times, this job.

He grunted before asking, "You've made the necessary arrangements?"

"Of course. I spoke with Grant at the morgue and faxed the paperwork over to Tony for processing."

"And the funeral plans?"

"Mr. Cullen has been notified. He did mention a possible price increase, just to warn you."

The FALM had arrangements with three key partners on Exit day; Doc Grant Houseman would list the cause of death, almost always old age. Then Tony Asper performed his legal duty and executed the contract for payment. Lately, the funeral director, Mr. Cullen had been a problem. Even though he had been giving a kickback to the FALM for years for the exclusive business rights, Pat Cullen began pushing back on the negotiated price of each exit. "More workload demanded more compensation," he had argued.

"Damn," the man cursed, his volume rising. "This will not do. I'll call him myself."

"I can handle Pat, Mr....."

"No, I'll call him." His tone offered a few clues to Harriet. It did not sound mean. It was worse: a threat with a hint of malice.

"I'll make sure he sticks to our bargain," he said, as though he had an offer Pat Cullen could not refuse. Harriet sensed his grin over the phone. It felt waxy and wicked. She hung up the phone and was glad for the moment of peace. It did not last long, as Julia from Marketing buzzed in.

"I have a Miss Winnie Ahearne ready to fill out the resident paperwork. She's sitting outside your office."

"Thank you, Julia, I'll be with her momentarily." Harriet groaned as she lifted her frame from the seat and headed towards the bathroom, stretching her aching back as she walked. She would onboard Miss Ahearne. As soon as she washed away the oily residue from the last call.

"Kennedy?" rasped Harley Benton. His lungs were unable to produce the forceful voice of his youth. Yelling at the help was an old habit he had not yet broken. "Kennedy?" He reached for the button on his wheelchair to summon his butler, missing it entirely, causing his hand to flail by the wheel of the chair like a tree branch in a high wind. On the next attempt, he made up for the whiff by pressing the button repeatedly, a bony finger mimicking the little cocktail bird, beak up, beak down, repeat, as if once would not be enough. He had the button installed as his voice began to fail him. The button a disappointing, but effective replacement for losing power he once possessed.

"Yes, sir?" asked the butler as he stepped into the bedroom of his master of twenty-plus years. "What can I do for you this morning?"

Harley coughed a large wad of phlegm and spit it into a handkerchief he kept in his pajama pocket for this purpose. He dropped it on the floor before answering. "I'll need you to make a phone call after breakfast." His frail voice did not carry, forcing Kennedy to move closer to better hear the commands of his employer and to retrieve the used handkerchief. He took a few clean ones out of his jacket, stuffing them into the old man's pockets. "Yes sir, to whom should I call?"

"An old friend of mine has a grandson. I'd like to speak with him about a business arrangement."

Kennedy nodded, asking his next question, "Would sir care to get dressed? I can call the car around once you've finished breakfast."

The old man went silent, eyes pinched in contempt. Although he could not yell as in the past, his anger had not diminished. His tirades, the bane of the staff, frightening the weakest to quit.

Benton was a man who suffered no fools. But now, without a firm voice, he could still signal his displeasure with a withering stare capable of melting permafrost. Kennedy received the message loud and clear. "Yes, sir. Let's get you ready for breakfast and then I'll make the call."

This communication placated the old man. Age had taken his vigor, but there was not much he could do about it. He had Kennedy push him to the elevator, and the two rode in silence until the doors opened into a corridor leading to the grand entrance. Kennedy pushed Benton's chair into the dining hall, the only noise coming from his black leather shoes echoing through the large and mostly empty mansion. Once Benton was placed at the head of the table, Kennedy rang a small bell, prompting the cook to come out with the master's breakfast. They had served Benton the same breakfast his entire adult life; One egg, sunny side up, a slice of burnt bacon, and two slices of white toast with a small dish of peanut butter. Benton spread the paste on himself, never liking the way anyone else did the task. He washed the breakfast down with a cup of black coffee and a small glass of tomato juice.

As Benton ate his meal in silence, Kennedy stood by awaiting his next order. Benton preferred his servants invisible until needed. He was not paying for their opinions, their companionship, and certainly not for any insubordination. He expected and received utter loyalty and subservience. It was how he was raised and once he took over the estate, continued the practice he had learned from his father. "This is our town and we need to make sure everyone understands this. Everyone." His father instructed him.

"Everyone," he mumbled, toast crumbs falling from his lips onto his lap, resembling a light snowfall. He sipped both his coffee and tomato juice before wiping his mouth and laying the napkin on his plate to signify he was through with breakfast. Then and only then did Kennedy position himself behind the old man's chair and pull him away from the table.

The butler pushed Benton from the dining room into the office. There was not much else for Harley Benton to achieve in his old age, but habits are hard to break. He still maintained at least one hour a day at his desk, corresponding with the heads of his various enterprises, crunching the numbers with his financial adviser, giving advice to the mayor or even scolding the editor of the town's newspaper when an article appeared he didn't like. Harley Benton might be old and infirm, but to the townspeople of Benton Falls, he was still the man in charge. Even if it was behind the scenes; his bony fingers clasping the puppet strings.

He was not up to the challenge of being in charge today. Some days were better than others where his strength came back, his voice clear. But today, weakness enveloped him. He felt old. *Ancient.* He pulled another handkerchief and coughed up more phlegm, throwing the linen on the floor in disgust.

"Damn lungs," he murmured. Displeased he could not trust his body any more than an employee who slacked off or a servant pilfering the silverware, he wrote out the name of the person he wanted to call and the message to relay.

Kennedy dialed the phone. It took only two rings. "Good morning, this is Mr. Kennedy from Mr. Benton's office. Am I speaking to Mr. Axel Ahearne?"

The voice on the other end must have replied in the affirmative, causing Kennedy to go on with the message.

"Mr. Benton would like to meet with you to discuss an idea of his." He paused. Benton saw the look of concern on his butler's face, prompting an impatient hand wave at Kennedy, signifying for the butler to get to the point.

"No, sir," said the butler into the phone. "You misunderstand me. Mr. Benton doesn't want to come to you. It is he who requests *your* presence here at Benton Manor."

The butler awaited the response but did not get one. "Mr. Ahearne? Are you still there?" When the voice did answer, Benton gave his butler a stare. Kennedy, once again clear on its message, proceeded, "Mr. Ahearne, I can have a car sent around tonight at five thirty. Cocktails will be in the study with dinner at six fifteen." The way Benton liked it. This was not a request. It was a summons.

The butler hung up the phone and turned to leave his employer to his work when Benton coughed more phlegm. The old man pointed a frail finger upward, motioning Kennedy to take him back to bed. He needed more rest if he were to entertain tonight. It was important he save his strength for the meeting he had planned.

As he was being pushed back to the elevator, Benton dropped the used handkerchief on the floor of the grand entry-way. He looked at Kennedy to make sure the butler was aware there was something to retrieve before the guest arrived.

Winnie sat outside the office of the administrator with Julia Storey, the Marketing Director of the FALM. Julia, aware people referred to the home by the acronym, was not keen on the name. It sounded as if they were taxed with raising cattle instead of taking care of the elderly, but did find it easier to use. Not having a mouthful of words while explaining the many features of the place did have its advantages.

Her job title allowed Julia to paint the idyllic picture of keeping the resident's golden years shiny. Every resident was acutely aware of the hidden meaning but wanted to believe what made them safe, and she excelled at shielding the truth no one wanted to hear aloud. Senior living meant many positive things, but always ended in one negative.

"Thank you, dear, but you needn't worry. I can take care of myself."

"Miss Ahearne, my pleasure." Julia answered with a soft pat on Winnie's hand. "It's not a regular part of the job, but it should be. Welcoming our new residents is important."

"It is a nice touch," said Winnie. "Do you like this job?"

"Yes, I do," said Julia. "It's rewarding to see so many people who, although ageing, still have a place to stay active. I'm sure you'll love it here."

Winnie shifted in her seat. Julia saw it as a sign she was planning to ask another question. She was not wrong. "Does it pay, dear? If I'm not being too nosy."

Julia looked in her lap before answering. "The job? Yes, they pay me a fair wage for Benton Falls." She looked up and held Winnie's hand. "My real payment comes from meeting people like you."

"You are sweet to say. Does your husband mind your work? I know it's difficult *and* rewarding, having worked my whole life, but men…"

"Miss Ahearne, I'm not married." Julia smiled at the elderly woman's attempt to gain information.

"Really? A pretty girl like yourself? How can that be?" Now it was Winnie who was holding Julia's hand. "My, my, what is wrong with the men of this world? Man buns and lack of manners, thinking only of themselves while here you are ripe for marriage and dare, I say it?" Winnie leaned in conspiratorially before whispering the last word, "Children?"

"Miss Ahearne, you are a trip! I love your spirit. Trust me, I will find the right guy soon enough."

"Dear, men are clueless. Do you know why God made woman?"

Julia shook her head, unsure of what this interesting lady might say next.

"So men would have someone to give them a clue."

The two giggled as the door opened and Harriet stepped into the lobby to address Winnie, "Miss Ahearne, so glad to have you consider becoming a resident here, do come in." Julia stood to join them, but Harriet raised an unwelcoming hand. She never let Julia sit in on the onboarding meetings. Her job was to find new residents and turn them over to Harriet. The hand showing a clear division of power.

Still holding Julia's hand, Winnie said loudly enough for Harriet to hear, "Dear, you've been kind to this old woman. Let's speak again soon. I may have a solution to your...um, problem."

This announcement caused Julia to blush, "Miss Ahearne..."

Winnie stopped her. "Dear, my friends call me Winnie."

"Yes, Winnie, we'll talk soon."

The administrator waved a hand inward, prompting Winnie to enter. "Winnie, please come in and have a seat."

"Ahem," pronounced the old woman. "It's Miss Ahearne." She then turned back to wink at Julia, who tried unsuccessfully to hide a smile. Harriet, a frown on her face, shut the door behind them.

Hector Gonzalez towered over everyone at the FALM. The nurses, other orderlies, and especially the elderly. For his size, one would assume him to be rough and clumsy bordering on the uncontrollable. This was an easy assumption to make, but wrong. Hector was what people called a gentle giant. He had a soft touch and a subtle finesse with the residents, which surprised many at first. Lifting an arthritic resident from bed to wheelchair at first scared the patient, but after the move, made it clear no one other than Hector would handle the task going forward.

"You're not a gentle giant," he had heard occasionally. "You're *our* gentle giant." This pleased him to no end. Hector loved the work, and the residents loved him. Even some FALM management team members walked the halls with a hearty greeting, "Hector! My man!" as he tended to the infirm.

Hector needed this job. He had the grades to go to college or could have entered a profession paying more but needed to stay under the radar. He had not planned to live with his parents for the rest of his life, but the obligation was strong. Born in this country made him a naturalized citizen but did not shield him from seeing the fear of extradition on the faces of friends who had come into the country illegally. He also lived with this fear, but not for himself. He stayed under the radar for a different reason: his parents were not legal.

He pondered this very issue as he prepared to make his scheduled rounds when his face brightened. He took special care of those in the 'Passing Lane,' making those resident patients as comfortable as possible as they awaited an extradition of their own. Polite and caring, yet keeping a safe distance from getting too involved with these people, understanding his tenure here would be longer than theirs. He did, however, make friends with people who came to visit. A casual wave turned into an introduction and soon a discussion on the health and well-being of the patient they visited.

This afternoon, Hector grinned because of the sight of one of his favorite visitors. The man had no family here but still came to visit the sick and elderly on his own time, which Hector found inspiring. "Hi, Mr. Ahearne," he said in his inside nursing home voice. "How's it going?"

"Fine, Hector, it's a great day to be alive," said Axel. "How's the family?"

Another trait Hector admired about this man. He was always asking after his family. An unselfish attitude Hector tried to emulate.

"Mr. Franz passed this week. But everyone else is fine, thanks. Except for Mr. Montley here. Been having a few rough days. Pneumonia," he said, thumbing at the door to his right.

"I'm sure you're doing all you can to make him comfortable. You're a good man, Hector."

"Thanks, Mr. Ahearne. Wait, you're here early today?"

"Good catch, Hector," Axel said. "I have an early dinner date, so I thought I'd duck out of work and do my visiting beforehand."

"A girl?" Hector asked, smiling as he drew the word out. It sounded like guurrrlll.

"No, you misunderstand. More of a... Come to think of it, I'm not sure how to describe it. Let's just say, it will be an interesting evening and leave it at that, shall we?"

"Sure, Mr. Ahearne."

Axel frowned. "Do me a favor, will you?"

"Sure, Mr. Ahearne, whatever you want."

"One, please call me Axel. And two, keep an eye out for any residents who don't get any visitors, and I'll make it a point to stop in, OK?"

"Sure, Mr.- I mean, Axel. Sure, I will." As Axel disappeared into Mr. Montley's room, Hector thought he would emulate Mr. Axel one day. Kind, successful, but still willing to make others feel special. How *he* always felt whenever Mr. Axel was around.

The moment did not last. As he turned a corner, he bumped into Benny Palz, another orderly working at the home. One not as nice as Mr. Ahearne. Or anyone else.

"Jesus, watch where you're going, ya big goon. Are ya trying to kill me?" said Palz, a sneer etched across his face.

Benny Palz had been a bully to Hector ever since he had come to work at the FALM. He was a wiry man with short greasy hair, a pencil-thin mustache, and an attitude akin to a rattlesnake. Hector did whatever it took to avoid the man, but a small building was bound to create run-ins.

"Sorry, Benny, wasn't looking where I was going."

"Then you better start, Rat Boy. Cause if you do it again, I'll kick your ass from here to the next county, got it?" Hector did not care for the nickname given to him by Benny. In fact, no one on the staff did. The rat should not have been in the building and it scared the female staffers, but Hector had come to the rescue, quickly disposing the rodent. Kill one rat and you get labelled as 'Rat Boy?' It was not fair. But neither was Benny.

Palz, slight and smaller than Hector, attacked him from the beginning and when Hector did not fight back, pushed forward as most bully's do. Hector wondered why Benny was so mean. Perhaps it was due to a bad childhood experience or poor adult supervision; the possibility of constant beatings wasn't out of the question. In his head, he listened to his father's warning, "Son, there are some people in this world that are never happy, unless they're miserable."

Whatever the reason, Hector was concerned. He was not afraid of the guy, only afraid of what he might do. When avoidance did not work, deference did.

"Sorry, Benny. I'll be more careful."

"You better be, Rat Boy. You better be," threatened the smaller man as he walked down the hall. Hector inhaled and then let out a sigh of relief. Another explosive encounter avoided.

After all, he had to keep a low profile.

aking Winnie's advice, Axel had been going to confession at St. Paul's church. He tried to tell himself it was uncomfortable telling his friend, Father Tom, his intimate secrets. That may have played a small part. Rationalizing confessing to a perfect stranger made him feel less like a turncoat, a cheater on his own pastor. But despite the excuses, none helped to deny the truth. Axel found he preferred telling his sins to a priest who was deaf.

The experience in the confessional was odd. The setup of the confessional booth, similar in every Catholic Church, had the priest sitting behind a curtain in the middle with two confessional booths on either side, to turn toward either sinner. A small door in the booth window offered not only privacy but anonymity when opened. The difference happened inside the confessional. When Axel knelt, he saw a switch with a sign above it.

When the door opens, please flip the switch to ON.
When done confessing, flip the switch OFF
and wait for your penance.

Evidently, this sign proved Father Champlin could not hear. The switch turned on a tiny bulb in the priest's booth announcing the next parishioner had arrived. Axel found it ingenious and liberating. In his youth, he softened the terms of his sins. 'A white lie' would become 'a small untruth,' 'a stolen cookie,' spun as 'taking without permission.' But the most difficult term, 'masturbation,' was described as a less embarrassing 'Abused myself.' With Father Champlin, no softening of terms necessary. Axel plowed ahead with the bare truth and its stark terms.

Given his penance, Axel stepped out of the booth and knelt to say his prayers. When finished, he stood and genuflected before heading out the door. He still had to change his clothes and freshen up for his dinner date with Harley Benton. He did not want to be late.

At precisely 5:45 p.m., Kennedy opened the large mansion door. An older gentleman with great posture, nose lifted slightly into the air and a gaze which looked past Axel as if seeking another incoming car. Axel's first impression was the butler's propensity to open the door before he had a chance to knock. "No need, Mr. Ahearne, the driver informed me of your arrival," the butler explained, without the benefit of being questioned.

Axel, feeling foolish with both his assumption and his hand in the air, dropped it to his side. He stepped into the grand hallway, where he was surprised by one of the largest rooms he had ever seen.

Two staircases mirrored each other as they wound their way upward, meeting at the next floor where a large picture window spilled the late afternoon sunlight through the spindles of the railing, breaking the sunbeam into several pieces as it landed upon the marble floor in front of him.

"Please, follow me," Kennedy commanded, without eye contact. Axel fell in behind the butler, following him under the staircase arch and through a pair of large wooden doors opening to the study. Behind it were floor to ceiling shelves filled with books. Axel immediately took in an aroma, something between ancient books and pipe smoke. Very comforting and fitting for a distinguished room such as this.

Kennedy offered him a seat near the window, the long drapes covering it sheer enough to let a small amount of light in but not enough to harm the precious volumes housed there.

"Mr. Ahearne, a drink before dinner perhaps?"

"Do you have any Irish whiskey?" Axel questioned. With the nod of the butler's head, he said politely, "On the rocks, please." Then adding nervously, "Can you please make it a double?" The urge to have a glass of liquid courage before meeting the great Harley Benton was powerful.

As he sat alone in this large room, Axel pondered how many generations of Benton's spent time here, and the conversations each shared between these walls. He stood and walked toward the shelves, glancing at titles with his hands clenched firmly behind his back, fearful of touching anything. Kennedy returned with his drink.

"The Master will be with you momentarily. He is rather weak today, so you'll have to sit close in order to listen."

Axel took the drink from the butler, thanking him before he exited. Sitting up in the chair, he took a sip. He could not decide which he enjoyed more, the whiskey or the leather chair enveloping him in comfort. He did not give himself the answer before Kennedy came through the study doors, wheeling in the master of the house and positioning him right next to Axel's chair.

"You'll have to forgive my absence from your arrival," said the old man, his voice barely a whisper. He was dressed in a dark grey pinstriped suit, a pressed white shirt, and silver tie. A silver handkerchief stuck fashionably in his breast pocket completed the ensemble. Axel noticed a sharp contrast to the original aroma of the room. A faint, yet pungent smell arose out of place.

Urine.

"The pleasure is mine, Mr. Benton. Thank you for the invitation. But you needn't have sent a car, I could have driven myself."

"Nonsense," whispered Benton. He coughed and paused before swallowing. Axel saw how old age had claimed the man and did not look forward to the time in his life when he met the same fate. "Let me ask, how is your grandmother doing? Well, I hope. She is a fine lady."

"She is indeed," Axel said, proud Mr. Benton actually knew Winnie. But then again, powerful men such as Harley Benton made it their business to know everyone in their fiefdom.

"How do you know my grandmother?"

Mr. Benton took his time as he recalled how they were introduced. A feint smile crossed his lips before disappearing; Axel could have sworn the man looked years younger for those brief seconds.

"We've both lived here our entire lives. I was a few years ahead in school, but during the summers and vacations, age never played a role in who you spent time with."

Axel could not believe Mr. Benton and his grandmother were a mere few years apart. His grandmother was aging gracefully, while Benton was not.

The old man coughed again, this time with the face one makes with something unsavory in their mouth, something bitter. He swallowed again before continuing. "I have great respect for your grandmother. After your grandfather died, she never remarried, did she?"

"No, she never did. I guess taking care of two boys and running a restaurant gave her enough to handle."

"Yes, a sad day for the town when your parents were ki—" Benton stopped in mid- sentence before correcting himself. "Perished at such a young age. Very sad."

"Thank you, sir. You're kind to say so. Winnie proved to be a great caregiver. As a parent, she taught me a lot. I'm still learning from her."

"Indeed. And spirited, too." Again, the old man coughed. This time it took longer for him to swallow. Axel finished his drink and placed the glass on the coaster provided on the table when Kennedy entered the room announcing dinner was served. Axel noticed the old man give the butler a searing look. *It wouldn't be pleasant to be on the end of that temper,* he thought. Axel also noticed the brief glance the butler returned to his employer. It was subtle; Axel could not decide if it was deference or defiance.

Kennedy wheeled the chair to the dining hall with Axel in pursuit. Benton was slid into the head spot, and as Axel began to take the chair next to him, the butler gently ushered him to the far end of the table. "This should be more comfortable," Kennedy explained as he pulled the chair out for Axel. "Wine with dinner?"

"No thanks, water, please. But another whiskey after dinner, if I may."

Kennedy nodded as he left for the kitchen to inform the cook. The two sat at either end of the table in silence. Axel wondered why he had to sit far away during dinner when he had to sit close enough to hear the old man's words. On the other hand, glad to be out of range from the old man's urine issue.

They ate in silence and once Benton had thrown his napkin into his plate, the cook entered and began clearing the table. She had swiftly snagged Axels plate even though he was not finished. He attempted to spear one last piece of his chicken but only managed to click his fork against the china, coming up empty.

Kennedy returned to his master to wheel him back to the study. Axel followed, pleased to find a glass of whiskey on the rocks placed on the coaster by his comfortable chair.

"Would young sir care for something else?" Kennedy asked, once again under the searing gaze of his employer. This time, the butler did not break character, his nose stiffly pointing upward.

"No, this will be fine. Thank you." Axel said, prompting the butler to leave the room to the two men.

Axel shifted in the chair as he made himself comfortable and sipped his drink in anticipation of an after dinner discussion. He stared intently as the old man once again coughed. A deep, rasping wet cough. The same sour expression crossed his face before swallowing.

Axel wondered why he did not have a drink himself to clear his throat and was about to ask when the old man spoke. "I understand you are an accountant. From my sources I understand you have a way with numbers?"

Axel nodded as he swallowed a mouthful of whiskey. "Yes," he answered, the liquid still stinging as he spoke. "I'm good with numbers. They never lie."

"I, for one, find it admirable you found an honest profession. I have an idea which requires your services." Benton reached into his coat pocket and pulled out an envelope. Axel leaned in and took it from him, again catching the faint whiff of urine as he did. He struggled not to let on, forcing a smile instead of scrunching his nose in disgust.

"Wow, Mr. Benton," he said as he opened the envelope. His mouth dropped in shock as he saw the name on the check was his. Then counted the zeros with a one in front. Five of them. Seven if you counted the cents.

"What is this for?" he stammered.

"As I said, I need your services. This, my boy, is not a gift but a new era for me. And more where that comes from, but there is a request attached."

Axel eyed the old man suspiciously before asking, "How much more and what is your request?"

The old man's smile showed crooked, yellowed teeth. Axel imagined it had been perfect years ago. Time had a way of destroying the best of things.

"My plan is to leave something for the town to remember me. Perhaps a statue? A street named after me? And definitely a charitable organization. Something that says, "Harley Benton thrived here." A faithful servant to the town. A shrine of sorts for the town folk to benefit. Alas, there are no Bentons left and I'm too old to bear offspring."

The old man continued, his voice squeaking. "In my remaining days, I'd prefer to make myself useful. And for it to happen, I'll need help with budgeting, city permits, construction. And of course, your own compensation. Surely, you can understand?"

"I suppose, but it's odd you want a perfect stranger to help, don't you agree?" Axel countered, still unconvinced.

Benton cleared his throat and the sour expression crossed his face once more before he swallowed. "Let me tell you a story which might clarify things. When a young man, I had wealth and good looks. A perfect combination to get anything one wants. This included women. I had multiple girlfriends, each wanting to take their place as Mrs. Harley Benton and a piece of my fortune."

He lifted a scrawny ancient hand and waved it as if brushing away a lazy fly. "But I used them and threw them away as if taking out the trash. I'm not proud of my behavior, but it's what I desired at the time. Each woman who came into my life, I used and tossed. With the exception of one." Benton paused before continuing. A look of wistfulness crossed his face, briefly softening his hardened features. "You see, one woman rebuffed me. Me, Harley Benton, the most eligible bachelor in town and she said "no" to my advances. And do you know who?"

Axel thought he did, but did not let on. It sounded like something she would do.

"Your grandmother, the only one who said 'no.'" Benton paused, and the wistful look returned. It occurred to Axel the only woman this man had ever loved was Winnie, the reason for the generosity coming into focus.

"Why did she turn you down?"

"Your grandfather. He came along and she was smitten. For the first time in my life, someone had said no to me. At first, it angered me, but over time the anger turned to respect. She is a woman who knows her mind."

"Did you still love her?" Axel asked, curious.

"Never stopped," the old man replied, as he looked towards the window. Axel felt sorry for the man rebuffed by his grandmother, but could not help wondering what life might have been like born into the Benton lineage.

"You see? You are not a stranger, are you?"

"I guess not. You know she's moved into the FALM." Axel said, noticing a slight change of expression on the old man's face. Like the poker player who had been caught in a tell as he looked at the four Aces in his hand. Surprise.

"Has she?" Benton replied slowly, his ancient fingers pressed together in a steeple of a child's game. "How nice to be with friends her own age."

Something about the way the old man drew out the words gave Axel discomfort, causing him to shift in his chair. Disrupting the moment, he said, "OK, if I agree to your plan, what's the next step?"

"First, quit your job and come work for me. Work from home at your own pace. This is a down payment for the setup. Then, you'll meet me for dinner once a week to discuss our game plan progress to better advise you. Once our business is concluded, we can sit and talk of the outside world. It gets rather lonely in this prison of a mansion." The old man looked forlornly at Axel, and he did not have the heart to say no. If he visited the nursing home and the other places, why not find time to share with this man? The acknowledgement of one hundred thousand other reasons both thrilled and embarrassed him.

"Of course, I'll help you with this plan. Next week then?"

"See? A smart boy. You've made an old man happy," he said as Kennedy entered the room. "Call the car for Master Ahearne. He has a few important things to contemplate."

"The car is waiting out front, sir." Kennedy responded. But before he could usher Axel out of the study, Benton had a coughing attack, the worst one of the evening prompting Kennedy to rush to the wheelchair.

"I can find my way out," Axel said. As he opened the door to leave, he turned around to see Kennedy pull the handkerchief from Benton's front pocket and hold it under the man's mouth just as he spit a large amount of grayish yellow sputum, forming thin lines to the handkerchief. Before the butler had the chance to wipe the old man's mouth, Benton snatched the handkerchief away, wiped his own mouth, and threw the linen on the floor as if it had insulted him.

Axel quickly shut the door, and as he walked through the front hallway, his throat began to clench with the urge to vomit his dinner. He slipped out the front door and into the car. As it drove away from Benton Manor, Axel's throat clenched again, causing short staccato gulps of air. It wasn't the old man's appearance making him sick, nor the stench of his urine. No, Axel had realized what caused the old man's sour expression. Each time he had to swallow.

Mrs. Irena Jones was an eighty-nine-year-old widow now residing in the Passing Lane. Her latest visitor knew her story well. She and her husband had led a simple, yet pious life. They worked hard, making sure to share their good fortune by tithing to the church. Irena and Winnie had not only been friends but served in the Altar Rosery Society, worked the church breakfasts together and helped fill and distribute the food stuffs from the parish sponsored food warehouse for the needy. Yes, although Irena and her husband had been faithful to her church, the visitor was all too familiar with the old woman's questions for God. "Why?" she would ask aloud. "When I had delivered on my promise to be a good Christian, didn't you bless my husband and I with children?" As a woman of faith clinging to life, she wanted answers. The visitor had listened calmly to these questions. Although God never took the time to answer, the visitor felt there was one. It began with patience.

On earlier visits this person had to speak loudly in response to her musings, having lost her hearing along with her youth. Today's visit was quiet, as Mrs. Jones no longer spoke. In the last stages before death, she had gone silent the week before. Like a play prior to opening the curtain, the audience turned mute in anticipation.

Looking down at the old woman, the visitor recalled their previous conversations. Those of her long and faithful marriage to her deceased husband. Her complaint about having no one left. The lack of understanding why God allowed young people to die before her. As a remedy, a hastening was called for. Send this woman to her justly deserved reward and end her misery. What God wanted.

The visitor watched as the woman slept. It wouldn't take long, but length of time is different between people like Mrs. Jones and her visitor. One had an eternity before their own death. For Mrs. Jones, today a good day as any.

At her bedside, the visitor pulled a small packet from a pocket and poured it into the water glass on Irena's nightstand, stirring the mixture with the straw to make sure it dissolved.

The contents of the package contained Vitamin K, a normally good vitamin aiding in blood coagulation and adding calcium. Mrs. Jones suffered from blood clots and prescribed a blood thinning agent. When combined with this vitamin, it proved to be a bad addition to Mrs. Jones' daily requirement, enhancing her chance of blood clotting leading to a stroke. And one could not be expected to hasten with a pillow every time. Each hastening, like the recipients, should be treated differently. *Special.*

After the powder dissolved, the glass was placed back onto the nightstand. The visitor nudged it close to the old woman, allowing her to reach it in the middle of the night. Just in case, the straw was pressed to Irena's lips, praying for her to finish it.

"This will help, Mrs. Jones. Soon, you'll be able to ask God all the questions you want," came the whisper.

Irena startled the guest as she awoke. "Lionel?" she asked, reaching out a hand for her dead husband.

"Yes, my darling," came the response. Smooth as silk and comforting as a quilt in winter. "Here, drink. You must be parched."

The old woman drank through the straw emptying the glass, more than enough to help her on her way. "Thank you," she croaked, a hand wiping the dribble from the side of her mouth. She rolled over and went back to sleep. The visitor kissed her on the forehead.

"I hope you get the answers to your questions."

The hastening complete, the visitor took a moment to pray. *O Lord, welcome Mrs. Jones to everlasting life in your presence. Go with God. Amen.* Then made the sign of the cross over her forehead, careful not to touch her before finally saying, "It'll only hurt for a moment. A small price to pay for an eternity of bliss."

The visitor slipped into the bathroom and laid the straw on the counter, rinsing the glass thoroughly before filling it again and placing it back on her nightstand.

"Good journey, Irena," said the Hastener before leaving the room. Stepping into the hallway, a smile appeared for a job well done. If outside, the Hastener would take the chance to whistle a happy tune. But inside, out of deference to the other residents, smiling sufficed.

CHAPTER
– 5 –

The sleeper awoke bathed in a cold sweat. The dream had been dormant for years. Research showed reoccurring dreams foretold a transition. A subtle reminder much was yet to be done.

This one had not changed since childhood. In a dark bedroom, the sleeper sat on the bedside, dressed in pajamas and robe with bare feet placed flat against the cool hardwood floor. Gazing down, two ancient, wrinkled hands arise through the boards as if made of water. Veins bulged with black blood oozing through them. Yellow pointed nails filled with cracks led the way until they covered the two small feet. A scream wants release yet never escapes. There was no movement to flee, only fear at the apparition of gnarled hands as they began to pull the feet of the child through the floor to the darkness beneath.

Before the child's ankles fully disappeared, the bedroom door would open, splashing fresh light from the hallway. The child raises a hand in an effort to avoid the glare.

Stepping into the doorway is a figure blocking most of the light, the halo surrounding the figure giving off an ethereal glow. No words spoken, no reaching out to one another. Only silence. Although the identity of the savior indiscernible, the relief is not. Prior to awakening, the dream child would glance downward again. The feet once again on solid hardwood, the ancient and withered hands disappeared. As did the figure in the doorway.

The adult dreamer rose from bed. The coolness of drying sweat, clammy against skin.

There is still much to be done. Time was of the essence. Redemption sought a job to erase the vile sin committed with another who should have known better. The acts had not been initiated by the child. But neither had it been stopped. God watched, and the shame burned upon the face as if near fire. God knew,but had not responded. No devastating plague or swarming locusts came to the sinner. No, it was worse. God exacted his vengeance slowly, painfully. Through searing guilt, a wound far worse than plague or locust. A vengeance which tore the sinner's soul apart bit by bit each moment of the day.

Deafening silence was the response to continual prayers asking forgiveness.

"Talk to me, please!" came the plea. "I beg of you." The sinner knelt bedside and wept through prayers. Redemption had to come, but how? The mind raced with questions, but no answers.

God helps those who help themselves, came a whisper in the mind. A subtle hint from the voice of conscience. *Blessed are the merciful, for they shall be shown mercy.* With understanding came acceptance.

"Thy will be done."

Realizing there would be no more sleep this morn, the sinner dressed and headed for the one place to find an ounce of peace from God's torment. Even if most questions went unanswered.

⤳

"Someone has been talking out of school," Winnie said, as she sat near the window, the afternoon sun weakening its harsh gaze. Axel sat in the rocker next to her. The room was spacious for one, but a little cramped had there been two residents. A sitting area, bathroom and of course, the neatly made bed to make a marine proud.

"Too much talk out of an *old* school," she repeated, the tone both playful and chastising at the same time. "You ought not to listen to the aged. They like to ramble on about nothing."

"I listen to you," said Axel.

"Number 1, no you don't. You pretend to listen. And B, I detect a hint of sarcasm. I'm not old. I'm mature."

Axel rocked as he placed hands on his knees. Every time he visited Winnie, he expected her to plead with him to leave this place, to bring her back home. Part of him wished she would because he missed her. But with each visit, she seemed to be enjoying herself more. She was still the independent woman he had known, now exerting her fiery spirit in a different place. She thrived in this environment, which made Axel proud.

"No one is telling tales out of school. I've been having dinner the past few Tuesday evenings with Mr. Benton."

"What?!?" Winnie sat up in her chair and dropped the book she was reading. It lay on the floor like a bird with a broken wing. "You stay away from that evil man. Nothing good will come of this."

"Relax," Axel said, patting her hand in an attempt to soothe her. She pulled it away as if a snake strike were imminent. "We're merely having dinner and good conversation. I'm working with him on a new project."

A dark expression hung on Winnie's face like a mask made of stone. "I tell you from experience, the man is not to be trusted. Stay away from him, please!"

"Winnie, he has nothing but good things to say about you. Why are you acting like this? And he's paying me handsomely. More than I was making at my old firm. The work I'm doing is for a good cause. You don't want to take that away from me, do you?"

The old woman looked hurt. Axel could see she was conflicted by the way she bit her lip on one side of her mouth. One of those telltale signs he had learned over the years.

"Besides, Benton has powerful friends in town, and I'll be getting introductions. Great networking, wouldn't you say?"

Winnie stopped chewing her lip and sighed. "He also had powerful enemies."

Axel looked at her side eyed at the word "had."

"Listen, son. You're a grown man, and I can't tell you what to do, but heed my advice. The man cares only about one thing: Harley Benton. He'll use you like everyone else. If you are going to continue to work for him, do an old lady one favor. Be careful."

Axel did not have time to answer as there was a knock on the door interrupting the old woman's lecture. Julia poked her head in and asked, "Is it OK to come in?"

Winnie waved her in, "Of course my dear, come sit next to me," she said, poking Axel to give up his chair.

"This is my grandson, Axel. A good boy. Has a new job, goes to church regularly and a gentleman to boot. But not much of a listener. I'm working on it. I believe he's trainable."

He offered his seat to Julia, noticing the warmth of embarrassment as the pinkish color appeared on her face. He shook her dainty hand and let go quickly.

"Winnie, please," he cautioned her with a stare that said, *No matchmaking.* She ignored him.

"Julia is the Marketing Director. She's very important around here, aren't you, dear?"

"I don't know about that," Julia said, the pink turning a light shade of red.

"And modest." Winnie complimented. "Very smart as well." The old woman put a finger to her cheek and looked off into the window in contemplation. "Tell me, I can't recall if you're married or not?"

"Winnie!" Axel scolded. "Don't embarrass the girl. Stop nosing around in other people's business. Stay in your own lane, please."

"Oh dear, have I embarrassed you?" she said, taking Julia's hand in hers and patting the top of it. "I'm a curious old woman." For effect, she batted her eyelashes at Axel, then winked at Julia.

"You know I'm not, Mrs…, ah, Winnie," she said, a sly look aimed at the old woman. "You wouldn't want to be accused of causing trouble this early in your stay, would you? I might have to call Hector to come in for punishment."

Winnie beamed at the suggestion. "Oh, send him in and tell him I've been very bad. Very bad, indeed." The two girls giggled. Axel did not.

"You two are quite the pair. I don't know if I can trust you together. No telling what mischief you'll get into." Then as an afterthought said, "Oh, did you hear about..." Axel was about to finish the sentence when he saw the stern gaze Julia threw at him. If it were a punch, Axel surmised it would hurt. A lot. He began again, "Did you hear about... um..."

Winnie watched as Axel struggled to come up with a different line than the one intended. She raised an eyebrow, "Well? Spit it out?"

Axel hung his shoulders, caught in the act of deception. Try as he might, he had never been able to fib to her. Or shield her from bad news.

"What was that look between the two of you?" she asked.

Now it was Julia's turn to blush again. This time from embarrassment. "He was going to tell you about someone's passing. I tried to warn him against it."

"Hmm, you two think I'm old, but I'm not stupid. Or senile. If you're talking about Mrs. Jones, I already knew. C'mon, I was born at night, but not last night."

The last line caused both younger folks to smile. "She doesn't miss much, does she?" Julia asked Axel.

"No, nor does she suffer fools lightly."

"I'm right here, ya know," said the old woman. "I ain't deaf neither."

Axel looked at his new ally. "Don't we know it. On a brighter note, Mr. Strong came out of his coma. He's a nice gentleman. Perhaps you two..."

"I'm gonna stop you right there, Mister. If any match-making is to be done, I'll take the lead. Nosy grandsons make poor neighbors."

Axel sighed at Julia, "She has a habit of mixing up sayings."

"Once again, right here," stated the old woman. "I get it. This is a home for old folks, none of us make it out alive. Face it, Old people die. The way God intended. But not me, and not today. Can we move on to a different and more pleasant topic? Please?"

Axel paused at her use of Leif's expression. He was about to question her when she beat him to the punch.

"How about we discuss where you two can go for a bite to eat and leave this old lady to play Mahjong with her friends?" Winnie pursed her lips and head nodded towards the door. Axel saw that as a direct invitation for them to leave.

"I don't have time for that," Axel said, giving his grand-mother another stern gaze.

"I do," said Julia softly, looking down at the floor.

"See what I mean?" Winnie said to Julia. "Clueless."

"You're incorrigible," said Julia, shaking her head.

"No, I'm corrigible. I'm a work in progress. It's not me that needs the reformation. It's him." Winnie pointed a thumb in her grandson's direction.

Axel took a deep breath. His grandmother had a way of getting what she wanted. Sort of like Harley Benton. No wonder they never got together. Like two same poles of powerful magnets, they spun away in opposite directions.

Still standing, he reluctantly put out an arm and Julia took it. As he opened the door for her, he turned around to wave goodbye.

"Bye!" Winne said, waving back. "Have fun!" Before the door closed, Axel thought he heard her say, "Blessed are the matchmakers…"

⌐͡ᴐ

If Winnie thought that Julia's lunch with Axel would go well, she could not have been farther from the truth. At first, Julia believed she herself was to blame. They sat in an awkward silence after they ordered. She not knowing what to say and he seemingly preoccupied elsewhere. By the time their sandwiches came to the table, she knew it wasn't her fault but something else. Even though they were four feet apart, his preoccupation deepened, taking him farther away from her.

If she was going to break through, she had to do it now. "Is there someplace else you'd like to be?" she asked. The volume of her voice must have startled him. He shook his head as if trying to rid the cobwebs inside.

"Uh, no. Not at all. I'm sorry, I just took on a rather large task and find my inner voice a bit negative today."

"Tell me about it. I might be able to help."

"I'm working with Harley Benton on his legacy. He wants to leave something behind for people to remember him by. It's time consuming, but not very exciting."

So, he was worried about disappointing his benefactor. She could deal with an old man. She was just glad it wasn't another woman.

She tried flirting, reaching out to touch his hand at certain points of a comment or question. When that didn't work, she challenged him with topics that might interest him. Nothing.

Julia watched as he took a bite of his sandwich. She wasn't sure if it was because he was hungry or if he really did not want to talk. She wracked her brain to come up with some way to change that. To spur the dialogue. She remembered a quote from somewhere that stated, "The more I talk about myself, the more I like you...."

She waited until he swallowed before she asked a question that required more than a one word answer.

"How did you get started giving eulogies?"

Axel gazed at her, his eyes squinting and biting the inside of his lip. A good sign. She took that to indicate he was thinking.

"What an odd question. No one has ever asked me that before," he said.

She put her elbows on the table and hands to her cheeks, leaning in towards him and forcing him to answer.

"It began with a story." Axel put his sandwich on the plate. "A neighbor of ours had a long struggle with cancer and finally passed away. Winnie and I went to their home to console his widow. She told us that she was going through the closet to find a proper burial suit. In one of the suit pockets she found a bottle of perfume. There was a note that read: *"When you wear this perfume, remember our love was as sweet as the air we breathe. PS keep looking, there are more surprises."*

Moving to his sock drawer, she found a box containing a locket and another note which read, *"My darling, when you wear this, think of my hands clasping it around your lovely neck. PS, keep looking."*

She peeked in his underwear drawer where she found a note with the words, *"Why would I leave something amongst my underwear?? There is nothing here but this note. I'll love you forever. PS, keep looking."*

Her search continued, and she kept finding little trinkets that he'd left and always with a note. Finally, she went into his home office where she found a bow on top of paperweight with a quote from A. A. Milne. *"If you live to be a hundred, I want to live to be a hundred minus one day so I never have to live a day without you."*

The note underneath read, *"I want to apologize for leaving you so soon. I had little to say about it, but that didn't stop me from leaving you with some lasting mementos that will keep me in your heart.*

PS, that should be the last of the trinkets I purchased for you, but not the last of the treasure life has to offer. So, don't ever stop looking over your shoulder because when you watch a sunrise, it is my light shining down upon you. When you see a beautiful flower, know the beauty represents what our love has meant. When you look out into the back yard garden, remember how we not only grew vegetables there, but three lovely children who took root and flourished because of you.

When you see the moon at night, know I will always be there in the moon light, watching over you. Death doesn't have any power over us. It never did, never will, and until we meet again, I will forever be in your heart.

And when your time comes to leave this world for the next, Do not be afraid, because as you step into the heavenly realm, there will be no fear, no worry and no more surprises because I will be there to greet you."

Julia was enraptured. "That was beautiful. You memorized that?" The more he talked, the more she liked *him*. She was hoping he got her clue.

He looked directly into her eyes. "How could I not? A story like that needed telling. I only hope I can find a love like that someday. One that transcends time. And death."

The faraway look returned, breaking her spell. If she wanted to get him to ask her out again, Julia knew she had her work cut out for her. She could hear Winnie now. "Men are clueless."

Perhaps it was time to give him a bigger clue. One he could not miss.

The next morning, Axel was working on an excel spreadsheet doing a cost analysis for a statue, a charity, and the formation of a Benton Museum in town when his phone rang. He did not recognize the number but pushed the call button anyway.

"Mr. Ahearne?" a voice on the other side interrupted.

"Um, yes, I'm Axel Ahearne."

"Axel, Veronica, here. Veronica Bucholtz. You knew my older brother, Richard."

"Yes, of course. I remember you. It's been a long time. Do you still live in the area?" Axel asked.

"No, I moved shortly after I got out of high school."

"How is Richard doing these days? Last I heard, he was based in California and doing well."

"It's why I called you. Richard died yesterday. A car accident on his way to work."

The news shook Axel. "I am so sorry," he managed to get out.

Richard Bucholtz and Axel were high school friends. Axel did not have many during those years, but Richard was an exception to the rule. He vaguely remembered Veronica, having been a few grades behind them. High school ended, as did the friendship. They each drifted down the streams of their own lives. And now Richard was gone.

"Mr. Ahearne? Are you still there?" Veronica asked.

"Uh, yes. Of course. And please, call me Axel. If there's anything I can do, please name it." Axel gave the response like many do when faced with a tragedy. Most people do not expect to honor the 'anything I can do' pledge. That's why her next request surprised him.

"Again, why I'm calling. My parents died a few years back and are buried in the church's cemetery. They also bought plots for both Richard and me. My plan is to bring him back there, have the service and bury him next to Mom and Dad."

"Sure, but what is it I can do?" he asked.

"You knew him better than anyone else. I wondered if you would give his eulogy?"

Another eulogy. It had been years since he had seen either Richard or Veronica. What last word could he possibly offer to the man?

"I'm not sure I'm the best guy for the job," Axel protested, hoping he might get out of this task.

"You're the perfect guy. You two used to be best friends and Father Tom suggested you for the job." She sounded sincere.

Axel felt a mixture of sorrow and pride. Sadness for his old friend's death but honored to be asked to take part in his farewell.

"I may need to talk with you about his later life, OK?" he asked. "We haven't spoken since high school."

"So, is that a yes?" she asked, closing him on the job. "Great, the service is scheduled for Thursday. I'll be in town tomorrow. How about dinner?"

They made plans to meet at the Razzi's Italian Restaurant at 8 pm causing Axel to wonder, *Three days to prepare. Do I have enough time?*

"And Axel," she added before she ended the call. "Say something nice about him."

He sat as his desk gazing absently at the spreadsheet in front of him, his concentration on Benton's task broken. It would have to wait. He opened a blank word document on his computer. *Say something nice.*

Axel began to type.

The Visiting Angels went to the FALM for their weekly visit. When Axel asked about the frequency of the visits, Helen said, "You never know when they'll pass and who you'll never see again."

"It's good for one's soul," Gil added softly. It was clear he still felt the sting of their jokes.

"Afterwards, I always feel better," said Becky, patting him on the back. He pulled away.

Axel thought about those statements as he had his patience tested by Mr. Brown and his constant complaining. Today, the topic centered around the conditions at the FALM. Axel tuned him out, bringing Veronica and their upcoming dinner to mind instead.

Mrs. Kalling was next on the list. She asked Axel if he was one of her sons. He held her hand as he told her no. "But they'll be by anytime, I'm sure." The white lie irrelevant as the old woman continued to speak to Axel as if he were her first born.

Mrs. Walsh gossiped to him as if one of her regular bridge club girls. He listened intently as she quipped, "Did I tell you about…?"

Axel found Mr. Strong in a jovial mood, enjoying this reprieve from death, and eating a sandwich as Axel stepped into the room.

"My boy! Come in!" Strong waved a hand in greeting. With the other, he pointed his sandwich outward. "Would you like something to eat?" Axel noticed crumbs falling from his mouth to his night shirt, but did not comment, glad to see the old man in great spirits.

"No thanks, already eaten," he claimed.

"Then come, sit. Life is grand, is it not?"

They spoke briefly. The old man talked between bites; grateful he had been given a second chance to tell his family how much he loved them. He spoke rapidly, and Axel could do nothing more than sit and listen. He did not mind at all.

"Axel, I also appreciate you coming to visit me. Our conversations have shown me what a kind soul you really are. And a talented storyteller to boot!"

Axel gave a half bow before answering. "Sir, it's been my pleasure."

"You're a good boy, Axel." The old man leaned in and in a lower voice stated, "Don't worry, when I get to the pearly gates, I'll put in a good word for you." Strong placed his plate on the table with the other, before brushing the crumbs off the bed and settled back. He was about to speak once more when a confused expression crossed his face as his eyes drooped. "I'm a bit tired suddenly. Perhaps we can pick up the conversation at a later date?"

"Of course. Get some rest and I'll see you next week." Axel opened the door and stepped into the hallway, almost running into Gil, who was coming to visit the newly awakened old man.

"Not now," he cautioned his fellow Angel. "He wants to nap."

Gil put his hands up. "Got it. I'll meet you out front in five. Gotta hit the head," he whispered.

Axel headed for the lobby where he would wait for the rest of the Angels. Recalling the earlier discussion with his friends, he realized Gil was right. *This group's deeds truly were good for the soul.*

The hallways were always quiet after visiting hours, a time when Hector was finishing his shift. He enjoyed the solitude after the hectic day of answering the same questions from those with dementia, assisting the funeral home after an exit, and cleaning after residents who had soiled themselves. This was his quiet time before he prepared to leave for the night.

This last chore of sweeping the hallways with the long dust broom was comforting. It made no noise as he pushed it along the corridors, depositing piles at the end of each run and sweeping the pile using the conventional broom and dustpan. It was quiet and mindless. Hector needed this time alone at the end of each day to recharge his batteries from a job where all he witnessed was the march toward death. The peace did not last.

"Hey, Rat Boy," said Benny Palz as he walked around a corner, kicking a pile of the dust, and spreading it up the hallway. "You missed a spot."

"Benny, you walked through my dust pile," Hector said, annoyed.

"Yeah, I guess I did." Benny smirked. "You may want to check the other hallways as well. Seems a dust storm erupted."

Hector raised a fist and took a step in Benny's direction but stopped. *Did he just flinch?*

What he really wanted to do was pulverize the little bastard but knew better than to engage with this horses' ass, so he kept his temper in check and his mouth shut.

"Let me finish. I want to go home," he said wearily.

"Oh, you'll go home when I tell you. It's your turn to sweep, so I suggest you do a better job of it." Benny had already changed into his street clothes: jeans, work boots, and a plain black hoodie. With the toe of his boot, he kicked more dust. "Looks like you'll be awhile here, don't it, Rat Boy?"

Hector sighed and pushed his broom along, sweeping the dust into the corner. *Benny will get his someday*, he mused. *And I hope I'm around to see it.*

Benny, not yet done creating more work for Hector, again kicked the pile Hector had created. "What is your problem?" Hector asked, the edge in his voice sharp.

"You, Rat Boy, are my problem," Benny said with a finger pointed at the tall orderly. Hector struggled to keep his anger in check, the worry causing his brow to furrow.

When Hector did not respond, Benny put his hands into his hoodie pouch and brushed by the orderly, in an attempt to push him aside. It failed as Benny bounced off Hector's large frame and into the wall. Benny turned in anger, but Hector already put his hands in the air in surrender.

"Sorry, my bad!" he claimed, although it was not. Benny accepted the apology with a "Better believe it was your fault,

Rat Boy," before walking down the hallway where he reached another dust pile. Turning to smirk at Hector, he placed a work boot into the pile and spread more dust before exiting, his middle finger held high, arm outstretched until it disappeared around the corner.

Hector sighed. Caught in this trap was painful. What he really wanted to do was punch the little punk, but the safety of his parents came first. He took a few breaths to calm down. Then cleaned the first mess, pushing the broom along, relishing the quiet once more.

CHAPTER
– 6 –

They met at the restaurant. Arriving first, Axel sat at a table by the window, the white tablecloth in stark contrast to the approaching darkness. He ate a slice of bread from the wicker basket with one hand while wiping away the crumbs from the table with the other when he saw Veronica enter the restaurant.

"Here," he said, waving his crumb filled hand, causing the bread morsels to spill back onto the tablecloth. Embarrassed, he managed a weak smile, as he once again tried to tidy up.

"Starting without me, I see," she commented, pointing to the breadbasket.

"I worked through lunch," he explained.

"No worries, I've done it many times." She reached into the basket, grabbed a slice, and pointed at the butter dish. Axel slid it over towards her. As she buttered the bread, commented, "Ooh, it's still warm. I love the smell of freshly baked bread!" Then, remembering why she was there, took a more solemn tone. "I'd like to thank you for agreeing to do this. I still can't fathom he's gone. He left a voice message on my cell, and I never got the chance to call him back. I can't get myself to erase the message either. Hearing his voice is my way of keeping Richard's memory alive."

"Why don't you tell me more about him. I'll listen and take notes," Axel told her while he pulled a small notebook and a pen from his pocket. "You can start anytime."

Veronica took a sip of water to clear her throat. "He was a gentle guy. Not arrogant like some guys I dated." As an aside she added, "In my youth I had a bad boy complex."

When she bit into the bread, he asked, "And now?"

"Gawd, I hope I'm over that phase. They all caused me a ton of trouble. I hope I've matured. Anyway, enough about me. Richard lived a relatively normal life. Work, home, liked to hike, fish. Does this help?" She paused and scrunched her mouth to one side. "I guess, the only extraordinary thing he did was his last act. The police investigation showed he was driving home from work. He was coming up to a bridge when he saw a woman standing next to a car with a flat tire. He pulled in behind her and put on his own flashers. She claimed he asked her if he could call a garage or towing service. She said she had no money, so he began to change the tire for her. After noticing she had a child in the back seat, told her it was safer to get him out and for both to stand in the grass away from the car and the busy road. As he was pulling the spare from the trunk, a car struck the back of his vehicle, crushing him between both and pushing the first vehicle over an embankment and into a river."

"Oh, my lord," gasped Axel.

"The driver of the second vehicle, a young girl, was driving fast and texting. Now two lives are ruined. My brother paid for his good deed with his life and the girl, arrested."

"I'm very sorry," Axel said, haunted by the story.

"But here is my take on it. Do I wish my brother had spent the money on a tow truck? Yes. Do I wish the girl had not been texting? Of course. But remember the child in the back seat of the disabled car? My brother, the gentleman helping a lady in distress, was also a hero because he saved the life of a child."

As they ate, she talked on a variety of topics. He listened attentively, catching himself leaning in when she spoke. Every so often, she reached across the table and touched his hand. He found it exciting and wondered why he had not noticed her when they were younger.

He felt a bit guilty about the feelings he was experiencing and tried to focus on the reason they were together. It did not work. The more she spoke, the more she captivated him.

On the way home after dinner, he contemplated what he would do at her doorstep. Should he shake hands? Ask for a second date? Was it too early for a goodnight kiss? Never comfortable around ladies, Axel was nervous. He really liked this woman. Smart and witty and although grief could explain her chatty disposition, he still found her fascinating. He would not wait long to find out.

Because she had taken a ride share to the restaurant, he insisted on giving her a ride home. Once at her hotel, she instructed him to park out front. Before he got out to open her door, showing he could be gentlemanly, she put a hand gently on his arm to stop him.

"Thanks for a nice evening," she said, hastily exiting the car on her own. Before closing the door, she stuck her head back in, "We should do this again sometime."

"Again?"

"I was thinking of staying. I'm a nurse and if I can get into Benton Memorial, it would clinch the deal."

If that was not an invitation to move forward, Axel didn't know what was. "I can put in a good word if you need it," he said, trying desperately to keep her talking. To keep her near.

"Not necessary. I can handle it. Goodnight." He watched in appreciation as she walked towards the hotel.

He drove home, whistling a tune; the name he could not remember. It did not matter. He had finished dinner with a beautiful and smart woman. *We should do this again sometime.* The phrase, magical like church bells at Christmastime. A wonderful feeling of being lighter than air carried him home and as he pulled into the driveway, he wondered when 'sometime' would arrive.

⌒つ

Dinner with Mr. Benton was not as Axel had imagined when the idea was first presented. The food was delicious, being waited on hand and foot was a treat, and the topics with Benton after dinner were interesting. Their discussions ranged from politics to world affairs and then to what was happening to the old man's town. Axel discussed the progress with Benton's legacy and the old man gave his advice.

Axel had grown fond of the stories Benton told of a younger and wilder version of the grandmother Axel had known. Even the sharp aroma of urine did not diminish the young man's enthusiasm. It was a small price to pay.

"Before I begin," started Benton. "I need to apologize. Age has a way of making one infirm of body, but also sometimes unaware of those around him. Would you be kind enough to move the waste basket closer to my chair?"

The master of the house had grown comfortable enough around Axel to use the handkerchief to dispose of the phlegm his weakening lungs discharged. Axel was grateful for the courtesy and complied with the request. Instead of dropping the soiled linen to the floor for Kennedy to pick up, Benton deposited it into the waste basket.

"Did she ever tell you about…" Was Benton's way of setting up a recollection and Axel lapped it up like a starving man with a full soup bowl. He marveled at Winnie's adventurous streak, a stark departure from the steady influence she had been to the boys.

"Did she tell you about how she once stole a car?" Benton waited for Axel to react.

"Winnie, a car thief? Impossible! Did she get in trouble?" The questions spilled from Axel's mouth like the ammunition from a machine gun.

"Well, she said she didn't steal, only borrowed it. She claimed she would return it with a full tank of gas. In fact, the police caught her at the gas station."

"What happened?" Axel said, enthralled.

"First, she made the officers wait until she'd topped off the tank. Then made them follow as she returned the borrowed vehicle to the rightful owner."

"Did she go to jail?"

"No, it was her good fortune the owner wouldn't press charges saying he'd lent it to her. The police had no other alternative than to let her go."

"Wait, why did she do it in the first place?"

"She wanted to learn how to drive."

"Wait, you're telling me Winnie stole a car even though she didn't know how to drive?"

"Precisely. The essence of your grandmother. When she wanted something, she pursued it with gusto!" The old man choked but recovered. Conversations of the past brought a gleam to his eyes which made him seem years younger. When he stopped, he fell back into the role of the aged benefactor. This transformation prompted Axel to continue with more questions so he could watch the years melt away from the old man. Even if it was brief.

"Do you know why the owner never pressed charges?" Axel asked, not finished with this story.

"I do." Harley Benton looked off into the distance as if back to the moment the police questioned the auto owner. "He was in love with her."

"*You* were the car owner!" Axel said, pleased he had figured it out.

"Guilty. I couldn't let the police take her away. Your grandmother was quite a woman."

The two men sat in silence, one remembering a time gone by with a wisp of a smile upon ancient lips. The other, nestled in a favorite chair, reveling in the stories told of a woman he thought he had known, but didn't.

Benton pressed a button on his chair and the butler arrived with another drink for Axel and more handkerchiefs for his employer. "From now on, a basket for my handkerchiefs, Kennedy. I am amazed *I* had to think of this. More sanitary, wouldn't you agree?" The sarcasm was not lost on Axel, who felt pity for the butler. Benton did not yell, but his words still had the intended effect. Supremacy.

"I pay you to do your job, not for me to do it for you. Otherwise, it would make you more redundant than you already are, wouldn't it?"

The butler, eyes front, head slightly tilted, bowed to his master, and replied, "As you wish, sir." He exited the room, his stoicism intact. Axel had seen glimpses of this behavior from the old man, but surmised if you had the money, you could treat anyone how you wished. He was glad Benton was more of a benefactor than a boss. There was no way he would tolerate being treated like a servant.

"There," said Benton, as though he had hung up on a telemarketer rather than berating an employee. "Where were we? Oh, yes, I was about to tell you another story about your grandmother."

Axel jumped in before the old man could continue. "Something has been bothering me. Although I appreciate the opportunity, the dinners and comradery as you help me see a clearer picture of my grandmother, why did you wait this long? Why weren't you around when we were younger?"

Axel watched as the old man's face darkened. It lasted a brief moment as Benton regained his composure, a telltale sign to Axel the old man was willing to share certain parts of his life but keep hidden those he deemed private.

"'Tis a long story for another day, young man. Let me say your grandmother and I didn't always see eye to eye."

Axel had the distinct impression *another day* would never arrive.

"Let's get back to the story, shall we?" Benton said, the smile weak. Behind it a tinge of annoyance. An expression one gives when trying to be nice while hiding their true feelings.

Axel listened more attentively. He had seen a different side of the old man, uncomfortable about how he had treated Kennedy, and the insincere expressions.

As Benton droned on, Axel decided to choose his words carefully, keeping an eye out for clues. The last thing he wanted was to upset the man… And the flow of his money. If Benton could turn on an employee of over thirty years, he wondered how long it would take for the old man to turn on someone he had just hired.

The smile returning, Mr. Benton began again. "Did she ever tell you about the time…"

"Look here, the prodigal son returns." Axel was sitting on his front porch with a glass of iced tea. It had been an unseasonably hot spring, and he welcomed the cool evening air. He also welcomed his brother, who came walking up the drive.

"It is I, Don Quixote, back from another adventure!" Leif said, punctuated by a sweeping hand gesture.

"Where were you this time?" Axel found it difficult to keep up with this brother.

"Here and there. I'm trying to get an idea for a new book, looking for inspiration." Leif sat in the rocking chair and pulled a cell phone out of his shirt pocket and began typing. Without looking up he asked, "Man, we had some memories here, eh?"

"We sure did," said Axel, then again softly, "We sure did." They sat in silence, Leif making notes and Axel looking out into the street at nothing in particular before asking, "Do you want sweet tea?"

"Isn't there anything stronger in the house?"

Axel remembered the whiskey bottle in the kitchen he and Winnie had shared. He had not touched it since that night. "Nope," he lied. He made a mental note to hide it somewhere no one would find it. "Only tea."

"Damn. Nah, I'm good," Leif said with a wave of his hand. "Look, I'm going to be in town a few weeks. Gotta do an outline on the new book. I was wondering if I could crash here."

Axel let the silence linger a little too long. He sighed in resignation, knowing full well he couldn't make his own brother sleep on the street, "Sure, no problem. You can take your old room. I'm now using Winnie's."

"Oh, you get the big room, eh?" Leif complained.

Irritated, Axel reminded him. "It's my house."

"Yeah, I see. Or I see how I got screwed."

"Not again, please. If you don't like my hospitality, you can always stay in a hotel," Axel stated, a swift change of mind with the firm conviction if Leif didn't like his sleeping arrangements, he was free to find his own lodgings, guilt free.

Leif slipped into silence, his phone to his lip as if pondering a story arc to a next novel. "Looks like a storm coming."

"How can you tell?" Axel did not see meteorology as one of his brother's strengths.

"Look at the leaves on the trees. With an impending storm, the leaves turn over."

Sure enough, the leaves on the trees showed their pale green backs. Axel wondered why every time Leif made an appearance, a storm followed. Sunny day or not.

"All right," Leif said, breaking his leaf gazing. "I guess my room will be fine as long as you don't bother me too much while I'm working."

"I may need your help to find worthy causes for donations."

"Really? C'mon." Axel noticed the discomfort on Leif's face. His brother was not one who hobnobbed with the poor or less privileged. Unless there was alcohol or a financial advantage involved.

"Yes, really. It'll do you good. A small price to pay instead of room and board."

"All right," Leif said, tapping the arm of the rocker. "At least you're branching out. I like it." There was no hint of malice or sarcasm, which caught Axel off guard.

"What do you mean by that?" Axel remained skeptical having been burnt too many times by his brother to do otherwise.

"Little brother, you haven't exhibited any wanderlust. The only two places you frequent are your church and work. I'm glad to see you widening your horizons, is all."

"Not true," Axel claimed, embarrassed that it was. "I do plenty of things outside work and the church."

"Name one," challenged Leif, unwilling to let go.

"I visit the sick and infirm," Axel said, puffing out his chest.

"With your church group."

A look of concern crossed Axel's face. "I help people with their taxes at tax time!" He knew this was a stretch, as did Leif.

"Which is an extension of your career."

Axel had yet to tell his brother about his new career. Leif shifted gears. "Tell me, when was the last time you took a vacation?" When Axel stumbled to come up with an answer, Leif drove his point home. "See? You need to branch out, do something out of your comfort zone. Or this will be your epitaph: 'He lived an uninspiring life.' On your tombstone? He was inconspicuous, a ghost in life *and* death."

"Stop it," Axel barked.

Leif continued, "Don't you want to see the rest of the world? Make a bucket list? Find out what frightens you?" Then he paused before throwing out the last and most damaging line. "Ask yourself, what the hell defines you?"

"Please stop." The question hung around him like cigar smoke. The only way to dissipate was to answer it. "The *church* defines me."

"Well, it doesn't define me," Leif slapped back, clapping the arm of the rocker in defiance.

Axel argued back, "It most certainly does! You stopped going to church, believe in nothing but yourself, and are a proclaimed atheist. If that definition doesn't derive from your experience in the church, nothing does."

"And you put your faith in spirits and miracles, like a lemming following those in front as they jump off the cliff to certain death."

"You've been angry ever since our dismissal as altar boys. Let it go."

"You have no idea what real anger is!" Leif leaned forward, breathing heavily.

Where did that come from? Axel thought as he watched with concern as Leif tried to compose himself.

"What I meant to say was," Leif said slowly and through clenched teeth, "you point your finger at the drowning guy but let the lifeguard do the work to save him. At least I'm doing something with my life and not sitting in the cheap seats."

"What the hell are you talking about?!?" Spittle flew from Axel's lips.

Leif leaned in close enough for Axel to smell the alcohol on his brother's breath, "You're the pointer, I'm the lifeguard."

Leif looked down at his phone and typed while he spoke, "I'm a doer, you're a watcher. In the end we'll both be dust but you keep believing in your spirit in the sky. I'll enjoy my life here on earth while there is still time. Everybody dies, but not…" Axel cut him off as he rolled his eyes.

"I know, I know. Not me, and not today. But the day will come, and if I'm hoarding cash, you should start hoarding something else before it's too late."

"As in?" Leif leaned in.

"Prayers for your soul."

Leif turned his gaze back to the street before uttering, "If the lies you tell yourself make you feel better, so be it."

"What? I don't tell myself lies."

"Of course, you do," said his brother matter-of-factly. "We all do. But those lies hold you back from your true purpose. Break through the lies and you'll find it. I guarantee it."

They sat in silence once more. Axel fidgeted with the condensation on his glass while Leif typed notes in his cell. He looked up and broke the impasse, "Look, all I'm saying is to go out and have a little fun. You deserve it. Life is way too short to live it uninspired."

"OK, Tony Robbins, enough of the rah, rah. My life is good, and it suits me. Quit trying to lecture me on how I should live it."

"Who else but the author of a self-help book. God helps those who help themselves, according to your good book." Now Leif was mocking him.

"Would you stop with the quotes? For an atheist, you're full of religious quips. Besides, God *is* helping me. He helps me every day."

"Yeah? In what ways does God help you?"

Axel chewed on the inside of his lip as he contemplated on how to answer the question. "He gave us rules to follow. I follow them; thus, he helps me make the right decisions according to his laws." *Most of them, anyway.*

"You're telling me God intercedes on your behalf?"

"Yes, he does." Axel said.

"And do you accept the concept of free will?"

Axel showed confidence in his answer. "Certainly. Another gift he gave us."

Leif sprung the trap, "You are ridiculous. You can't have it both ways. Either God guides us, ergo, no free will or he doesn't *because* of our freedom to choose. Which is it?"

Axel's confidence wilted as he pondered the conundrum. Leif bolstered his argument, to drive his point home. "There are people who possess the unnerving capacity to convince themselves of anything to suit their own needs. They take the responsibility out of their lives by placing it under the control of an almighty and picky God. Take an earthquake, for example. It kills one thousand people and after a few days they find a baby alive. Suddenly, it's a miracle. If God appeared and warned the one thousand soon to be dead citizens to move to another place a week prior, now *that* would be a miracle."

Axel snapped at his brother, "Smart aleck comparisons don't make you right. Instead of questions, maybe you should come back to the faith and get back to practicing your religion again."

"Brother," Leif stated, slowing his speech. "Self-help is the *new* religion. I've realized if you want something out of life, imagine it and then take action to get it. You can't rely on anyone else, even God, because in my experience, he's not listening."

Axel countered using his brother's own words against him, "I'm sorry for you then. If spending eternity in Hell makes *you* happy, then so be it."

"At least I'm not a hypocrite. My book sales are rising, seminars are in the works. Next comes the audiobook and even a podcast. Then I follow it all up with another book and the wheel continues to roll. All of which I got through hard work and no help from God. Everyone is looking for something. I plan on delivering."

Leif began writing again while Axel was left to his own thoughts. Without looking up, Leif asked, "Do you at least have a girlfriend?"

Axel turned to his brother. "Where is the hotel you're staying?" They both chuckled, breaking the tension, giving Axel a chance to ponder aloud a question nagging him since Leif returned, "Tell me, why do we argue so much?"

Leif put a hand to his chin, reflecting on the question, "Maybe it's because we're opposites. Sort of like Cain and Abel."

"Good analogy. You realize Cain kills Abel?"

"Damn, you've found out my plan to get Winnie's house and the rest of the estate," Leif said as he rubbed his hands together in mock greed.

Axel shook his head and responded, "You, my brother, are incorrigible."

Leif leapt out of his chair and bounded down the porch steps. "I am. But right now, I'm going to grab my bag. Unless you can summon God to bring it up for me?" He walked a few steps up the drive before turning and asking, "What's for dinner?"

"Crow," Axel responded with a smirk. "This debate is far from over, as you'll be eating a lot of it tonight!"

"Good," replied his older brother, waving his cell phone in the air. "Because I need more of this material for the book!"

Axel watched his brother walk towards his car. Great, just what he needed, an evening full of arguments, debate, and fodder for Leif's publisher. One particular question nagged at him as he rocked back and forth.

What lies do I tell myself?

CHAPTER

- 7 -

"Jules," Axel said. "What are you saying?" He started calling her Jules, a nickname she abhorred. Since they met, he had been the only one who got away with it. Others tried, but only once. After the searing stare, no one tried it a second time.

"Nobody calls me that," she said. Just a statement. No glare, no anger.

"It's a cute version. Although, I didn't mean to offend."

She put two fingers to her lips to hide the thrill at the word 'cute.' Looking at her feet whispered, "But you can."

He dismissed the permission, referring back to his original question. "Again, what are you saying?"

Axel had stopped into her office. A sparse room with a desk housing a phone, small lamp, and a laptop. No pictures were present, and one file cabinet stood out of place against the inside wall. A window facing the manicured lawn and large maples made for a calming view. Today, the view failed her.

"Don't you find it unsettling there has been a spate of deaths lately?" she asked. "I've been here for a few years now and never seen this many in such a short period."

"I hadn't noticed. How many?"

She did not need to look at the list on the desk, acutely aware of those who had exited. "Two in the last week. Nine over the last month. C'mon, you're a numbers guy. Doesn't that sound unrealistic to you?"

"Jules, they're old people. Old people die. When we're old, we'll die too."

Jules liked this man. He was matter of fact. Dependable. *Humble.* She told herself it was a little crush. "It seems there's been a lot of these old folks dying." She paused before continuing, "I love most of my job. This part? Not so much. You never get used to it. Now I have to recruit to fill the empty rooms. It's so…" She struggled until she found the right word, "Unfeeling."

"You shouldn't worry, I'm sure this is nothing."

Jules pursed her lips to one side. "Worry is what spurs people to act."

"They say ninety percent of what you worry about never happens," Axel countered.

"Yeah, but it's the ten percent I'm concerned about. And it seems as though nine dead residents might agree with me." She corrected herself, "If they could."

"Alright, I'll give you that point. What were the causes of death?" Axel asked, the curiosity sneaking out.

"Not sure. We don't discuss the exits. It's an unwritten rule: the employees don't talk about the deceased. One minute the person is a resident and the next minute, poof, they're not. The only ones who discuss it are the residents."

"To ponder their own mortality, I guess."

"Yeah, but not good for business. It's why we wait awhile before scheduling any visits from potential residents. Gives the current one's time to adjust."

"And when was the last time you showed the place to a new resident?"

Julia recognized he was fishing. "I've spoken to prospects but haven't brought anyone in lately. With one dropping after another, it hasn't been easy. I have a few scheduled for early next week. Got a quota to hit. Hope we don't have any more for a while." A thought occurred to her, "Why, Mr. numbers guy, are you seeing a pattern?"

"Maybe. Let me ask you a question in two parts. One: Has this ever happened before? And Two: Why haven't you spoken to the coroner to see how each died? Old age can find many ways to kill, but if they are all similar, then I take it you are suggesting something more sinister…"

"Wait," she said, waving a hand in the air. "I'm sorry you have to listen to these ramblings. This is ridiculous. To consider a few deaths in a nursing home suspicious would mean someone was intentionally murdering old people. It's called the 'Passing Lane' for a reason. Please forget I said anything at all."

"Hey, no worries, it's forgotten. I have to stop in to see Winnie first, then give a eulogy later today. I'll see you around?" Axel stood up to leave and headed for the door.

"Sure," she said, waiting for another invitation to go out. It never came as he closed the door behind him. Disappointed, she went back to her work. Her phone rang. It was Harriet.

"Julia, we've had another Exit. Mr. Strong passed. How are your interviews coming along?"

"What?" Jules said a little too loudly. "He was doing so well. What happened?"

"The doctor said it was a condition known as 'Terminal Lucidity.'"

"I've heard of that. It's when a patient comes out of a coma. The lucid part." Julia was unfamiliar with the knowledge those patients do not survive long after they reawaken.

"This was the terminal phase," the administrator said without emotion. "Looks like you have to step up the new resident search."

Julia sighed as she hung up the phone, the weight of this latest exit heavy as a wool winter coat. *Mr. Strong. Axel will be very upset*, she thought. "Axel," she whispered as she ran to the door to look down the long hallway. It was empty.

She went back to her desk and picked up another application, about to make the call when she cradled the phone back into its place. "Another one makes ten," she said to the phone. Three in the past week, but this one had a rational answer. The others? Still heaped in suspicion. *Ten percent of worry spurs one to action. But what can I do?*

Detectives are paid to believe there is a crime around every corner. But a murderer in her nursing home? She pushed the idea away, focusing on the work of replacing dead residents with those very much alive. At least for the time being.

Hector walked into the changing room, throwing his keys into the air like a juggler with only one ball. Opening his locker, the stench hit him in the face as though someone slapped him, causing him to drop the key ring with a clatter. He wiped his stinging eyes and covered his mouth. Disbelief took over. Hanging from one of the hooks, its fur peeled back from its skin exposing rotted flesh, was a dead rat.

Hector turned away and almost retched but held his throat, forcing the bile to stay put. He kept a hand to his mouth, wondering who would place the rodent in his locker. The answer was clear. There was only one person sick enough to do this. Benny Palz. Hector's anger rose, but he pushed it back like the bile. Unwilling to risk causing a scene for fear of exposing his parents, he calmed himself. To make it seem all was normal. Maybe if he showed the ass hat he had no effect, Benny would give up.

Hector trotted to the bathroom and grabbed a handful of paper towels to extricate the vermin. He placed it on the floor before putting on his orderly scrubs. He then picked up the rat carefully, but not quite enough. The animal slipped out of the brown paper and began to fall. He grabbed the vermin with his bare hands, squeezing the bloated belly. A deep purple liquid ran on either side of his hands, one rivulet cascading across his right arm like the spidery vein on one of his elderly charges. He stuck his foot out to catch the offensive globs before they touched the floor, causing Hector's breakfast to attempt another escape.

Regaining control of himself, he surmised it better to get germs on his hands and not in the changing room. Placing the rat in the paper towels again, he ran through the employee entrance, bolted through the door, and leapt from the steps before tossing the rat into the dumpster.

He turned to go back inside, holding his soiled hands at arm's length until he could scrub them thoroughly. The hope to rid him of any diseases the rat may have carried. No amount of hygiene would erase the memory of what had taken place.

As he stepped back into the changing area, Benny Palz appeared, blocking the entrance. "Whatcha doin,' Rat Boy? Hanging with you rat friends?" The sneer on his face made Hector want to throttle the man. Instead, he decided on a different course of action. He gave Benny his biggest grin and said, "Just taking out the trash, I can help you into the dumpster if you want?"

Benny was not amused. "Why you little rat bastard, I ought to kick your ass right now!" He took a step to show Hector the threat was real. Hector did not move, but held his grin, prompting a puzzled look from Benny. Palz, like all bullies, did not like it when their victims did not back down.

Hector was not afraid of Benny kicking anything. Benny was in no position to talk to his supervisors. Those discussions would lead to questions about how a certain rat got into Hector's locker in the first place. Cleanliness was of great importance in the FALM, and news of a dead rat intentionally introduced would be cause for dismissal. No, Benny would do nothing. *This* time.

Hector decided it was safe if he did. He reached out and grabbed both of Benny's hands and began rubbing his wet fingers all over the bully's. "No!" Benny screamed, realizing the big man had handled a dead, putrid, smelly, disease ridden-rodent. "Stop it!!"

"We're rat brothers now," Hector whispered as he rubbed the back of one foul hand onto the bully's while holding onto the other allowing for no escape. When satisfied they both shared enough rat DNA, he released the horror-stricken Benny, who rushed into the changing room looking for a sink.

But Hector was wrong about standing up to this bully. Following Benny, he found the little man at a sink furiously scrubbing his hands, the soap foaming around his hands like the mouth of a rabid dog.

"You think this is the end, don't you?" Palz said into the mirror as Hector turned on the faucet of the sink next to his tormentor to wash his own hands. He smirked at the angry mirror image, which seemed to have a calming effect on Palz, not what Hector had expected.

"It's not, you know," Palz went on, his voice lowered but with a hint of malice. Hector noticed the corners of the man's mouth upturn. "No, it's only the beginning. Everyone has a secret, don't they? An Achilles Heel." Palz eyed Hector in the mirror, but Hector made a crucial error in front of the bully. He flinched.

"There. Right there, you just told me you have one too. An affair with a married woman, perhaps? An arrest record?" Sweat formed on Hector's forehead as he looked for the towel dispenser. He averted his eyes from the mirror.

"No, your secret is more personal, isn't it, Rat Boy? I'm good at finding these things out." Palz whipped his wet hands in the air, the moisture flying off into the sink basin and against the mirror, leaving droplets to run down and leave streaks. Hector turned and headed towards the door.

"And when I do, and I will," Palz threatened, "Watch out, Rat Boy."

What have I done? Hector thought, realizing he had overplayed his hand. Benny would not go to his supervisors about this incident, but if he dug deep enough, he'd find out Hector's secret. Bending over, he picked up his keys off the floor and stuffed them in his pocket.

Slamming his locker door, he headed towards the door to begin his rounds. Before Hector exited, he heard the evil cackle from his bully and a malevolent warning behind him ringing in his ears. "Watch out!"

⌇

"Are you ready?" asked Father Tom, smoothing out the wrinkles in his white and gold vestments. He prepared for mass in the sacristy, a small room right off the altar. It housed a table with two closets on either side. Father Tom's Bible, worn from years of use, sat on a small podium by the altar door.

"As ready as I'll ever be," replied Axel. It had taken all three days of writing and polishing to finish Richard's eulogy.

"You'll be fine. Have you practiced?"

"Only for the past two days," said Axel, unsure if he had practiced enough.

"Good. I find the absence of anxiety is directly proportional to the presence of practice." A concept Father Tom must have known well, having delivered mass, homilies, and eulogies in this parish for the last ten years. "Come then, we have a funeral to perform."

The two men walked onto the altar, genuflected together, and then proceeded down the aisle to the rear of the church. Axel noted the sparse crowd. Those who may have known Richard were either deceased or lived elsewhere, too far to return in time for the service. Most were the elderly parishioners with nothing more to do than show respect to the fallen.

They reached the back of the church as the funeral employees wheeled the casket on a gurney up the wheelchair ramp. Veronica followed the men as they moved the casket into the aisle. She gave a small nod to Axel before he and the priest stepped behind her. The organist began signaling their procession. Ambling slowly, they reached the altar where the funeral employees moved the casket into place perpendicular to the pews. Veronica sat in the front row, Father Tom behind the altar, and Axel sitting next to the podium.

Wringing his sweaty hands with an occasional rub against his slacks to dry them, Axel's thoughts drove his anxiety, a slight buzzing in his ears, and the constant pounding of his heart highlighted his fear. *Why am I this nervous?* He tried visualizing himself doing a masterful job, going over the introduction again and even the suggestion of seeing the congregation in their underwear. Axel pushed the image away, as most of the parishioner's present were all over seventy years of age.

"Ahem," the priest said, breaking Axel out of his self-imposed spell. Axel stepped up to the podium, pulling the three by five cards from his jacket pocket. As he cleared his throat, he remembered a trick a teacher had offered when he had to give a speech in school. *Look for someone who smiles at you. Then at least you'll have one friend.*

He scanned the church, some old faces recognizable, others not, all meeting him with solemn expressions. His gaze moved to the front pew where he stopped at Veronica. She gave him a weak smile, but it proved enough.

"If you visit any cemetery, you'll see headstones for the deceased. They all have one thing in common. Their date of birth and the date of death etched into the stone separated by a hyphen. This puzzles me because when a child is born, it has yet to accomplish anything. When a person dies, they can accomplish no longer. My conclusion is, on the headstone, it's not the date which truly matters... but the hyphen. The timeline in between birth and death.

Richard's was the life of bookends; the beginning of his hyphen began with promise where he excelled in school and a comfortable life in his chosen profession. The hope of marriage and family, all very normal.

An exciting life was not in the cards for Richard. Like myself, the middle of his short hyphen, uneventful. And while most of his hyphen was unremarkable. The ending? It was spectacular.

Despite his outcome, Richard found himself at the right place and the right time... for someone else. He chose to be a gentleman, assisting a lady with car trouble. But he had the foresight to make sure she and her child inside the car were moved to safety. By this act, he did not just lose his life, he also saved one. Or, as his sister put it, a gentleman, and a hero to the end.

An uneventful hyphen with a spectacular ending. We should all be so blessed.

As Axel finished, he looked back at Veronica, smiling through her tears. He left the podium and sat next to her, taking her hand in his. As Father Tom proceeded with the mass for the dead, Axel leaned over to whisper, "Nice enough for you?"

"No," she said, wiping her tears with a handkerchief. "It wasn't nice, it was perfect."

On the way out of the church, a crowd of the elderly awaited him. They all congratulated Axel on a job well done. Father Tom bent to whisper in his ear. "Looks like you have a permanent job."

Axel was not sure if he was joking or not.

The home was a modest three-bedroom ranch. It sported a nice-sized lawn with a forest on one side and a cornfield on the other. Living in the countryside proved too secluded for some, but it provided the freedom a rural existence offered.

No noisy or nosy neighbors. Peace and tranquility. An abundance of wildlife. Although only a short distance from the Benton Falls town line, it felt miles away.

The Hastener rocked on the porch as a flash of red whizzed by the railing. A cardinal landed on the branch of a large oak tree. The bird's bright red body, with black eyes and mask, reminded one of a bandit, scoping out his next unsuspecting victim from his perch. Some old wives' tale spoke of a cardinal sighting after someone's passing as a sign the soul of the deceased had entered the bird and made itself known to the bereaved. A sign they were fine in the next life.

Mr. Strong, perhaps? The old man was next on the list. Wasn't Terminal Lucidity supposed to end in Termination? If so, why wait? Evidently, God had other plans. A new method unnecessary as the old man succumbed to his condition naturally. The Hastener could not help feeling a bit disappointed.

The bird flapped its wings, then settled on the branch. It stared at the rocker who tried but failed to break the bird's gaze. A laugh arose at this silly game.

Cardinals were the inspiration for the color scheme and name of the upper echelon of the church; the bishops who chose popes. A tinge of satisfaction formed on the reflection of the black eye the church had given itself during the sex abuse scandal. This thought faded quickly away by guilt. *Those in glass houses.*

Not prone to wives' tales or other superstitions, a call went out to the bird anyway. "Whoever you are, thanks for letting me know you're OK."

A vehicle approached from the direction of town, the hole in the muffler announcing its approach long before the sight of a front bumper would. A pickup truck barreled past the house at a high rate of speed, causing three events to occur. The first was a shout by the homeowner for the driver to slow down. There was no need to speed by the house, the driver's disregard of the law an annoyance.

The second occurred when the young man driving the vehicle stuck his middle finger out the driver's window. The first two were not entirely out of character. A homeowner protecting their turf, while young men with power behind the wheel, flaunting theirs. The third incident happened after the young man passed by. A squirrel darted into the road, rolling under the back tires of the vehicle before exiting the rear like a gray tumbleweed rolling across the mesa. The driver sped on, leaving the crushed animal twitching on the pavement.

Jumping off the porch, the homeowner sprinted to the road. Careful to look both ways before stepping onto the asphalt. An interesting thought occurred. Getting hit and killed at this moment would prompt both human and animal to enter the gates of heaven together. A chuckle rose at the irony, recalling a conversation on this topic with father so long ago.

"No, animals don't go to heaven," he'd scolded, "When they die, there is nothing. They're dead."

Mother had a different opinion, "It seems the church has waffled on this subject. A few Popes have said, no, animals do not go to heaven, but I'm not sure. Between you and me, pets are so lovable, faithful and give companionship to their owners, how could God *not* want them in his kingdom?"

Mother was wise and comforting with her analysis, it made more sense. This caused the adoption of the idea, her logic sound.

The poor squirrel struggled. The back legs and tail lay flat and motionless against the road. Guts leaked from its abdomen like water from a slit garden hose. The eyes darted in terror; ears twitching, paws scratching at the pavement. A futile attempt at mobility.

The homeowner realized the squirrel was destined to die soon, even if the animal was not convinced. Both parents, each with differing views on animal afterlife, did agree on one thing: never let animals suffer. True mercy was a gift to the dying as well as the Hastener. The merciful should not carry their actions as a burden, but as a badge of honor.

Blessed are the Merciful, for they shall be shown mercy.

"Say hello to my mother when you get to heaven, little one," was whispered to the squirrel who was now only making short paw movements, its eyes looking off into the distance, blackness overcoming the shine.

The homeowner said a brief prayer before putting a foot over the squirrel's head and pressing hard enough to crush its skull. "Tell her I love her."

The Hastener walked back to the porch, wiping the bottom of the shoe on the grass. At the first step, a glance towards the tree to see if the cardinal was still there. It was.

The homeowner did not believe in the wives' tale but found it comforting to see the red bird perched on the branch, anyway. "Love you, whoever you are." Then taking the steps one by one until reaching the front door. Once inside, the homeowner turned executioner used two fingers to move a window shade out of curiosity to look back at the tree.

The bird was still there. As was its black-eyed stare.

CHAPTER
– 8 –

As the body count and Jules' suspicions grew, so did the opportunities for Axel to eulogize the dead. Father Tom's prophecy about a "permanent job" had come true. Parishioners called upon Axel to deliver fond memories of the deceased. To give them each a last word with the understanding funerals were a way for the living to begin the grieving process. Axel was found to be quite competent, garnering the reputation as an excellent storyteller. Everyone in the parish agreed he was perfect for the task, especially Father Tom, who welcomed having Axel lighten his own workload. And for the first time in his life, Axel built confidence, as people would wave hello while out on a daily walk or call him to ask a favor. His reputation grew like the flowers in a well-tended garden. It blossomed.

Those who Axel afforded the last word were not so lucky.

With the help of the internet, the Hastener was able to devise creative methods to use on the residents in the Passing Lane. Find an issue on their chart and apply a readily available product to move the resident along.

For Mrs. Hunter, who suffered from Hyperkalemia, the Hastener employed an unhealthy addition of Potassium into her drinking water. That did the trick.

Mr. Brown, after the administration of a healthy overdose of the old man's Digitalis, complained all the way to a fatal heart attack.

Mr. Strong needed no such creativity, succumbing to Terminal Lucidity.

Axel, unaware of the Hastener's methods and without any search engines, proved equally creative in crafting the deceased's final words.

For Mrs. Hunter's eulogy, Axel used a common theme from the bible. "A meek woman, always thinking of others first, especially her husband, whom she has now rejoined. And as the good book says, she will be one of those who shall inherit the earth. A much-deserved prize for a life well lived."

Due to Mr. Brown's grumpy attitude, Axel found his last words difficult to construct. What does one say about constant complainers? He wondered if God had allowed the old man to linger to a ripe old age because He had little patience for those types? Axel settled on the virtues of speaking one's mind, of truth setting him free. He surmised what Mr. Brown's first comments would be to Saint Peter at the gates of heaven, prompting a laugh from the parishioners familiar with the old man's disposition.

The next resident death pained Axel greatly. Struggling with Mr. Strong's passing, Axel eulogized him by utilizing the last name. "Strong. An appropriate name, for although his body weakened, he was strong of heart, strong of faith and most of all, strong in his commitment to his fellow man. God needs strong souls in heaven and he has received another." The deceased's family were comforted and thankful for Axel's stirring tribute.

The circle of life and death proceeded without interruption. Old people die, and Axel proved up to the task to make sure they all got a final word with the exception of one.

The Hastener had another creative task ahead, but under different circumstances. This hastening would need to be special. No last words required.

The lobby of the FALM was quiet as all the residents were in the dining room having lunch. Julia took this time to meet with Harriet Gordon, the administrator of the home. She was competent, patient, and had a head for profit generation. All attributes for running a successful business.

Julia understood her own best attribute was of a steadfast seaman on board and no boat rocking. Attributes she found unappealing and against her better nature.

"Harriet, do you have a minute?" asked the younger woman.

"Barely. With all these exits, I have much to do. What's up?"

"It's why I wanted to talk to you. Something tells me these deaths aren't random. First Mr. Franz, then Irena, Mrs. Hunter, then Mr. Brown, and finally Mr. Strong. Doesn't it occur to you this trend is unusual?"

Harriet sighed weakly and her shoulders slumped. "Dear," she said, brushing an errant lock of hair away from her forehead. "We run a nursing home. Call it assisted living, call it a retirement home, but when it comes down to the bare truth, it's a nursing home. In such places, people, *old* people, die. It's the circle of life thing. All we can do is comfort those residents with us and bring in new ones. Circle of life, see?"

Julia did, but also saw the circle getting unnaturally larger on her watch. "Yes, this I get. But you can't argue with the numbers. We haven't had a string like this since I've been here. Have you ever seen this many deaths in such a short period?"

"To my recollection, we had a virus rip through here ten years ago. But that was the only time. Wait, what are you suggesting?" Harriet's errant lock of hair was back. She ignored it; a stern expression aimed at Julia. "Well? I'm waiting."

Julia bit her lower lip and thought hard on how to explain this. "It's more of a gut feeling something is amiss. Not quite right." Julia knew her gut was telling her one thing, but lack of evidence was another.

"Do you trust your gut?" came the administrator's next question, It came out hard like a slap in the face. "Is it telling you foul play is going on in our little neighborhood? Or is this your imagination talking?"

Julia, under pressure, tried to explain but could not string the right sentences together. "It's just... I mean to say, when I spoke with Axel, I..."

"You spoke to whom? Are you telling me you have spoken to an outsider about a conspiracy theory your gut is telling you? Are you out of your mind? This is an assisted living facility and your job depends on bringing in new residents once others depart. How would it look if we went about spreading rumors of foul play? How would the marketing slogan go?" Harriet's voice changed from angry to sarcastic as she spelled it out, "Come and enjoy your golden years with old friends but don't make new ones because you won't be here long. We have a pool, outdoor space, and our very own resident euthanizer on staff."

Jules took a breath while marshalling the courage to ask the next question. "What about the security cameras I asked for?" She had put in a requisition for security cameras after Mr. Long had been found downtown in the least expected place for an elderly man. A strip joint.

"Denied," said Harriet, the hair now a distraction like a mosquito you could not quite swat away. "People come here to be independent as long as they can. They don't want Big Brother looking over their shoulder."

"Or the expense of watching over the safety of our residents," Jules blurted out, her face turning a crimson in frustration.

"Now you listen here, missy." With voice lowered, Harriet leaned across the table. "You will cease and desist from any talk of conspiracies, murder or anything else having to do with harming our residents, understand?"

Julia held her gaze with the boss before lowering her head at the admonishment. A forced, "Yes, Ma'am," escaped through her teeth.

"Good," said the administrator, sitting back in her chair and folding her arms. "Now get back to work and no more 'gut feelings.' And never speak to outsiders of our internal affairs. Am I clear?"

Julia stood up, her face still crimson, her gut exposed. "Crystal," she said before heading toward the door.

At lunch, the table was surrounded with spirited conversation. Or her spirited conversation. Veronica, excited about her new job at the hospital, never took a breath. Axel, content on eating and listening. *She's going to stay!*

"I've been too busy at the hospital. I never expected it to be this hectic. Emergency room duty is tough. Don't even get me started on the weird things I've seen."

Axel, not accustomed to the attention of pretty girls, fidgeted uncomfortably, his heartbeat hammering in his chest. The way the sweat dampened his shirt, sticking to his skin, made him self-conscious. Even trying to match the woman's conversation caused feelings of inadequacy. But despite all the uncomfortableness, he was in heaven.

"Tell me about your visits to the home and hospital," she asked, taking a bite of her salad.

Other than the Visiting Angels, Axel told her as little as possible because he did not like to talk about himself. He enjoyed listening to her speak, loving the sound of her voice. She commented easily on different topics, as if a humble expert on them all. No bragging, just the facts, ma'am.

"I am impressed with the work the Angels are doing," she said. "I'm very proud of you."

Axel blushed. The only time he wanted to be the center of attention was when delivering his eulogies. It was not about ego. Allowing the deceased to have a last word in this world was a noble deed. He was merely the conduit.

She talked all through the salad phase, telling him about her ideas for the hospital. When their entrees arrived, she mentioned looking for a new house. The apartment she had found did not suit her.

"I could help in your search," he said. Anything to be near her.

"Oh, I can handle the search myself. I don't want to be a bother." She put him off with a wave of the hand he did not find dismissive. It signaled he could offer help from his experience in other areas.

"I've finished my projects at Winn... My house. I could show you what pitfalls to avoid. What do you say?"

Veronica toyed with her chicken. "I guess it would be all right. Don't want to monopolize your time, seeing how busy you are."

Monopolize. Please monopolize, he thought, as he envisioned a future of the two of them finding the right house. Something cozy. A house with all its problems solved, one turned into a home. Like his.

"This was delightful, but I need to be leaving. Got lots to do!" she said, breaking his daydream. She raised a hand to the waiter for the check. When placed on the table, she grabbed it first. "On me this time."

He fought to be valiant, but not too aggressively, not wanting to offend her. "I'll get it the next time. Like for dinner?" This was calculated. *Next time. Dinner.*

"Hmm?" she said, as she signed the receipt. "Oh, yeah, next time. Sure."

Focusing on the term 'next time,' a familiar voice at the side of their table spooked Axel.

"Hmm. What have we here? Finishing a little lunch and I wasn't invited?" Leif said, placing both hands on the table and wearing a smirk on his face. "And who is this lovely creature?" he added, extending his hand to Veronica, who took it a little too quickly for Axel's liking.

"Veronica, this is my brother, Leif."

"Pleased to meet you, Leif. Axel and my brother were friends."

Leif held on to Veronica's hand, "I'm very sorry for your loss. Such a tragedy." Then brightening quipped, "But I heard little brother here did a bang-up job at his service." Axel winced at the reference. "I would have come, but I had a meeting with my publisher." Leif paused and Axel saw it was for effect, so he jumped in.

"My brother wrote a book, and it consumes his every waking moment."

"Wow, how wonderful," exclaimed Veronica, missing Axel's sarcasm. "Not sure I could do something like that."

"It was a lot of hard work, and now they want a follow up."

Axel broke the conversation. "We were just leaving." He got up, extending his own hand to Veronica. She slipped her fingers out of Leif's hand slowly and took Axel's.

"It was a pleasure meeting you," she cooed.

"Likewise," Leif claimed as Axel hurried Veronica out the door and into the car for the drive back to the hospital. When he dropped her off, she turned down his offer to drive her home after her shift.

"I'd rather walk tonight, if you don't mind," she said. "The evening air will do me good. Maybe next time."

Disappointed his brother interrupted their date, but exhilarated by their time alone together, Axel drove to the FALM to visit his grandmother with a solitary thought on his mind as sweet as the juice from a Georgia peach. *Next time.*

"Come in, son! Look who dropped by for a visit." Winnie beamed as she patted Jules on the knee. "My favorite Marketing Director." Jules blushed as she ran the toe of her shoe across the floor.

"Hey," Axel said, still pondering lunch.

"Julia and I were having a nice little chat." Winnie got up and moved to another chair forcing Axel to sit next to Jules. "But I'm sure there are other things to discuss, right?"

"Yes," said Jules. "I need your help. Could I pick your brain on something?"

Winnie's eyebrows raised. "Sure, pick away."

"I could use your detective prowess," she began.

"Oh, no you don't," Axel interrupted. Turning to Winnie, he explained, "She has a wild theory someone may be killing the residents here."

"Axel!" yelled Jules. "I was only going to ask her to keep an eye out for anything suspicious!"

"A murder? Oh, do tell." The old woman said, clasping her hands together as she leaned forward. "I love a good mystery."

"What are you worried about? If anything, the bad guys are the ones who should be concerned. There's a lot of fight in this one." Axel countered, wagging a finger at his grandmother.

Jules reluctantly described the rash of recent deaths and without a good explanation, needed to either learn the truth or live with the suspicions.

"OK, question one, what makes you suspicious at all?" Winnie asked.

"My gut tells me there's something wrong. I can't quite put my finger on it, but we've never had this many deaths so close together. It's... unnatural."

"Powerful stuff, women's intuition," Winnie said as she nodded in deference. "Have you spoken to the coroner?"

"That's what I asked her." Axel interjected.

"Shush you," Winnie scolded. Then to Jules, "Go ahead, dear."

"I can't, my boss told me to back off. Said it wasn't good for business to be spreading rumors or unproven theories."

Axel jumped in again, "Without proof, all you have is conjecture."

Winnie turned and said nothing. She didn't have to. Her glare did the speaking for her. Axel puckered his lips in a "OK, I'll shut up now" expression.

"Dear," the old woman began, "Don't discount woman's intuition."

"What about a man's intuition?" Axel interjected.

"Like Santa and the Easter bunny, it doesn't exist." Winnie snapped at him impatiently. Turning back to Jules she asked, "Tell me what your intuition is telling you."

"It's telling me people are dying, but it's not telling me how or why."

"They're old and old people die," said Axel. Winnie gave him the withering stare again, causing him to close his lips. Tighter this time.

"Motive?" Asked Winnie, getting into the game. "Are there any feuds going on I should know about? A good feud equals motive!"

Jules bit her lip, "Not that I know of. And as far as a motive, I don't have an answer. Like I said, it's a gut feel."

Axel opened his mouth but shut it again as Winnie glared once more before speaking next. "Then we must be vigilant and come up with clues why this is happening. Julia, can you do research without your boss finding out?"

The young woman bit her lower lip again before answering, "I think I can, yes."

"Good, and I'll keep my eyes and ears open here. It's good to have an inside source. Do you have surveillance cameras?"

Jules bowed her head as she spoke. "I'm embarrassed to say no, we don't. I've asked, but I was turned down."

"Too cheap?" Winnie said, raising an eyebrow. "Jules, what I'm hearing is your boss doesn't want the residents to find out. Killing the customers is bad for business, correct?"

Julia nodded her head, causing Winnie to sigh.

"And you want me to do some snooping?"

"Boy, you are a good detective," Jules said. "Can you use discretion?"

"My middle name is discretion. Don't want to hamper our sales quota, do we?" Winnie said, tilting her head and grinning.

"No, it's not. It's Pearl," Axel corrected.

Winnie ignored his comment and tapped a finger to her forehead. "OK, Nancy Drew, I'm on the case. I'll ask a few innocent questions to a few of my friends and keep an eye out for suspicious behavior."

"But what if the residents gossip amongst themselves?" Jules looked worried the plan would not work.

"They won't," said Axel. "She has a way of extracting information without you knowing about it. Years of practice on my brother and me. Then turning to his grandmother, warned, "Don't mess it up, Columbo."

Winnie took the last statement as a compliment. Axel had not meant it in this manner. He was far too young to remember the TV detective who disarmed his suspects by feigning incompetency.

He was also unaware Columbo solved every single case.

Dinner with Leif had gotten interesting. He had called her after the lunch with Axel and asked her out. At first, she hesitated, but he convinced her it would be fun to get acquainted. Besides, what harm could come from one dinner?

Veronica liked interesting conversation and over Italian, she was in the middle of a doozy. No discussion of banal topics such as work, extracurricular activities or books being read, all boring but usually accompanying a first date. Not today. Veronica came right out of the gate and asked about the relationship between Axel and Leif.

"He's got a normal job, stays in his lane and goes to church regularly. You wrote a self-help book, travel extensively, and are an affirmed non-believer. How did this happen?"

"I see you don't care for small talk," Leif responded. "And if we were all the same, this world would be a boring place."

"You didn't answer the question." Veronica was nothing if not persistent.

"Perceptive and bold. Outstanding qualities for a health care provider." He paused and Veronica guessed it was to ponder his next sentence, choosing his words carefully like picking out the right piece of steak at the butcher shop. "The book thing just happened. I was inspired. I travel because I can't sit still in one place very long. And the religion thing? I don't see how there can be a benevolent being looking over his children. Especially with all the shit happening in the world."

When Veronica did not answer, he did. "It's my belief you have one life and should live it to your fullest."

"Now don't give me your life lesson mumbo jumbo," she protested.

"Sorry, but shouldn't a person try to reach the potential within? It's my belief religion was created to keep man in line.

Don't create havoc, get rewarded at the end. No thanks, I want it all now."

"Sexist, aren't we?" When she noticed his look of puzzlement, she explained further. "You said, 'Keep *man* in line.'"

"Another apology. Humankind in line. When was the last time someone came back from the dead? No proof exists of a life after death. None, nada, zip. Why not have a blast while you're here?"

"This is where you'd be wrong again. As a nurse, I've witnessed plenty of stories of near-death experiences."

"That, my dear, can be explained scientifically by neurons in the brain. Doesn't count."

Undeterred, she pressed on, "OK, your argument is life occurred randomly on earth? We crawled from the ooze, stood upright, and Voila! Here we are?"

"If you mean to suggest evolution as a plausible theory, you'd be correct. Solid proof exists."

"OK, what do you make of ghosts? Many instances of people have claimed to have seen them."

"If I haven't seen it, I don't buy it."

She went in for the kill. "Have you ever seen an atom? A quark? A neutron? All unseen by the naked eye, yet all exist."

"Now you're playing with semantics," he countered. "Do I detect a religious bone in your scientific body?"

"I find it hard to accept all this life, this consciousness, was caused by chance. When you experience the miracle of birth or watch a child learn, or even the technological achievements we've seen so far, it makes little sense a higher intelligence *wasn't* involved."

"Maybe your god is from an alien race. Like ghost stories, those of abductions exist as well, right?"

Veronica shook her head, not buying into the 'evolution is the only answer' theory. She was firm in her beliefs and in letting others have their own. She had to admit Leif was engaging, personable, and if truth be told, easy on the eyes.

"Call me a lapsed Catholic," he said. "Call me a heretic, it's all the same to me. The pragmatist in me says man invented God. Not the other way around. Like the automobile."

"You're arguing God could be a Volkswagen Beetle?" she teased.

They both chuckled at this vision. Veronica took a sip of her wine before continuing, "So, this is your philosophy of life, or should I say death?

"It is. Life is all we have. If there is an afterlife, there's no definitive proof. Me? I'll go with what I can sense as real for now and deal with the consequences later… much, much later."

"Let me get this right, you have no faith in God?"

"Nope. I may have been born into a catholic family but doesn't mean I need to follow blindly."

"A very jaded opinion. What made you change your mind from Catholicism to atheism? College? The opportunity to be a lightning rod? Or from an event too painful to discuss?" She joked.

Leif put down the forkful of pasta and seemed to squirm in his chair. She noticed his discomfort as he searched to find a suitable answer. "Well," he began, "When your parents die early in your life, it forces skepticism. Again, why would God allow such a thing to happen?"

"Wait, didn't they die when you were like, three years old?"

"Yeah, but it's hardly the point. I still remember them, and they were taken from two small children."

"Is there any other reason for your skepticism?" She suspected he was leaving something out of the conversation. Something important.

"Yes. Reason itself." The waiter came by and he ordered the Crème brûlée and two spoons.

"Two?" she asked semi-suspiciously.

"If we can share opposing viewpoints like rational adults, why not dessert?" She silently added chivalry to his list of qualities.

The waiter returned with dessert, placing it and a spoon for each in the middle of the table. Leif allowed her to dig in first. "I used to be a practicing Catholic," he said, allowing for her previous question.

"So, what happened?" she asked, right on cue.

He took a spoonful of the dessert but answered before popping it into his mouth, ending this part of the evenings Q&A.

"I quit practicing."

CHAPTER
– 9 –

Becky Root called Axel with a request. "Hey, we have a job to do and I need an Angel. I heard Father Blake is in the hospital. I've called the others but none can go, can you?"

Father Blake, instilled as priest at St. Simons during the time of altar boys Leif and Axel, had two consistent quirks distinguishing him from those arriving later. His first was not to hail the boys with a regular salutation such as "Hello," but asked, "What did you have for dinner?" as if making this small talk led to deeper conversations of other personal habits. It never did, at least with a shy Axel, who would give mono syllable answers to any adult questions.

The second idiosyncrasy the priest exhibited was unpleasant. He had a habit of splashing too much cologne on his face, neglecting to wash his hands before delivering communion. From the altar, Axel amused himself by watching the faces of the parishioners as they cringed at the fine smelling, but foul tasting host.

Axel chuckled at the memory, but soon frowned as he recalled how abruptly his service on the altar ended as the boys were relieved of their duties. Soon thereafter, Father Blake transferred to a different parish as another priest took his place at St. Simons.

"I can go this afternoon," replied Axel. "What's he in for?" he said, grinning at his small joke. Axel wondered what was worse, being healthy and sentenced to prison, or sickly, sentenced to a hospital bed. Neither appealed to him.

"He fell and broke a hip. Let me warn you, though. He's in the grip of dementia. He repeats himself often and doesn't always remember who's speaking with him," Becky warned.

"No worries. I'll head over there soon."

When he got to the hospital, Axel asked the nurse where to find the old priest. She gave him the room number and pointed in the direction. Axel knocked on the open door as he walked towards the hospital bed, its sheets as white as the priest's pale complexion.

Afternoon sunlight lit the room as the aroma of disinfectant and past occupants hung in the air. Today, a whiff of the priest's cologne would be welcomed.

"Father? It's Axel Ahearne come for a visit. Is now a good time?"

The elderly priest shifted in the bed, wincing in pain from the repaired hip. "Of course, my boy. Do come in. Let me look at you." His gnarled hand shook as he waved Axel into the room; it reminded Axel of a crab claw. "Tell me," Father asked. "What did you have for dinner?"

Axel nodded. *Some things never change.* "I grabbed a quick bite on the way. But let's talk about you, how're you doing?"

The priest shifted closer to Axel, wincing once more. The old man clasping his arthritic claw hand around Axel's. "I've been better," Father Blake said. "It's terrible growing old. How are your parents faring these days?" Reminded of Becky's warning, Axel paused. Father Blake should be acutely familiar with the family history. "Fine, they're fine." he responded calmly as to not upset the old man.

Axel listened as Father Blake spoke of the many parishes he had been assigned since leaving St. Simon's, smattered with a few complaints of old age issues. Axel found it odd the man's memory, although faulty, conjured all these places. Assignment to so many parishes did not seem possible.

"And your parents?" the priest asked again. "How are they?" The repetition was frustrating, but Axel answered each question in the same patient manner. *It's not his fault.*

As Axel's visit neared its end, the priest reached out his clammy hands to clasp Axels again "Thank you for coming to visit me. I have no family of my own, and it's nice to see a familiar face... Leif."

Axel was poised to correct the man, but given his condition, replied instead, "It's my pleasure. Hope they release you soon. Get better."

The priest squeezed Axel's hand, holding tight as he looked around the room as if to find anyone else listening. "Thank you for the visit, and also..." He loosened his claw grip and wagged a 'come closer' finger at the young man before whispering, "For not letting on to our little secret. You're a good boy, Leif."

Axel froze by the bed. *What the hell did he mean by that?* The question arose in his throat but never came out as the priest waved his claw hand farewell, his voice resuming its jovial volume, "Tell your parents I said 'hello.' Please come back and chat soon."

As Axel walked from the room and out of the earshot of the old priest, he dialed his brother on the cell and when Leif picked up asked, "Are you home? I visited Father Blake. We have to talk." After the call, he jogged to his car and drove, his mind asking millions of little questions. No answers came.

He parked in the driveway. Axel noticed the look of sadness on his brother's face as he stepped onto the porch. Leif never said a word of greeting, instead turned towards the door. Axel followed him into the house and sat at the kitchen table. Leif pulled two glasses and the bottle of whiskey Axel had hidden. "No, it's too early and I'm heading over to Benton Manor for dinner." Axel protested. But Leif ignored him, clapping the glasses on the table, and pouring the brown liquid into each one. "Yes." A firm reply to show he was not asking.

Axel explained the conversation he'd had with the priest at the hospital. "Weird, huh? The repeating was easy to deal with, or not acknowledging the death of our parents. But mistaking me for you was weird, and when he said *secret*, it kinda freaked me out."

Leif lifted his head and sighed before taking a sip of his drink. "I never wanted you to find out. Winnie and I decided it best to steer clear of him after, uhm…"

"After what?" Axel hunched his shoulders, his hands raised in question. He slowly lowered them as realization struck. He now knew what his brother meant. And what terrible secret he had kept.

"Oh my God," moaned Axel in disbelief, turning to horror. "He, he—" Axel choked on the word. *Molested.*

Leif nodded. "Did you ever ask yourself why we stopped being altar boys? I told Winnie we needed to protect you. I didn't want what happened to me to affect you. And after he left, we buried it. No further discussion as though it never happened."

"And you've kept this secret all this time?" Axel asked.

"I did. But It doesn't define me." Leif said, showing a fierce look of defiance.

Axel now understood why Leif would always hover around him whenever Father Blake was in the vicinity. Also realizing the reason their differences on religious beliefs were so far apart. Who would not shy away from a religion where you lost your innocence and had faith shattered by the lust of a trusted leader of the church? Axel felt the blood rush to his face, its heat burning as much as his guilt for not recognizing his brother's pain. Oblivious all these years, he maintained a firm belief in his religion. One that allowed this foul behavior. Even *protected* the abusers.

He wondered if he would have reacted in the same manner had *he* been the victim. His faith shaken to the point of turning his back on religion… and God. A concept he found unfathomable. Until now.

"Now you know why I quit practicing," Leif joked, trying to lighten the mood. "I mean, how could a benevolent God allow the abuse of children at the very hands of the people he's entrusted to protect them?"

Axel struggled with the question. His mind filled with contradictions while his heart felt the pain his brother endured and how he had protected Axel from this secret and the abuse all these years.

"And no 'free will' crap, either." Leif appeared relieved to expose the secret, sounding like himself again. Axel supposed the whiskey may have played a role. "Do you realize in several years I'll have outlived Elvis?"

This caused Axel to smile. "You have a way to go there. He died at forty-two."

"Yeah, my goal is to live forever. Everybody dies, but not me and not today!"

Axel knew his own journey towards eternity was a marathon littered with many roadblocks to test his faith. To Leif, it was a sprint; a race to outrun death and every ghost from his past.

"Where are you off to next?" Axel asked.

"I meet the publisher in New York on Friday. He wants to discuss a follow-up book."

"Here's a title idea for you. *When You Climb Your Tree, Don't Fall.*"

They both laughed as Leif poured another round before silence surrounded them like a dense fog. Quiet. Opaque.

Axel attempted an apology, staring into his glass, "I'm very sorry this happened to you."

"Don't," warned Leif. "Don't even."

"I have to. You spared me this pain and took it on your shoulders. So, thank you."

"Don't get sappy with me. What's done is done. Oh, wait, before I forget." Leif reached into his pocket and pulled out a wad of bills, laying them on the table. "This is a partial payback for what I owe you. I got my advance."

Shock rendered him speechless. *Leif with money and paying me back? Will wonders never cease?* He took the money off the table, knowing it likely a onetime offer, and stuffed the bills into his pocket.

"Well, it's over now," Leif said, ending the difficult discussion. "No sense worrying about an incident from years ago." As an afterthought added, "Say, what hospital did you say he was in?"

Axel lifted his head sharply at the question to find Leif smiling. "Sucker. The guy is old. He'll be dead on his own soon."

Relieved at the joke, Axel rose, the two brothers shaking hands. He headed out the door as an unchristian thought materialized. *I hope sooner than later, brother. Sooner than later.*

⟾

"What is it, my boy? You're distracted this evening." Harley Benton asked his dinner companion as they settled into the study for a drink and discussion.

Axel waved a hand as if brushing lint off a jacket, "It's nothing. I found out some disturbing news and am trying to process it."

"Tell me, perhaps I can be of assistance?" Benton seemed sincere in his offer, and Axel had no doubt he had the where-with-all to help, but what kind, Axel had no clue. Besides, Benton had enough problems of his own. The old man pulled out a handkerchief, anticipating another cough. Three linens already crumpled in the waste basket by his wheelchair, resembling a pile of dirty diapers. Axel waited until the fit ended and he had dropped the fourth. He hoped Kennedy would enter soon to remove the soiled mess before his own gag reflex kicked in.

"No, it's something I need to work through on my own," Axel said. Uninterested in sharing the details with anyone, especially the old man, he changed the subject. "Can you tell me another Winnie story?"

"Certainly, my boy. I would be delighted. But first comes business." Benton reached into his desk drawer and pulled a manilla envelope, pushing it across the desk to Axel. "I need your signature on these papers, power of attorney for the charity, you see." The old man pointed to where Axel needed to sign, and the distracted young man obliged.

Benton closed the folder and placed it into the drawer. Gone was the greasy grin and mean demeanor. Was it because Kennedy was not present? Or did the old man have a bad day on his last visit? *Who wouldn't have a bad day in his condition?*

"You realize, the best way to keep a person alive after they've gone is to remember accounts of their life." Benton offered. "Keeping their memory alive, *gives* them life. Remember this when both your grandmother and I have left this life. Have I told you the time our Winnie jumped off a bridge?"

Axel looked at his host with surprise. "What? Why?"

"Teenagers do the craziest things believing they are immortal. There used to be a railroad trestle over the river, past the falls where the train came into town. It's long gone now." Mr. Benton gazed towards the window as he recalled the memory. He shook his head back to the present to continue the story. "It was summer, and we were walking over the trestle, a feat unto itself. You didn't want to be in the middle when a train approached. As I recall, it was a warm afternoon and as we reached the center of the trestle, a few of the boys stripped to their undershorts and jumped into the river." The old man caught his breath before continuing. "One boy dared your grandmother to follow suit. When she paused, the boys began taunting her. One even had the audacity to tell your grandmother she wouldn't jump because she was frightened AND a girl." Benton chuckled at the memory.

"Uh oh, you never questioned Winnie's bravery. What happened next?"

"Much to the shock of everyone, she stripped to her undergarments and said, "I'm not afraid." She stared at her tormentors, claiming, "We girls can do anything boys can do." Her willingness to jump did not surprise me, for I knew her to be fearless. The taunts merely added to her determination." Axel waited as the old man reached for a handkerchief and coughed. Wiping the corner of his mouth, the old man continued, "The surprise came right before she leapt. She pulled her panties to her knees, exposing her buttocks! You younger folk call it 'mooning.' The act was shocking and wonderful at the same time!"

"And scandalous as well!" Axel added, laughing.

"The whole town spoke of nothing else for weeks. I was proud of her for her courage. So proud."

Axel finished his drink, a satisfying conclusion to the visit. Benton's story had taken his mind off his other worries. He said his goodbyes and as Axel stepped out of the mansion, he wore the look of contentment. As long as the old man told him stories of his grandmother, Axel felt even after she was gone, he could keep her alive for a long time.

Leif walked Veronica back to her apartment. "I had a lovely dinner," she said, bringing her eyes to his while crossing her arms to ward off the chill in the air.

"Yeah, it was… interesting."

Veronica tucked her chin into her chest pouting, "What do you mean?"

"What I meant was you are a very interesting person. It was a compliment." He took his jacket off and slipped it around her shoulders.

"Oh," she replied, pulling the jacket closer, the warmth comforting her. "I'm sorry, haven't done this in a while."

"Done what, had dinner?" He teased.

"No silly, you know... dating. I'm a little rusty."

"So," he said, stepping closer to her and taking her hand in his. "This is what you're calling it, rust?"

He kissed her gently on the lips, brushing the hair from her cheek with his free hand. *That certainly felt like a dating kiss,* she thought, catching her breath.

"Only if you want to continue the evening." She desperately wanted him to say yes. The butterflies had been missing for a long time. It felt good to have them return. Rust or not.

"Do you have a suggestion?" he asked, feigning chivalry.

Veronica looked at her feet and whispered, "The best I can do tonight is ask if you'd join me for a drink at the bar on the next block. It's a short walk."

"Sure, I was hoping for *coffee*, but a drink will have to do," he said, both understanding the significance of the term as they walked the block to the bar and ordered. A merlot for her, a beer for him.

After a brief, yet awkward pause, she apologized. "I'm sorry, but I'm old fashioned and you seem to be sort of..." She hesitated before finishing the sentence, giving Leif time to jump in.

"Sort of what?"

"A lost boy."

"A lost what??"

"Boy. You know, one of the boys from Peter Pan. A lost boy."

His puzzled expression was clear. "Not sure how to take that."

"Leif, we've had a lot of fun tonight. But I've just moved back here. I don't want things to get... complicated."

Leif frowned, but it didn't last long.

"Yet," she said into her drink, her eyes looking over the glass rim as Billy Joel played from the speakers in the bar.

Leif sang along, the timing perfect. "Catholic girls start much too late…"

She took over. "I'd rather laugh with the sinners than cry with the saints." Together they finished the song before laughing, causing Veronica's drink to spill.

"Ahh," she said, wiping a laugh tear from her cheek. "See? We have fun together."

"We do. And I'd be up for more. Can we do this again soon?"

"I'd like that. But for now, I have an early shift tomorrow. I need my beauty sleep."

"Impossible," he said.

She rose from the barstool and finished her wine, placing the empty glass back on the bar top. She grabbed his face with both hands and planted a firm kiss on his lips, lingering a moment too long before breaking off. "Catholic girls start at the time of their choosing," she said and as she turned to leave added over her shoulder a little too loudly, "And we *love* coffee." She grinned as she walked the length of the bar, knowing her new lost boy had watched her stride all the way out the door.

It was past calling hours. A time when only the overnight staff was on duty. The perfect time for an intruder to enter the hospital unseen. Opening the door and sliding into the priest's room found the old man fast asleep, a saline drip attached to his withered hand. The unpleasant smell of old people and disinfectant filled the intruder's nostrils.

At first, the plan was to perform the hastening and get out fast. But once inside, the plan changed. With anger mounting, the intruder vowed not to release the man in his sleep. This pervert should have the distinct displeasure of seeing the end coming.

Standing at the edge of the bed, a nudge of a knee poke to the hip insured the priest's full attention. He awoke with a start. "Wha... You?" he questioned, recognizing his visitor.

"Yes, it's me. I've come to talk of our little secret."

The old man rubbed his eyes and shook the cobwebs of sleep from his head. Recognition put a new expression in the man's eyes. Fear. *Good.*

"This was our little secret. No one needs to find out," the priest began, his hands beginning to shake.

"You're correct," said the intruder. "No one needs to know but you and me. And God, of course. He knows."

The old priests' eyes grew larger, prompting the intruder to poke harder, enjoying the reaction to the pain. "Do you believe God will forgive you? I mean, it wasn't the only time, was it? Or with one child? No, I'm sure it wasn't."

"I, uh," the old man sputtered, trying to form an argument to release him from the accusations. "I apologize for any hurt I may have caused you. It was a weak moment on my part. People make mistakes. Please forgive me?"

The defense was lost. "Stop it. You were in a position of power and took advantage of a young child. I did my research and guess what? They moved you from parish to parish because you repeated your sins wherever you went. How many children did you molest? How many did your sick mind corrupt?"

The fear now caused the old man to thrash around in bed, wincing as he did. He searched for the nurse call button lying by his side, but a swift hand interceded lifting it and hanging it on the oxygen valve behind the bed out of the old man's reach. The notion this decrepit sinner was attempting to avoid his fate produced a chuckle. Try as he might, tonight there would be no escaping justice. The Hastener thought about gagging the priest. The wretched mouth that kissed and did other unspeakable things but decided the old man's begging was worth the risk of exposure.

"You used your authority to damage those innocents for good. Including me. But there will be no more children for you to prey on. Tonight, I will settle the score."

The intruder pulled a small black case from the hoodie pocket, opening to expose a hypodermic needle. Lifting it in the air in the full view of the shocked priest, said "Oh, don't worry, I have nothing to put in it. I want you to ponder your transgressions, your sins." The evil grin on the Hastener's face showed pondering as the starting point.

"Questions for you," asked the Hastener. "Is it possible to perform one last confession on yourself? Will an Our Father or a Hail Mary get the job done? Will God offer absolution?" The priest squirmed, gasping for breath.

Grabbing the groping hand against the bed rail, the needle was inserted into the port above the saline tube. The old priest's attempt to counter with his free hand proved useless as the Hastener pushed the plunger in and out a few times, sending air bubbles directly into the priest's blood stream.

"No," Father Blake whispered, the fight in him now gone.

"Oh, yes," came the reply, the finality of the plan clear. "Consider it penance. I'm not certain God will forgive you.

Perhaps Satan allows pedophilia in hell. We sure don't approve of it here."

"Please, have mercy," pleaded Father Blake, but the phrase fell on deaf ears.

"Like the mercy you showed me and countless other innocents? No, when a priest is guilty of a crime, the church should defrock the priest, not shelter him. No mercy given. De-frocked."

As the air bubbles travelled to their destination inside the priest's brain, a firm grip continued to hold the man's arm. The priest weakly lifted his other hand, attempting to point a broken finger at his assailant, but dropped it when the aneurysm struck. A wet bubble escaped the old priest's mouth and popped. Like the blood vessel in his head.

"Consider yourself defrocked." The final word sounding bitter. The Hastener let go of the man's arm, extracting the needle and placing it in the small case before checking the drip for any leaks. There were none.

"Go and sin no more," came the final comment, a hard edge to it. This time, no prayers were offered. There would be no joy today. Hastening someone evil was serious business and some secrets one had to take with them. Heaven or hell, it was up to God to sort. Today, the safe assumption would be hell.

CHAPTER
– 10 –

Hector was at the tail end of his shift. He was tired and getting hungry, but knew mama had his dinner ready for him when he got home. Tossing his keys in the air and catching them mindlessly, the thought of her home-cooked meals made his mouth water. He looked at the clock from the nurse's station and decided he would spend the last few minutes checking on his patients. He turned the corner and stopped. Benny was leaning against the wall, a smug look on his face. He wore his black hoodie ready to leave at the end of his shift. Hector pushed his keys in his pocket, like a squirrel protecting its stash of nuts.

"Rat Boy," Benny called out, "after the last stunt you pulled, you and I have business to take care of."

"I don't have time to argue with you today. I have too much work to do." Hector wanted to get away from the man, so he brushed by Benny, who grabbed him by the arm. Instead of pulling Hector back to him, Hector dragged him a few feet before Palz let go.

Recovering, Benny said, "For years, everyone always told *me* what to do. Not anymore. No sir. Now it's my turn to give the orders."

Hector ignored the last sentence as he walked down the hallway. Palz yelled after him. "How are your parents doing?"

Hector stopped in his tracks. He turned slowly, the fear creeping into his throat. "Excuse me?" he said.

"I asked you how Manuel and Juanita were doing. You still live with your parents, right, Rat Boy?"

Hector began to sweat; afraid this day would come. Determined to protect his parents at all costs, he would do anything to prevent them from being extradited to their home country.

"I know what you're doing," he said, his voice above a whisper.

"Yes, I'm sure you do," Benny responded, a sneer plastered across his face. "Now, don't you want to ask me a question?"

Hector took his time before answering, the sweat forming across his body leaving telltale wet marks under his arms. "Yes," he began. "I do. What is it you want?"

"Now we're talking. Come with me."

He led Hector to the medication dispensary room door. At this time of night, it was quiet; residents getting ready for bed and the night shift settling in. Benny pointed at the door before pulling a slip of paper from his pocket and waving it at Hector.

"I can't. I'll get fired," Hector said, backing away.

"Let's see," Benny answered, a grin showing a few rotted teeth. "If you don't, someone will have to alert the authorities about your parents and their immigration status. Now which would be worse? The chance you *might* get caught? Or the certainty your parents will? And don't tell me you don't have your keys, because I saw ya playin' with 'em."

Hector wanted to kill this man with his bare hands but knew he had to protect his parents no matter what. If he lost this job, he would always find another one. Losing his parents would be unthinkable. He gritted his teeth, took the slip of paper from Benny, and unlocked the door.

"Good, Rat Boy," purred Benny.

Hector filled the prescription order and placed all the bottles in a rubber glove box. He'd put a pair on and shoved the remaining gloves in his pockets to throw out on his way home. He locked the door behind him and handed the drugs to Benny. "Are we done here?" Hector asked, the contempt in his voice evident.

"Sure, for now," Benny responded as he made sure his order matched the contents.

Veronica Bucholz had a dilemma. She understood Axel enjoyed their time together; she saw it in his eyes. He was asking her out to spend more time together. It did not take a rocket scientist to figure out he was enamored. There was a slight problem. She was not. Sure, she found him nice and kind and she respected the work he was doing with the eulogies and Visiting Angels, but it did not mean they would work as a couple.

This was where the larger problem entered her picture. Although she did not feel Axel was the right match for her, she did see herself dating someone else. Relationships were complicated, but when you yearn for the brother of the man who is enamored with you, complications multiply.

Leif was interesting, a bit of a rogue, and had strong opinions. And to top it off was now an author. She guessed it was a reoccurring case of "Bad Boy" syndrome, but she did not care.

"The heart wants what the heart wants," she said as she got ready. If this relationship moved on the right path, she would have to let Axel down easily. In fact, it should happen before it became heated between her and Leif. She was daydreaming on how 'heated' it might get when her cell rang. It was Axel.

"Hey," she said, still daydreaming about Leif.

"Hey back. I was wondering if you wanted to get together after my visitations tonight?"

"Jeez, Axel. I'd like to, but…" Veronica searched her mind for an excuse that wouldn't sound lame. "I already have plans for tonight."

The next question was not a surprise. "With whom?" he asked.

She demurred, "Now aren't we the nosy one. I'm meeting a friend for drinks, then straight home to bed. Workday tomorrow." It was not a lie. She and Leif were friends. For now.

"Sorry, just really wanted to see you." Axel sounded clingy to her, a trait she found unappealing.

"I…" she stopped herself from telling him the whole truth, "I need to get some rest. Haven't had much sleep since… you know."

"Of course, you still mourn your brother. We all do. I totally understand. Ok, I'll see you soon."

"Sure," she said, getting ready to hang up.

"Unless," he jumped in. "Unless you want to go out before then?"

She pretended not to hear the last part. "Bye," she said, disconnecting quickly. He was a nice guy. Just was not *her* kind of nice guy. She made a mental note to sit with him and tell him about Leif at a later date. Better yet, she would get Leif to do it. This was a brother to brother discussion. It also meant she would not have to face him. Veronica confronted people in the hospital every day, but that was business. She hated the fact she was in a predicament of having to hurt someone in her personal life. His feelings might sting for a while, but he'd come around, eventually. She did not want to be the cause of the pain.

Brushing the thought aside, she put on the rest of her makeup, noticing a good job so far. She wanted to look especially nice for the upcoming evening events. And where those events might lead.

Around midnight, the door cracked open as Winnie slid her head out, looking down each side of the hallway, like a child sneaking out of bed for a midnight snack. She closed up her housecoat and tied the soft belt around her waist. She also wore a pair of slippers belonging to her late husband. They looked like cloth loafers. She kept them for sentimental reasons, wearing them when nostalgic. But not tonight. This evening she wore them for a more practical reason. There was no flop, flop noise like her own slippers. These were silent as she glided along the hallway towards the common room. They were quiet but too big for her feet and occasionally one would slip off, causing her to bend over, hook her finger into the heel and pull it back in place.

Winnie had begun this nightly habit since Jules had first explained her theory and Axel shaking his head and rolling his eyes in skepticism, "Sorry, but old people die. Especially in a nursing home. It's a numbers game. Numbers are infinite in most instances, but in life, when your number is up, it's about as finite as it gets."

Finite or not, Winnie loved a good mystery and was curious to find out if Jules' theory had merit. And she had a vested interest if the allegations proved true, Didn't she? She would never forgive herself if harm came to a fellow resident, and she had done nothing to prevent it.

Determined to do what she could, she slipped into the corridor. Keeping an eye out was a good use of her time. An area where she excelled, being nosy.

As she walked through the quiet hallways, she would touch each door and whisper the name of the resident, "Mr. Egleston, Mrs. Hart, Mrs. Kneckler…" Each life she would touch like the doors she brushed her fingers against. *If I was going to kill someone here, where would I begin?* she asked herself, slipping into the shoes of the killer. Was there a pattern? She'd thought long and hard about the answer and had come up with one. From Mr. Franz to Mr. Strong they all had two things in common, all had medical conditions that could easily explain their demise, and those conditions left each with little time.

Winnie had yet to tell her theory to Jules or her grandson. He would shrug it off, anyway. But to be sure she was on the right track; she roamed the halls near the residents most likely to be the next victim. Those in the Passing Lane.

She came to the common area, the chairs arranged around tables for pinochle or other such games, the fake plants standing sentry. "A lot of good they'd come to in an emergency," she said under her breath, approaching the wing where only the most terminal or needy residents lived. The hallway's recessed lighting gave off a faint yellow glow providing enough light to see, but not harsh enough to seep under the doors to bother the residents. One light at the end of the corridor blinked on and off like a hazard light. "I'll have to point it out to Hector in the morning," she whispered to herself. Again, she named the residents as she skimmed along, touching one door on her right, then crossing over to do the same on her left.

She reached the end and touched the wall before turning around, confident the wing was safe. This point gave her mixed emotions; glad all was quiet, but somewhat disappointed there was nothing out of the ordinary. Nothing exciting.

Walking past Mrs. Ramble's door, she called it a night. She was sleepy anyway. Her right heel came out of her slipper again, causing her to stop and bend over.

"I'm about over you," she complained, hooking her finger into the offending slipper. She was still fidgeting with the heel when she was pushed from behind, face planting on the floor. Looking up, she was shocked to see a figure running down the hall. She could not tell whether it was a man or a woman because of the black hoodie covering the intruder's identity. But she was left with a whiff of something that did not belong there.

Shaken, but now fully awake, Winnie got up and slipped into Mrs. Ramble's room. She found the woman snoring peacefully. "Dorothy? Are you ok?" Winnie shook her arm and the old woman roused with an answer. "Kurt?" she said drowsily. "Don't forget to let the dog out before you go." She then drifted back to sleep, no worse for the visit from the hooded stranger. Again, Winnie noticed the faint aroma.

Winnie left the room and headed back to her own, cautious at every corner in the event the intruder was still lurking in the building. Stepping into her room, she sat on the bed and called Axel, rubbing the carpet burn on her chin. She then spent the next five minutes looking for something to defend herself, acknowledging she would get no sleep this night. She settled on a lamp.

The apartment building Veronica lived in was not quaint; a red brick square sitting on the corner of two busy streets, the street noise loud, trash littering the corners of the sidewalk. But it was inexpensive for her first living space back home. *Home*, the word sounding foreign as she walked back from the restaurant alongside Leif.

"Hey, Lost Boy?" she said when they got within eyesight. "How do you like my new digs?"

"I've only seen the outside. Plus, I don't have to live here. The question is, how do *you* like your new digs?"

"It's fine for now," she said as she slipped her arm into his, pulling herself closer to his warmth. "When I get bored, I'll find someplace larger. A little cottage, perhaps?"

"Jeez," Leif responded drawing his face inward in mock sorrow. "What'll you do with me once I bore you?"

"Not a chance. But don't piss me off to test the theory. One never knows what'll happen."

"Here, this isn't boring," he said as they stood in her doorway. He pulled her towards him, kissing her passionately. They held the embrace for a short while and when they broke, he kissed her on the forehead. He was about to step off the landing when she whispered, "You could come up for coffee?" She turned her head towards him, accentuating the last word.

They both knew what "coffee" meant. But because she was playing coy, she noticed he played along.

"Not much of a coffee person this late at night. Keeps me awake."

She smirked, not taking the bait. "Isn't that the whole point?"

"You're not going to pull a Praying Mantis on me, are you? I like my head attached to my shoulders."

"Perhaps I will, perhaps I won't," she teased back. She enjoyed the game of cat-and-mouse. "There's only one way to find out."

"Are you sure you want a lapsed catholic to come upstairs with you? How scandalous."

"Listen, you said yourself, you used to be a practicing catholic but quit practicing. The only way to get better at anything is to practice more."

"We're going to practice religion tonight?"

"Nope, I have something else in mind," she said as she stepped towards the apartment entrance. "And it will take a *lot* of practice."

Leif put a hand to his chin as if in thought. "I could go for some practice."

Veronica took his hand. It was the most mature thing he'd said all evening. She unlocked the front door and led him inside. *There is hope for my lost boy after all.*

"Are you OK?" Axel asked, out of breath as he burst into the room. "I came as fast as I could. Jules is on her way, too." He noticed the lamp in her hand, wielding it at him like a police night stick, the shade off and bulb removed. "What in the name of?" he said, puzzled. "Do you think this little lamp is going to protect you?"

"Yup," Winnie said, thrusting the lamp forward. The motion was similar to poking an object with a large stick. Axel realized it was plugged into the wall socket. "Not much for hitting but will give them quite a shock they soon won't forget."

Axel shook his head in wonder at his feisty grandmother's resourcefulness. "But you're OK otherwise?" he asked, touching the rash on her chin.

"Ouch!" She said, pushing his hand away. "I'm fine. I was…" the opening door interrupted Winnie, who reacted by pointing the lamp in front of them to ward off the intruder. Axel reached out a hand and took the unofficial stun gun from her hands. It was Jules.

"What happened?" she asked, her eyes wide with fear. "Are you all right?"

"Fine dear, I'm fine," Winnie said. "And so is Dorothy Ramble." Winnie then told them her suspicions and the events of the evening.

"It makes sense," said Jules, scratching an eyebrow.

"I think it's time to call the police," said Axel, as he pulled the cell phone from his pocket.

"No!" the two women shouted in unison.

"We don't want scare the person away. We want to catch them," said Jules. "Besides, no one believed me before. What makes you think anyone would believe us now? Heck, even you doubt it."

"Blessed be the women, for they have the most sense," said Winnie, shaking her head in agreement. Then excused herself to the bathroom. "All this excitement and I forgot to pee."

Jules looked over at the lamp lying on the bed. "What's that all about?"

"She was using it for protection. Almost electrocuted me."

"Maybe she should have," Jules shot back. "It might've shocked some sense into you."

"What do you mean by that," Axel said, confused at her snipe.

"You know exactly what I mean."

Axel did not.

Jules turned her attention to Winnie as she returned from the bathroom. "Can you think of anything else you can tell us? Anything at all?"

"As a matter of fact, I can. Sitting on the john, I remembered something I found odd. When you're in a place like this, there are many odors. Some good, some not so. I noticed a distinct scent when the intruder ran past, and again a slight whiff when I checked on Mrs. Ramble."

"Go on," Axel prodded.

"It was an odor that didn't belong in either the hall or her room. But I know it because it belongs in only one place in this entire facility." She pinched her nose as if the scent lingered.

Axel interrupted, "I'm confused. What kind of place has an odor of its own?"

Jules had the answer, "A pool." Then addressing Winnie, "You smelled chlorine?"

"I did," said Winnie, a proud smile forming. "See Axel, I told you she was a smart one. Gonna make somebody a fine wife."

Jules blushed and tried to change the subject back to the chlorine odor. "Why would the person smell of chlorine?"

"Is there a lifeguard? Someone who maintains the pool?" asked Axel.

"As a matter of fact, there's both," answered Jules. "We employ two lifeguards but they're young kids, and I can't see either being killers. If they were, why not let the swimmers drown? But what's interesting is the orderly responsible for the pool maintenance."

"I didn't know Hector cleaned the pool?" said Axel.

"He doesn't. *Benny Palz* does. Let me find out when he clocked out today and if he had been in the pool area. In the meantime," Jules turned to Winnie, touching her arm, "It's time we put you to bed. You've had enough excitement for tonight."

"Oh no," Axel interjected. "She's coming home with me tonight."

"I most certainly am not," Winnie protested. "This is my home, and I'm not going to be scared off by some hoodlum traipsing around the hallways trying to get a peek of me in my nightgown."

"Winnie, please. I can't let you stay here. It's too dangerous."

"You can and you will." Winnie was adamant and Axel knew better than to argue with her. "Besides, I have my stun gun here to protect me." She raised the lamp and thrust it towards Axel. He took it away and put it on the table.

Axel gave Jules a look of concern, resigning himself to her decision.

"I'll stay in my office tonight if you need me," said Jules. "I think you scared them away, whoever it was."

"That's very kind of you dear," Winnie mumbled before stifling a yawn as she was helped into bed before Axel turned off the overhead light and the two headed for the door.

"What a cute couple you make," she said before closing her eyes.

As they entered the hallway, Jules whispered, "Now do you believe there's something going on?"

The evening's event wasn't electric but a shock, nonetheless. Axel was shaken and the realization Jules had been right scared him even more. Now, he could admit the answer to her question. There was no longer any doubt in his mind a killer was on the loose.

"I do," he said. "The question is, what do we do about it?"

CHAPTER
– 11 –

L ater that morning, Axel was fixing breakfast. His thoughts miles away from the frying bacon, he did not notice it burning until he smelled the acrid odor. He waved a dish towel around to dissipate the smoke so it would not set off the smoke alarms.

Burnt bacon was the least of his problems. He was ridden with guilt because he had allowed his grandmother to live in an unsafe place, putting her life in jeopardy. The helplessness magnified with her refusal to come home with him. And he was exhausted, not sleeping due to worry.

Leif came into the kitchen, a wrinkled expression on his face. "Are you trying to burn down the house? Gasoline is a much better accelerant than bacon," he teased. His facial expression changed when Axel did not respond. "Hey, what's the matter? You worried about something?"

The writer in Leif had developed an annoying penchant for noticing subtle changes in Axel's mood. *Evidently, I've been giving off more than smoke signals.* He put on a convincing face and answered, "No, everything's fine. It's a glorious day and I've made you breakfast. Here's some eggs. The toast is on the table. I'm saving the burnt bacon for the birds." *No need to get Leif involved, as if it would make a difference.*

Leif seemed to accept the explanation and sat to eat.

"Coffee?" asked Axel, the pot jiggling in his hand.

"Sure, I need caffeine after the night I've had."

"Out on the prowl again, huh?" Axel mused while he poured. "Anyone interesting?"

"Nope," Leif said, looking away from his brother, "No one worth mentioning."

Axel felt a twinge of suspicion, but did not press further because his cell vibrated. "Hello," he answered. He listened to the person on the other end, his shoulders drooping. Finally, he ended the call with a "Thank you." His expression remained grim as he turned to his brother.

"That was Gil. He seems really upset. Father Blake died the other night." He gauged his brother's reaction to the news and was not disappointed as Leif's expression turned sour. "Good," was the response as he mopped the eggs with a slice of toast. A few awkward moments of silence ensued. How should one react to the death of an old pervert priest? Brightening, Leif broke the silence, "It's a good thing priests don't marry. No evil spawn."

Axel wanted to quote the old axiom not to speak ill of the dead, but changed his mind due to what the priest had done to Leif. But the ambivalence in his brother's reaction to the old priest's death spurred a thought Axel quickly dismissed. His brother was no killer. How could he even conceive such a thing? Still, the nagging doubt forced him to test the waters further. "A priest is married to God. Wonder what God thinks of the man's infidelity now?"

Leif answered the question with a question, "Tell me you don't buy the horseshit about celibate priests? You're smarter than that."

"God's rule, not mine."

"Supposedly, God also turned into a burning bush to deliver ten commandments to Moses. I don't remember an eleventh, Thou shall not allow priests to take wives. Ridiculous."

Axel remained silent.

"Catholic priests and even Popes married like the farmer or the blacksmith. The problem arose when priests died. Leaving worldly goods to their families and not the Vatican was not well received. Lesson learned? A religion bleeding cash doesn't last long, regardless if God is on their side."

"Your argument is the Vatican changed the celibacy rules not for purity but for financial reasons?"

"Yup, No offspring, no loss of church property."

"Leif," Axel said, toning down the rhetoric. "The commandments are road signs to heaven. Father Blake went off roading and now he must pay for his sins."

"Ah, hell. I've broken most of those commandments, what's one more." Axel wondered which of the commandments his brother had broken. He hoped 'thou shalt not kill' did not make the list.

"It is kind of weird we were talking about the guy and he dies just like that." Leif said, munching nonchalantly on his toast.

As he searched Leif's reaction for any sign of his involvement, Axel said, "Yup." The previous sentence hanging in the air like the bacon smoke. *Just like that.*

"We've got a problem." Nurse May stepped into Julia's office. Jules had hoped today would be a good one, but by the expression on Nurse May's face, that hope disappeared.

"What is it now?" she asked the nurse, the dread creeping into her stomach, like vines encircling a tree.

"I was doing inventory in the med room and I found medication missing."

"Are you sure?" asked Julia. "Maybe they've been misplaced?"

"Yes, I'm sure. You know the protocol. I do a weekly inventory, then check the list against the usage report before I re-order. There is no mistake."

"Damn." Julia whispered. Nurse May was as efficient as they come. They'd had residents pilfer from the kitchen, family members take small mementos from the room of a deceased loved one, but while Jules had been there, they had never had meds go missing.

"Well?" May asked, her arms crossing her large bosom.

"We have to inform Harriet. Let's go."

The two women walked towards Harriet's office. On the way, Jules noticed Winnie sitting with another resident, Mr. Kinsella, in a wheelchair. *What a kind soul*, she thought. The two exchanged waves. *I'll check in with her later to see if she's heard anything.*

Jules knocked on the door to the administrator's office and walked in without waiting for a reply.

"Oh, no. something's wrong." Harriet said as she shook her head. "Out with it."

May explained about the missing meds while Julia plopped herself into a chair in front of the desk.

Pushing her glasses up, she warned the two women, "Not a word to anyone about this. I'll handle the investigation myself. We don't want to alarm any guests or potential new residents. Am I clear on this?"

"Isn't it time to invest in cameras?" Jules said, leaning forward in her chair. "If we'd had them installed, we'd be able to catch the thief or, at the best case, avoid the theft at all."

Harriet shifted uncomfortably in her seat. Her lips pursed before she spoke. "I've told you before, we don't want our residents to think we are spying on them. And it's not in the budget."

"I'm gonna have to throw the BS flag." May jumped in. "Until now, we didn't need them. Stealing medication hurts not only the residents who need them but shows our lack of ability to take care of the people who pay us!" May was leaning over Harriet's desk, her fists pressing into the wood, turning the skin around her knuckles white. "You might be able to fool some other folks, but I've been here a long time. Probably be here after you leave. We have a responsibility and it's up to us to see to it. And if it's not in the budget, it should be. Today."

Jules marveled at May's strong will and the power of her convictions. She wished she could exhibit some of the same courage. Especially when seeing how it affected her boss. She decided this was as good as any to step up. "I have an idea." Both Harriet and May stared at Jules.

"Well? What is it? We don't have all day," barked Harriett.

Jules straightened up in her chair. "I have a friend in the Benton Falls police department who may be able to help. I could give him a call and see?"

Harriet shook her head, but May stopped her before she had the chance to say no. "You got a better idea?"

Harriet sat back in her chair and sighed. "Alright, make the call. But for now, keep this between the three of us. Let me know what ideas your detective has." Jules noticed the grin on May's face. Calling in the authorities seemed to placate the angry nurse.

"May, you can go, but keep your eyes open." Turning to Julia, she said, "We need to discuss how the new resident search is progressing. We have to fill these rooms soon. Time isn't money but a full occupancy is."

Jules waited until May left the office before asking for information to aid in her investigation under the guise of selling new prospects. "Fine, I'm brainstorming novel ways to spin facts for pitching FALM to potential prospects. Do you have access to death records over the last few years?" Jules was all about the data. Mixed in with a dose of deception.

"What an odd request?" said Harriet, as she dipped her head, an eyebrow raised in suspicion, "You're not on the murder angle again, are you? You don't want to go down that path."

"Of course not," Jules lied. "I merely need some facts for this spin."

The administrator gave Julia a hard gaze, but Jules did not flinch.

Harriet answered, "We're required to report every passing to the state and yes, I have those records, but how would you spin death information to a prospective resident? It's not a topic people want to hear about."

"You're right, a sensitive topic. I want to see the data and develop an idea to assure the children their parents will be cared for. Not sure it will work, but I like to think out of the box."

Relenting, Harriet turned to her laptop. "I have the past three years on an excel. It's easier to email. No one wants paper anymore."

"Perfect!" Julia said, a little too eagerly. "Once I'm done, I'll keep you in the loop if I come up with anything." She got up to leave and was opening the door when Harriet had the last word.

"Anything *useable*," warned the administrator, reminding Julia of the sensitive nature of the information.

"Yes, of course, useable." Julia said, correcting herself.

Harriet waved Jules out of her office as she picked up the phone.

Usable, Jules thought. *Most everything is usable.*

"My boy? Harley Benton here. Do you have a moment?" Benton asked over the phone. Axel's silence told the old man the sound of his voice caught the younger man off guard. It was Kennedy's job to place the calls and, once connected, hand the phone off to Benton. But not today. Not with a call this important. "Axel, are you there?"

"Yes, yes. busy working on your Memorial plan. Is everything OK?" Axel asked.

"Of course," replied the old man, smiling as he toyed with his protégé. "Why wouldn't it be?"

"No reason," stammered Axel. "Yes, to answer your question, I have time. Need a break anyway. How can I help?"

Benton coughed and wiped his mouth before continuing. "There is a favor I have to ask," dropping the handkerchief onto the floor, a little reminder to Kennedy who was in charge. "I am receiving an award by the Rotary club and although I'd like to accept it in person. I am afraid it's not possible."

"Kennedy and I could get you there and back if you wish?" Axel offered.

Benton frowned. He hated suck ups almost as much as being wheelchair bound. Almost.

"No, you're very kind but quite unnecessary," he said in the most fake tone he could muster, unused to keeping his true feelings in check with subordinates. "I have an alternate idea." Benton let the sentence sit out there for a moment. To him, pauses were powerful.

"Yes?" Axel said.

Benton squelched the urge to grin, thinking, *the first one to speak always loses.* "My boy, I hoped because of your work on our charitable projects and your propensity for eloquence at the podium, you'd do me the honor of accepting the award for me?" Again, Benton paused.

"Why, uh…I'd be honored," Axel stammered. "Yes, of course I'd be happy to."

Good, according to plan, thought the old man before giving Axel the details of the event. They set an appointment for Axel to come to Benton Manor. Benton wanted to go over the speech. *Can't leave something this important to a mere amateur.*

"It's settled," the old man said, ending the conversation, the fake pleasing tone masking something else. Something darker. One more step towards the goal.

⇌

The Visiting Angels walked through the door of the FALM for an afternoon visit before dinner. All four signed in at the front desk, chatting with each other and the attendant.

"Who's in need today?" Helen asked. Because they had been coming on a regular basis, Jules had asked the nurses and orderlies to list those who needed a visit to lift their spirits. She had used this as a selling point to prospective family members. "If for any reason, you couldn't visit in a particular week, we have a church group come and sit with your loved ones to talk, or to listen." It turned out to be a great asset, and even though Julia spun it as a service offered by the home itself, and not the church, it was well received. Since the Angels had begun making their rounds, it also helped close quite a few sales.

"Good afternoon, our Angels," Jules said to the group. "A little early today?"

Gil was the first to respond, "Yes, a few of us had things planned for tonight, so we came in early. I also brought in some flowers for the nursing desk. They have been so kind to us."

"What a sweet gesture. It sure is good to have a few angels on our side," she said, hoping it sounded authentic, not wanting to make anyone in the group uncomfortable until her research was complete. "Have a pleasant visit," she said as she turned to walk back to her office. She stopped, turned around, and waited until Gil placed the flowers on the nurse's desk. When he looked at her, Julia wagged a finger at him. With his head slightly bowed and his eyes peering up at her, she thought he looked as if he was being summoned by a teacher for running in the hallway. "Tell me," she asked. "You come here on Tuesdays. Do you visit anywhere else?"

Gil's head rose, and a smile appeared on his face. "Yes, on Thursday we go to the VA home on Brinkerhoff and on Wednesday we hit the hospital. Seems like the middle of the week is the loneliest for most people." Julia noticed the smile disappear, only to have it return. To her, it seemed as though he enjoyed talking about the group and its mission.

"But that's why we do this. To make the unhappy, happy. At least for a day," he continued.

"And how long has this been going on?" she asked. *Ignorance is not bliss.*

"A little over a year at the hospital. Six months at the VA, I guess."

"God bless you and your friends for the work you're doing. It must be very comforting to the residents."

Gil looked as if the teacher had given him an A plus on an assignment. He beamed proudly as he walked back to his group.

"Here's your rotation list," said the nurse, handing it to Helen. As they looked it over, the attendant added, "Mr. Goggin's has a slight cold, so if you're worried about catching anything..."

"I'll see him," stated Gil, still beaming. "I'm not afraid of any cold."

As the four angels split up to do their rounds, Julia spied from the shadows, suspicious of the coincidences. She had done her homework and found since the group had been making their Tuesday night rounds, deaths had increased sevenfold in the same months year over year from the previous two. And not all, but most had occurred on either the Tuesday night or Wednesday morning after their visits. People died when it was their time. Axel could call it what he would, but coincidence or not, her residents were dying and on the same night as if going to a weekly bridge match. After the attack on Winnie and Mrs. Ramble, coincidence or not, it was hard to ignore.

The data did not lie. Which made her uneasy, but also a bit excited—now she found out where else the Angels had been visiting, which gave her another idea. A cross section of death by data. As she walked back to her office, she now could comprehend the thrill a detective got when investigating a crime. She did not have all the proof a crime had been committed; she was also unsure of a conspiracy. *Only way to find out is to dig deeper.*

She found Axel and pulled him into her office. "Any ideas on how to protect Winnie? I could ask Hector to watch over her."

Axel scratched his chin "But what about when he's not on duty? Who'll watch over her then?"

"We both will," said Jules, an eyebrow raised. "If Harriet won't pay for a surveillance system, we'll have to improvise." She brought out her phone and scanned, found what she was looking for online before texting to Axel.

He nodded when it popped up. "I'll go out right after my visits."

"Have at it," she said as she shooed him out the door, not wanting him to know what research she was working on yet. Once gone, she made four calls. The first to Hector.

"I spoke with Axel and we want to see if we can catch the med thief. Can you stay a little later today? I'll arrange it to get the hours back next week. Fair?" She trusted Hector. The only orderly she did trust. She was not sure who was stealing meds, but she was damn determined to find out. There was also an ulterior motive. To watch anyone coming into or out of the FALM.

The next two calls went to the hospital and VA home. She had contacts there who would provide the information she sought.

"What research are you doing?" was the question she received when she asked for the death records.

"My boss wants to make sure we're giving our patients the best quality care, and she's asking us to dig into mortality records to see if we're on par with other institutions. Everyone is so data driven these days." Julia did not like to lie but had a bigger motivation. Lives may be counting on her findings.

Her final call was to the Benton Falls Police Department. "Detective Gary Kepner, please," she asked the operator.

"Detective Kepner, can I help you?"

"Gary, it's Julia. How are you?"

A sigh came over the phone. "I'm fine, Julia, what do you want."

Jules frowned, "Is that any way to greet a friend?"

"So, we're friends now, eh? The last time we spoke was a few years ago. Remember how you called me about a stalker in your neighborhood. Said you had a hunch?"

"How did I know he was a contractor looking to buy houses to flip? He could have been a serial killer for all we knew." Jules hunch had been horribly wrong.

"Oh, friends only call each other every few years? I don't think so. Again I ask, what do you want?"

Detective Gary Kepner had been a friend to the family for years. Correction, her brother's friend from high school. Evidently, her use of the term "friend" was interpreted differently by the detective. Clearly, he was still upset about the mistaken identity of the contractor. She decided the best course of action was to dive right into the problem.

"We had medication stolen from our dispensary and we need help."

There was a pause on the line before Kepner spoke, "So this isn't a friendly call but a professional one?"

"Well," she answered. "It's sort of sensitive, so let's consider it a friendly, professional call."

"And how sensitive is this?"

"I need help finding out who the thief is. Can you help me?" She tried her hardest to sound like a damsel in distress. It worked.

Another sigh came across the line. "Alright, what do you need?"

She explained her idea, and he agreed to help, setting up a date and time. "But no more 'hunches.' I'll do the questioning and give you my results."

"Agreed," she responded, hanging up the phone. Smiling that she'd been successful on the phone, she turned back to the work on her desk filled with excel spreadsheets. The smile disappeared. Spreadsheets annoyed Julia. They had all these weird formulas and were at times unwieldy delivering the data she sought. But it was the best they could do and by late afternoon, she was comparing the death data between The FALM, Benton hospital and the VA home. She put each one on a new spreadsheet, each with its own tab so she could toggle between the three.

Each sheet organized by weekday and placed the date of deaths under each day, then tallied them at the bottom of the sheet. For each location she highlighted in green the days the Visiting Angels had appeared.

The task was arduous and gave Julia a headache as she worked. It would take time but she would either find a connection or, at the least, put her mind to rest.

As she sat at her desk mulling over coincidence versus conspiracy, she also wondered if they would have to put a call into the morgue tonight.

CHAPTER
– 12 –

"Hey, Rat boy, looks like a nasty spill in aisle five!" Benny Palz shouted to Hector from the end of the hallway, a yellow cleaning bucket on wheels at his feet. Placing a foot underneath, he tipped the bucket over and a greenish looking liquid with small clumps splattered across the floor.

"Hey!" yelled Axel, who stood behind Hector. On their rounds, he and Gil had come upon the orderlies. Benny's face dropped when he recognized Hector was not alone.

"What is wrong with you!" Gil asked, taking a step behind Axel.

Benny stood his ground pulling nervously on his sleeves as the three men approached him, the bitter aroma of the waste on the floor reaching their nostrils making all three men turn their heads but not stopping them. Hector put a sleeve to his nose to cover the stench.

"If you're expecting Hector to clean up, you better think again," Axel demanded.

"Yeah," said Gil, taking another step back.

Benny had regained his composure. "And what are you going to do about it?"

Hector intervened. "Mr. Axel, Mr. Gil, It's OK. It's my wing, I'll clean it." He headed to the storage closet, pulling out a mop and filling a bucket. The smell of disinfectant began to mix with the odor from the human waste, further nauseating Axel.

"No, it's not." he said as he pointed at Benny, "You made the mess? You clean it."

"Yeah, your mess, your duty to clean it." Gil snapped, taking a step forward.

Palz came closer to both men, sidestepping the mess on the floor. "And who is going to make me?" he asked threateningly, pushing a finger into Axel's chest. This time Gil took two steps back and leaned against the wall.

"Certainly not you, Rat boy lover," Palz said to Axel.

Axel held his ground as Hector passed him, already on his way to clean the mess. "Leave him be, Mr. Axel. Not worth it," he said over his shoulder.

Axel turned toward Benny, the two men glaring at each other.

"Stay outta my way, little man," he said before brushing by him and walking away. "If you know what's good for you." Axel watched him leave as Palz raised a fist towards Gil, causing his friend to flinch.

Axel had an urge to punch the little weasel on the spot, but decided it would not be the prudent thing to do so in front of the man cleaning up shit. He walked over to Hector and addressed him. "How long has this been going on?"

"Whaddya mean?" asked Hector, mopping without turning around.

"This guy has been bullying you. How long?"

"That guy has some real issues." Gil said. "Why is he such a, um, why is he so angry?"

"He's not too bad," Hector lied. "All I want is to be left alone, please."

"I'm going to report him. Who do I need to speak to? Jules?"

Gil chimed in, "Jules would be a good place to start."

"Please, Mr. Axel, it's nothing. Please do not make any trouble for me." Hector pleaded, looking back at Gil as he leaned against the wall.

Axel stepped back. *Not make any trouble?* Hector was the one being bullied and did not want trouble? "Do you want to tell me why you don't want any trouble?"

"Yeah, why not?" Gil said.

Hector shook his head and nodded in the direction of Gil. Axel took the hint. "Gil, I have this covered. I'll meet you in the car."

"Right," said Gil. He turned and headed back through the hallway. Axel watched his friend swivel his head back and forth, as if to stay on alert should the bully reappear.

Once alone, Axel asked again. "Okay, now tell me why you don't want any trouble?"

"No, Mr. Axel. I just want to be left alone to do my work. Please don't go talking to anyone about this. Please."

Hector's face said it all, his pleading eyes nearly ready to shed tears. Fear of something. Enough to allow a smaller and weaker man to bully him. To take this abuse, he held a secret he did not want to get out. A secret once escaped might result in dire consequences.

Axel decided if Hector did not want him to report the bully, he would honor the man's wishes. "Hector, bullying has consequences. Let me tell you a story and you'll understand." Axel recounted the advice of Winnie when a bully at school had been bothering him.

"How do you stop a bully?" she had asked.

"How?" young Axel responded through the hitching and tears.

"Punch him in the nose. A bully won't stop until you show him the consequences to his actions."

"But if he's bigger than me, he'll murder me!" young Axel countered.

"Ah, then you'll need a new strategy, because I like having you around."

The strategy was revealed the following day at recess as the bully came towards Axel with a menacing grin, his fists clenched and raised above his hips. Before the bully reached his target, Leif stepped in between the two. Making Axel no longer responsible for punching the bully in the nose. Leif did it for him.

"Remember this word," Leif mimicked Winnie as he pointed at the bloody nosed boy on the ground. "Consequences."

Every child in the school got the message. The consequence to any bad behavior towards Axel was Leif.

"But Mr. Axel, I tried that. Getting him to stop. It made matters worse. Please leave it alone."

He turned to Hector and said, "I won't cause you any trouble with Palz." He did not like to lie, but for now he had more important issues to deal with. "I have an idea, and I'll need your help. Can we meet later?"

Hector nodded, "Miss Julia told me you'd need my help, but we have to do it tonight. Can you stick around?"

"Sure. No problem."

Hector pursed his lips and blew out air in relief. "Thanks, Mr. Axel. Come around the back door by the garbage bins around nine O'clock, and I'll let you in. But remember, no talking to Miss Julia about Benny, OK?"

With roles reversed, Hector's problem became Axel's. This asshole was trash, and Axel decided it time to stop this bully. But not by punching him in the nose. There were more effective ways to teach Palz the meaning of the word 'consequence.' Axel would make sure Benny Palz learned the lesson. Damn sure.

Axel began his rounds in the Passing Lane by visiting Mrs. Hertzinger before moving on to Mr. Kinsella and finally slid the door open and walked into the next room. "Mrs. Ramble?" Axel inquired softly. "It's me, Axel Ahearne."

"Kurt?" she said meekly. "Is that you? Come." She waved a frail hand and patted it by her bedside. "I'm glad you came to visit your mother."

Axel pulled a chair up, too uncomfortable to sit on the bed. "How are you today, Mrs. Ramble?" he asked politely.

"Mother," she said, a bony finger wave admonishing him. "To you, I'm Mother."

Axel took the half full glass on her nightstand and felt it. Lukewarm. He took it into her bathroom and filled it with cold water before bringing back to her. *She thinks I'm Kurt.*

Kurt Ramble, the son, was a terror to a younger Axel. His greeting of, "Hey AXHOLE!" still frightened him upon thinking of the taunt, even after all these years. After Leif graduated, there was no one to protect him from *this* bully. Axel had not given much thought to the man since leaving high school, and even though he could excuse Mrs. Ramble from having Alzheimer's disease, he found it hard to swallow her ability to bear another disease... her son.

Axel wanted to correct the mistake. He wanted to tell her how badly he'd been treated by the bully of her son. But in the end, he made her drink a sip of water. He even granted her wish by calling her 'Mother.'

She spoke of times past, memories he would never recognize, people he'd never met. When it was time to go, he refilled her water glass with cold water and placed it on her nightstand. Patting her hand, he said goodnight and as he walked toward the door she said, "You're a good son." He did not respond as he stepped into the hallway and leaned against the wall, closed his eyes, and took a deep breath. God had a plan, but Axel wondered why he allowed his children to go through such pain and suffering before they could enter his kingdom. Perhaps it was sacrilegious, but when his turn to meet his maker arrived, it would be the first question asked.

"Hey Axel," said someone at the end of the hallway. Old fears returned enough to make his knees quiver. At first, he heard. "Hey Axhole." The voice chillingly familiar, prompting him to speak before opening his eyes to confront Kurt Ramble. "Hey, Hurt," he blurted out of habit, followed quickly by a "Sorry," when he saw the tired look on the face of his old nemesis.

Kurt gave Axel a sad smile. "I haven't been called that in years." The old bully leaned against the wall, sliding down until he sat on the floor. Axel followed suit.

"You haven't changed a bit," Kurt said, staring straight ahead while rubbing the stubble on his chin.

Axel wanted to utter, "You have," but didn't. He remembered Kurt as the tough linebacker from the football team. Tall, muscular, and mean. A cliché for the term bully, and no one messed with him. Back then, his nickname fit like a glove and a reputation he relished. But today, a different story. Kurt was still tall, his legs outstretching Axel's by a good foot. Now no longer muscular; his arms sagging thru his short-sleeve shirt. He had six-pack abs in high school but they had morphed into a keg, a beer belly protruding allowing a place to rest his arms. His meanness seemed to have softened too. "Visiting my mom, I see. How is she?"

Axel gulped before answering, another old habit returning in the face of an old nightmare. "We had a nice time chatting. She's a very sweet woman." He left out the part about the intruder.

"Was," Kurt corrected as he lifted one knee, his shoe flat against the floor. "She *was* a sweet woman. Now I don't even recognize her. Alzheimer's is a terrible disease. She's weak and frail. No way to live. I wish God would take her and be done with it."

The two sat silently for a moment before Axel spoke, "She was pretty lively tonight. She called me Kurt, mistaking me for you. Told me all sorts of stories before she tuckered out."

Kurt took a deep breath. "You're lucky. I'm always a stranger to her these days. She cowers anytime I enter the room. I hate seeing her like this. I did nothing but disappoint, an 'oops' baby and have been living up to the name my whole life."

Again, silence enveloped the men until Kurt put a hand out. "I want to apologize for being a dick to you in high school.

You're not the Axhole, I am. Thanks for visiting my mom. I really appreciate it."

Axel put out a hand, and they shook, sorrow overtaking him for this man who had one tough life. A saying popped into his mind; *Forgiveness is the gift you give yourself.* Now, the perfect time for such a gift. "No problem. I enjoy it."

Hector interrupted the conversation as he pushed his broom along the floor causing both men to stand. Hector nodded hello as he passed by.

"Aren't you going inside?" Axel asked.

"Nah, turns out she's already seen her son today," Kurt commented, a deep sigh of resignation. It seemed as though this bully had also endured pain. One much greater than a young Axel who had been bullied. Pain only relieved by the old woman's passing. One hurt replaced by another. The irony not lost on Axel. Had he not been consumed by the Ramble's issues, been a little more alert, he would have noticed a figure slipping through the door to the pool.

The water was as still as glass, the area always quiet at this time of evening except for the footsteps which carried across the calm water like a sonar ping. No one took late night swims or came to sit in one of the lounge chairs to read. Exactly why the Hastener picked the place. No one to snoop or ask questions. Hiding out for a few hours until all the residents were sound asleep was not the most comfortable, but the safest place to hide.

In the changing rooms, steel lockers stood in a row like sentries guarding their posts, their combination locks hanging like war medals. The Hastener walked through to the hiding spot in a storage room. It had become not only a place of hiding, but one of rest. The pool vacuum hose hung like a bedpost; orange life jackets offered a cushioned bed perfect for napping. The aroma of chlorine comforting the senses. Looking at the cell phone glow indicated a few hours left. Enough to take a short but restful nap. Plenty of time before heading to the Passing Lane. And freedom.

Hanging on a hook was a black hoodie. It had occurred to the Hastener early on to keep an identity secret; one needed a disguise. All superheroes had a costume, the hoodie an excellent choice. Especially coming in handy with the old Ahearne woman. Now, with identity still intact, the Hastener vowed to handle that loose end soon. But tonight, there was another matter to attend. One where suffering would end. This task made the Hastener glad. Performing good deeds, a worthwhile endeavor. Doing so anonymously without a thank you or accolades gave the process humility. The superheroes hood, fitting right in for this honorable emotion. Some people did not have any heroes. Another problem easily rectified. In the absence of heroes, there was only one alternative. Become one.

"Pssst, over here Mr. Axel," whispered Hector. The orderly was halfway out a door resembling an ordinary broom closet, his finger beckoning. Axel, a plastic bag in his hands, followed Hector through the door and walked into a dark room save for the faint light emitting from a ceiling lamp. It gave the room a gloomy appearance like a scene out of a horror movie or some creepy guy's surveillance of his ex-girlfriend.

"What's your idea?" Hector asked as Axel pulled the contents from the bag. It looked like a doorbell.

"Let's see what we're working with, shall we? It's like a James Bond film. We're protecting ourselves. Have you ever heard of a Vidbell?"

Hector shook his head.

"It's a video doorbell. This one works with a battery, so you don't have to wire it into your electrical system. Screw it in, set it up on our phones and we'll be able to get alerts on any activity."

"But Mr. Axel," stated Hector, a look of concern on his face. "I don't have a cell phone."

Axel reached into the bag once more. "You do now."

A big grin crossed Hector's face. He had never before owned a cell phone. All his money went to his parents. The smile was replaced when he scrunched his lips to the corner of his mouth, a thought occurring to him. "Where will we put it? Where it won't be seen? Miss Harriet won't like us spying, and if Benny finds out..."

"You leave him to me. I can handle Benny Palz." Benny was trash and now Axel's problem. *Time to take out the trash.*

Axel and Hector sat in the broom closet as they discussed the perfect place for the Vidbell in Winnie's room, offering her enough privacy but alerting Axel to any visitors.

"Why your grandmother's room?"

"She's very important to me. If your mom or pop were in here, wouldn't you want to keep an eye on them? To make sure they didn't fall or have a medical issue?" Axel fibbed.

"Sure, you're a good grandson, Mr. Axel."

Axel downloaded the app and put the settings on vibrate. They could be silent...and stealthy. He then added Hector's and Jules' phone numbers to the list to receive notifications on the 'motion detected' setting.

"You know what to do?" asked Axel.

"I guess," responded Hector. Axel could tell he was still unsure of the action plan, in enough trouble already with Benny and the break-ins to the med room. Now they were adding cameras, a necessary evil worth explaining again.

"Hector. You're still not sure of this plan, I get it. But let me ask you a question. Do you believe in God?"

"Of course, I do. As any good Catholic does." As devout as anyone, save Axel, Hector began attending St. Simons shortly after meeting Axel, transferring from the church his parents attended. Even they came around once Axel introduced them to Father Tom.

"And do you trust in *me*?" Axel asked.

Hector bent his head as if ashamed, as if he had not shown the proper respect to his friend. "Yes."

"Both God and I are here to protect you and Winnie. Understand?"

Hector nodded his head. Axel patted Hector on the back. "Let's get back to the Lord's work, shall we?"

Mrs. Ramble lay asleep, snoring lightly as the visitor approached the bed. Such a shame. But time to finish what the old Ahearne woman had interrupted. The police were not called and there was no chatter at the FALM suggesting anyone had believed the woman's story of an intruder. Or she had believed it to be a dream. Either way, God's work waited for no one.

Mrs. Ramble suffered from other maladies but especially low blood pressure. A sealed baggie containing a mixture of an over the counter diuretic combined with ibuprofen would lower it further and send her to sleep comfortably, before quickly exiting her system without a trace. Except for urinating in her own bed. A small price to pay for an eternity of bliss.

The powdery contents were added to a glass filled with water, then stirring the solution until mostly dissolved. "Mother?" came the question, holding the straw to her lips. "Time for your medication."

She stirred but did not fully wake, taking the straw into her mouth and sucking instinctively until it was pulled back when she began to cough. After the bout, the straw once again found her lips until she had consumed the rest of the liquid. The Hastener stepped into the bathroom to rinse the glass and fill it once more with fresh water completing the murderous task.

The Hastener began to pray. "O Lord, welcome Dorothy to everlasting life in your presence. Go with—" Mrs. Ramble interrupted the prayer inquiring, "Kurt?" A hint of saliva forming in the corner of her mouth. "Come sit by me. I'm scared."

Sitting in the chair next to the bed offered enough room to grasp the old woman's hand, patting the top of it with a free one in comfort.

The dying woman began to hum a song, soft and melodic, yet unrecognizable. "You're a good boy to sit with his ailing mother. But I'll be home soon," she claimed in between hums. "Home soon."

As the medication began to take its toll. Mrs. Ramble dropped her hand causing the arm to slump along the side of the bed. It was picked up and placed gently over her chest.

Blessed are the merciful for they shall be shown mercy.

After the deed was done, the Hastener remained silent the whole way home.

CHAPTER
- 13 -

The news of Mrs. Ramble's passing made the atmosphere at the FALM morose and shocked both Axel and Jules. After the initial attack, they were now convinced that hers and other deaths were not coincidental. Jules wanted to share the information she had collected to prove where the patterns existed. The guilt each felt for not protecting Mrs. Ramble weighed heavily. Determined not to let it happen again, Jules moved a folding chair next to her desk and pointed at it. "Here, sit next to me."

"Any word on the pool lifeguards?" Axel asked.

"Yeah, both are college students. No way they could do this."

"And Palz?" Axel would love nothing more than see the punk go to jail.

"He's next on my list to interview. I'll fill you in once I speak with him. Now, check this out." Julia pointed to the laptop and the spreadsheets she had been working on to show Axel what she had found.

She clicked on the spreadsheet entitled Operation Euthanasia. "There," she said, pointing to the green-shaded totals for FALM on Tuesday. "See the percentages spike on Tuesday nights and Wednesdays?"

Axel sat there with a bemused expression on his face. "OK, Watson, this Sherlock will play along."

She punched him in the arm, "This is serious. Now, watch when I click the VA home tab for Thursday. Compared to the other days, this shows another death spike."

"It still proves nothing. So far, only coincidental," Axel pushed. "We need more, something tangible. What else you got?" he said. His conversion to her theory had been shocking, scaring him as to who could be the next target. He also knew that if they were going to catch a killer, they needed hard evidence.

She clicked on the third tab. "Here's the hospital for Wednesday... and voila, another spike Wednesday night and Thursday."

"Whoa. These days all correspond with the Visits by the Angels. You think one of them is the killer?"

"I'm not sure, but it is a pattern. Although, it could also be someone who is trying to make it appear that way."

"Jules, this is an outrageous path. I know these folks, all good Christians. Besides, one can make data show anything one wants. We need concrete evidence like forensics to take to the police. Do you have any?"

Undeterred, Julia responded, "No, but I want to rule out anyone who enters the building."

"If you want to catch a murderer, you need more evidence. What is it they say, 'follow the science?' Which would mean..." Axel waited for her to pick up his hint. She did.

"Get an autopsy," she said, a solemn tone to her voice.

"Get an autopsy," he repeated, just as solemnly.

"Well, it might be difficult to get any of the families to agree to an autopsy. Families don't enjoy carving their loved ones."

"Guess there goes your theory," Axel said.

"Not so fast, ye of little faith," she said. "I'm sure I have a few more tricks up my sleeve. Not sure what they are, but don't underestimate me."

Axel did not. He wondered what tricks she was capable of manufacturing, and hoped her blouse, however filled with tricks, was short sleeved.

The phone rang surprising Benton. Gaining his composure, he let it ring once more before answering. "Axel, my boy," he responded, believing the young man had forgotten to update him or to ask a question. He was wrong. It was Harriet.

"Mr. Benton, we have a problem. Medication has gone missing."

Harley Benton hated it when things did not go according to plan. When one problem was solved, another popped up to destroy his mood. He scrunched his face and breathed through his nose before answering. "Harriet, this is what I pay you for. To solve problems for me. Do I have to remind you of this every time?"

"No sir, you don't. But this is a serious issue, and I need your council. Don't you think we should call the police?"

"I do NOT!" Benton screamed into the phone. "The last thing we need is to do is involve the police! You need to get your head out of your ass and do your job!"

"But sir?" Harriet squeaked, giving Benton the higher ground but also, he surmised, presenting him with another problem. He was correct on both.

"There are murmurings about these exits."

"Murmurings?" he asked. "What murmurings?"

"Some people are questioning the high number of the recent exits. If they are, how do I put this... natural?"

"Woman, what are you talking about? Idle chatter about unnatural deaths? Have you lost your mind?"

"No sir, I haven't. Others have suspicions a few of these exits could be, are, well, caused by—"

Benton yelled into the phone, "Out with it. Caused by what?"

He heard Harriet take a deep breath and then she delivered the one word he never thought he would hear from a nursing facility. Especially his.

"Murder," came the reply.

A few hours after Harriet had presented her murmurings to Benton, Jules stepped into her office.

Before Jules could speak, Harriet asked, "Any headway on the medication thief? I trust we're keeping a low profile on this?" She whispered as if they were in a crowded room rather than her office with the door closed.

"We are," answered Julia. "I've asked Detective Gary Kepner to assist with the employee interviews and then I'll go over the responses with him."

"Any early front running suspects?"

"Believe it or not, two are on the list. Benny Palz is one."

"Doesn't surprise me. There is something not right with that boy. But when the young folks are not breaking down the doors to work here, we have to take what we can get. Who's the other one?"

"Hector Gonzalez."

"What?" the administrator said with a tone of incredulity. "You can't possibly suspect Hector, can you?"

"No, But I want to be thorough. He is the only orderly with keys to the med room, but that doesn't convict him. We still need proof. Several people have been in the room since we discovered the loss."

"Time is of the essence, we can't have meds go missing every day now, can we?"

Jules cringed at the thought Harriet was more concerned with the loss of expensive medication than the prospect of danger to her residents.

The phone rang and Harriet shooed Jules out of the room with a wave of her hand, whispering a final word, "Discretion."

She picked up the phone, confident of who it might be. This would be the second call from him this morning.

"Harriet," said her boss on the other line. "Any updates?"

Harriet explained their investigative process and how they planned to keep it under wraps.

"Good, no need to upset the residents," Benton replied.

"I would agree," said Harriet.

"A few other things we should agree on. One, when found, the thief needs to be terminated. Have them escorted out the door, post haste."

"The other things?" she asked.

"Only one. Let's have no further talk of anything unsavory in my home."

"Like what?" she questioned, unsure where he was going with this thread.

The answer was brutal and direct. "Like murder."

Harriet hung up the phone and immediately went to the bathroom. After this second call, she needed a good scrub.

On Thursday, Axel and Gil met up with the other two Angels at the Veteran's Home in the neighboring town of Clawson. The town, smaller than Benton Falls, comprised a row of downtown shops, a park near a small lake and easy access to Highway 35.

"Why they put the VA here, is beyond me," commented Axel.

Gil answered, "The politicians said they wanted to give the people a direct route to go visit their loved ones, but I suspect the real reason was a direct route of cash to the politicians' pockets."

"Skeptical much?" Axel asked as they walked to through the front doors.

"You would be skeptical too, if you…" Gil stopped in mid-sentence. "My dad was skeptical. Maybe I got it from him."

Axel knew about skepticism. After speaking with Jules and the attack on Winnie, he had more questions than ever, a trend which frightened him.

Although the building was old, it had good bones. A clean facility despite news reports of homes such as these being dilapidated or in dire need of repair. The Murphy home, named after a WW II hero from the town who never returned, was not one of them.

The four Angels spread out to do their rounds. Fifteen minutes was not very long per visit, but enough to make sure several residents had at least a few visitors. Most were Viet Nam vets, others from conflicts or skirmishes in Central Asia. Older vets were easier to spend time with. They had lived through hell and grown old with their demons intact. The young men and women coming in with arms or legs missing were not so inclined and this bothered him. But it was the veterans who sustained brain damage that sent him over the edge. Service for your country should mean engaging the enemy in combat, instead of the cowardly practice of hiding devices to blow up unsuspecting troops. Still, he visited as many as possible, spending the time talking about anything other than the horrors of war.

One patient stood out. This soldier had been horribly disfigured in a helicopter crash in Afghanistan after extracting wounded soldiers from a position the marines wanted to hold. What should have been a hero's welcome turned into tragedy. While being ferried back to base, the helicopter was hit by a rocket-propelled grenade.

The hero was the lone survivor. He had lost both arms and legs, was burnt beyond recognition, and his lower jaw was missing. Despite the catastrophic condition, this marine was still breathing on his own. Axel marveled at the toughness of the young man, disfigured in a war waged far too long.

His chart told Axel his name was Specialist First Class Hobie Frehorst. He was born and raised nearby in a small farming town. Sturdy and strong, with a fierce desire to serve his country, SFC Frehorst had spent months at Walter Reed before coming home to be close to family. But each time Axel came to visit, Hobie was alone. After asking the nurse, he found Hobie *had* no visitors; he was apparently a sight too painful for the heartiest of souls. Axel discovered that within the first year of Hobie's injuries, his father had died of a heart attack. His mother had succumbed to cancer a year later. As an only child, this poor soul could not catch a break.

Axel spent more than his allotted fifteen minutes talking to Hobie about normal matters such as the weather and updating the young patient on how his local baseball team was faring. He even told him about his new friend, Veronica. Axel wondered if Hobie had a girlfriend nearby, but even if he did, it was doubtful a young woman could deal with a tragedy such as this..

The doctors did not talk directly to Axel, but the nurse indicated the prognosis of the young man. They would feed him intravenously, clean the wounds as best as possible but because of his dire condition and no one to take responsibility, there would be no skin grafts, no reconstruction. A grand way to thank a vet for his service.

Axel decided if no one else would help, he would. The plan began with a veteran-focused charity, asking their board to look at his personal recommendation. He sought other charities interested in assisting wounded veterans and then called his congressman and other politicians to hear his plea.

The news from the nurse about Hobie's future did not come as a surprise. Nothing more could be done for Specialist Frehorst, except make him as comfortable as possible. And wait.

Axel stepped into the young man's room and sat next to his bed. "It's a nice spring day," he said. "Hobie, there is a sweet smell of cut grass in the air and the sun would warm your face." There was no response as usual, but Axel moved forward anyway.

"By now you must know the end is near, and although I can't do anything about that, there was one thing I could do. My congressman and I contacted The Office of Army National Cemeteries, and you'll be heading to Arlington. It's an above ground Inurement. I hope that's OK. I was told not to say anything, but the congressman also informed me there's talk of you and your fellow soldiers receiving the Purple Heart soon." Axel saw a tear form in Hobie's eye and wiped it away before it hit the pillow.

Axel stood bedside and said his prayer, made the sign of the cross and whispered, "Thank you for your service, Specialist First Class Hobie Frehorst. Rest well." He saluted the broken hero before walking to the door.

As he stepped into the hallway, he found Gil waiting for his turn with the soldier.

"How is he today?" he asked, as if the soldier's condition might have miraculously changed in the last fifteen minutes.

"Same. But Gil?" Axel said, stopping him before he entered the room. "Can you catch a ride home with the girls? I need to stop in to see Winnie."

"No problem," Gil answered.

Axel grabbed his friend by the arm and nodded his head at Hobie's door. "Can you also do me a favor?"

"Sure, pal. What do you need?"

"Thank the man for his service to his country, would you?"

Gil slowly nodded. "Absolutely," he said and went in, a solemn expression on his face.

As Axel walked back to his car, he thought; *Old people are supposed to die. What is hard to fathom is when the young pass. But at least Specialist Frehorst would go to his Maker with full military honors from a grateful nation.*

⮑

After returning from the VA, Axel stopped by the FALM to check on Winnie. The Vidbell camera bothered her at first, but once Axel showed her his phone app, she saw it was placed in such a way not only to defend her from assault but to protect her privacy. "Seeing yourself on TV is kinda fun," she commented, "Until you think someone is watching you on the toilet."

"Trust me, no one will see anything of the sort. As if anyone would want to," came Axel's retort.

"Now, now, be nice. I'll have you know I was a looker back in the day. All the boys wanted to be my boyfriend."

"Like Harley Benton?" He regretted the faux pas as he watched Winnie's face darken.

"Definitely not that cold fish," she said. Axel noticed a change of expression before she spoke again.

"Blessed are the Righteous, for they shall be the fisher of men," she whispered.

"What?" Axel asked. "Did you say something?"

"I have an idea," said Winnie, a finger against her temple. "Where do you go to fish?" Axel was never much of a fisherman. "I don't know, a lake or river. A pond maybe."

"No silly, you go where the fish are. The Passing Lane is where people go to die in this place."

"Not sure I follow," Axel said, scratching his head.

"It's where the fish are located. For the killer. The easiest people to kill are the ones who can't protect themselves, right?"

"I guess?"

"Keep up, boy," she admonished. "We know where the fish are. What do we need next?"

"Um, fishing equipment? A license? A boat. I don't know, I'm confused by this analogy."

"Bait, son. We need bait."

It dawned on Axel what his grandmother was suggesting. "Wait a minute, tell me you're not suggesting—"

Winnie interrupted him. "For crying out loud, Jules would have gotten it a lot quicker. You need someone who's on the ball. Good thing for you she's available. And she likes you."

Axel turned his head quickly, "She does?" He caught himself and then turned the conversation back to her crazy plan. "I mean, you are *not* going to do this. It's not right."

"Of course, it is. Who else could do it? Like I said, blessed are the right. God doesn't care for those who are always wrong."

He wanted to correct her but only shook his head. "I forbid it. This plan of yours is too dangerous."

"Forbid, huh? I'll run it by Jules. She'll see the wisdom in it. As for dangerous, you can give me a fake disease, then put me in the Passing Lane with one of those doohickey cameras to watch over me. I can fake a deathly illness." She coughed a few times, and Axel had to admit she sounded convincing. "We'll call it 'Operation Chum.' Clever, huh?"

"It's not clever," Axel said, frowning at the idea. "It's reckless." It was dangerous, yet he could not shake the internal voice telling him she was right. If you wanted to catch fish, you had to first go where the fish were. He was uncomfortable with the fact that in order to lure a killer, his grandmother had to play the role of bait.

～⊃

Absolution comes in all shapes and sizes. Forgiving oneself or others is a difficult task to perform. The one place to receive absolution when all other avenues are blocked is the confessional. A place where you can sit with a priest and tell him what weighs heavily on your mind. Then, receive penance and be granted forgiveness, not by the man in the next booth but by God Himself.

It was the early morning before a weekday mass, the perfect time to ask for the absolution of sin from the deaf priest of St. Paul's. There was plenty on this person's mind, most having to do with the recent hastening of Hobie Frehorst. Even though the justification for the death came from good intentions, a good confession was in order.

The sinner sat in a pew a few feet from the confessional while others awaited their turn: an elderly man and woman, his old paw covering hers as they knelt in prayer. A mother attempting to calm her impatient son by pulling out a book for him to read. *Probably a first confession, a daunting task for any child.*

Although not the first time in the confessional booth, it sure felt like it. Sweat formed on palms. A jerk of the head towards any sound. Negative thoughts filled the mind. Regardless of the hard-of-hearing priest, nerves made their jangled appearance each time before telling the old man the latest transgression. Today was no exception.

An old woman sat in front, a scarf around her head reminiscent of days gone by when it was mandated that every woman's head must be covered upon entering the church. A sign of deference the younger women no longer followed, if they came to church at all. The church of these childhood memories was steeped in mystery. The history of saints and sinners and the touch of dread brought on by the prospect of choosing the wrong side. Cross God and risk banishment to a fiery hell where you would spend eternity in interminable agony.

The confessional door opened as the newly cleansed soul crept to the alter to recite penance with a promise to sin no more.

The walk towards the confessional booth was short. In the haste to close the door, the sinner flipped on the switch and began reciting the confessional opening, "Bless me, Father, for I have sinned—" The sentence halted when the light did not turn on. Flipping the switch several times produced the same result. Darkness.

Peering through the small, latticed window used for communication and designed for anonymity, the petitioner looked in horror. This priest did not have the cragged profile of the old, deaf priest but instead, he was a young man in the Catholic collar. His brown hair was neatly cut, his voice youthful and full of energy, not ancient and lethargic.

"Sorry, the light doesn't work anymore. I disabled it," said the youthful voice. "Go on, my child, tell me your sins."

"Where is Father Champlin?" came the reply, the mind clouded with fear.

"Father Champlin has taken ill. I'm Father Testa, and I'm pinch hitting for him until he recovers."

"When will he be coming back?"

"Hard to say. Might be a few days or longer. Please continue with your confession. We have people waiting."

The sinner took a deep breath and began. "Bless me, Father, for I have sinned. It's been a week since my last confession. I lied to a co-worker…" Listed were a few sins, all venial, all boring. No mention of mercy or hastening. Without hearing the final penance, the sinner slipped out of the booth and through the side door of the church. In the haste to exit and for the first time in this sinner's life, there was no genuflecting in front of the altar.

CHAPTER
- 14 -

Axel entered Mrs. Young's room. It was dark because the shades were closed, keeping the early evening light at bay. At first glance, he thought she was asleep, her hands resting at her sides, the blanket tucked under her armpits. He was about to leave when something about the stillness of the old woman changed his mind, and he turned back towards her. At the side of the bed, he touched her arm. It was cold. He then took two fingers, placing them on the side of her neck near the carotid artery like he'd seen many people do on TV. No pulse. Saddened, he took a deep breath. This was not good. Fear crept into his thoughts. *Is this another murder? Or just a natural death?* Then, *What if Jules caught me in here? She already suspects the Angels.* He was not about to take the chance of being discovered with the corpse of the old lady, whether she had departed by normal or nefarious means. He said a quick prayer and slipped into the hallway. *She'll be found soon enough.*

As Axel headed down the hall, he spotted Hector. He raised a hand in a silent greeting but lowered it when he saw who followed his friend. Benny Palz. Axel watched as

Palz patted Hector on the arm before turning towards the front hall, but the young man pulled away as if burnt by a flame. Hector turned and began walking towards Axel, his eyes squinting and mouth pursed. Hector flipped his keys in the air and snatched them in what appeared to be…what? Frustration? Anger? Agitation?

"Hector," Axel whispered. "Hector?" But the big orderly walked on, unaware of Axel's presence until he was right upon him. "Whoa, big guy. You almost ran me over," Axel said as he laughed at his friend. Hector raised his head, showing Axel a pained expression, as if he had lost a favorite pet.

"What's the matter, big man?" Axel asked with concern. When Hector did not respond, he asked another question, "Did that horse's ass pick on you again? If he did, God help him."

"He didn't pick on me," said Hector, a tear forming in the corner of his right eye. "He did worse. I need to talk to somebody about this. What am I gonna do?"

The pleading pained Axel. "You can confide in me. If you're in trouble, I'm here to help. You helped me with my grandmother; now it's my turn to help you."

"Really, Mr. Axel? Cause I'm in trouble deep."

"Yes, really," responded Axel as he touched the young man on the arm. "We should get out of the hall and speak somewhere more private." He motioned for Hector to follow him when the orderly stopped and grabbed Axel's arm. "Is Mrs. Young asleep?"

"Uh, yes. She's out for the night," said Axel. *She's out forever.* "Let's keep going."

"No, this is perfect," Hector replied, opening the door and stepping inside. Axel followed reluctantly.

"Hector, not a good idea. What if we wake her?"

"We won't, poor thing. Wouldn't hear us if we screamed, let alone talked."

Won't hear us, anyway, thought Axel as he tried to persuade his friend by pulling on his arm. "We should find a different place." His pleading fell on deaf ears, as Hector stepped into the room and headed to the bathroom, dragging Axel with him.

Hector closed the bathroom door, fondled his keys and told Axel the story: his parents, Benny's bullying threat and the scene in the medication room. When he finished, he looked at Axel with eager optimism, hoping Axel would come to the rescue again. "Do you have any ideas? Cause if not, he sinks my whole family."

"Not yet, but I'll come up with something. Did anyone see you?"

"No, but Benny will blame me. Plus, a detective is interviewing people this week, and I'm afraid he'll find out it was me." The keys jangled in his hands as if *they* were being grilled.

Thinking quickly, Axel said, "Look, the detective will ask you a series of questions about the missing drugs. You need your answers to be brief and to the point. Got it?"

"Yes," Hector answered, but Axel was not so sure.

"Hector, do you have the time?" Axel asked, now annoyed that Hector was still playing with his keys. Axel needed him to focus.

"What? No, I don't wear a watch, and I just got a cell phone. I wish—"

Axel cut him off and grabbed the keys from Hector, placing them on the sink. "I didn't ask you about a watch or a phone, only if you had the time. If you get questioned, answer yes, no or I don't know. Nothing more."

"Oh, I get it." Recognition appeared on his face. "Ask me again."

"Hector, do you have the time?"

"No," replied the orderly, puffing out his chest proudly, as if he had correctly answered a teacher's tough question.

"Good. Remember, yes, no or I don't know, only."

Hector's expression changed from pride to worry as he asked the next question, "But what if they ask me if I stole the medication?"

"Ah," Axel explained. "But you didn't. Benny did. Do you have the meds?"

Hector frowned. "No, of course not, Benny—" This time he interrupted himself as he realized Axel was testing him. "No," he replied.

"Right. If Benny has the meds, he stole them, not you." Axel took his friend's hand to broach the more serious topic. "You realize you may need to lie, don't you?"

"Yes," was the big man's answer.

Axel pushed him further. "Did you open the door to the med room?"

"No," Hector lied. Axel found it convincing.

"Good. One-word answers. Lie when necessary and you'll be fine. If you get nervous…" Axel tapped his wrist. "Do you have the time?"

Hector got it right away. "No."

"Good." The men were about to leave the bathroom when they heard someone enter the room. Hector put a finger to his lips to make sure neither made any noise. Footsteps made their way into the room, past the bathroom and then, silence.

Axel felt sweat dampening his armpits. The next-to-last thing he wanted right now was to get Hector involved in Mrs. Young's death. The last thing he feared was getting blamed for it.

Hector mouthed the word, "Housekeeping." Axel moved closer to the shower and stepped in. Hector followed suit. He closed the curtain as the bathroom door opened. The two men held their breath. The room darkened with a click as the night nurse turned the bathroom light off before leaving the room.

Relief covered Axel like a warm blanket on a chilly night. The two men stood silently in the shower stall for another few minutes before sneaking back into the hallway, closing the door on Mrs. Young for the last time. Hector's keys remained on the sink.

⌐⌐⌐

The Hastener watched as the two men exited Mrs. Young's room and walked down the corridor. *What were they doing in there?* A cold sweat broke across the brow. *"Do they know Mrs. Young has been hastened? Do they suspect anything?*

Feeling nauseous, the Hastener entered Mrs. Young's room. She still looked asleep, undisturbed by the toxic cocktail of fast absorbing naproxen and ibuprofen. This combination led to the heart attack that had sent her on her way. If they had discovered her, there would be a rush of activity. There was not, though; all was quiet.

Relief swept over the Angel of Mercy, who stepped into the bathroom for a splash of cold water to the face. Sitting on the sink were Hector's keys. "Hello," said the Hastener with a grin. Insurance was a concept designed to protect the insured. With these keys, an alternate plan appeared. One throwing suspicion on a different medication thief. These hastening's would point at one and only one suspect. One who was plausible and would not be missed. The Hastener placed the keys inside the hoodie pouch, pleased at the new insurance plan. This one paying two dividends. No one likes a bully. No one.

⬥

Winnie began by practicing her cough. Then she toned down her personality so people would suspect something was amiss. Next came putting on a drowsy act or taking an unplanned nap in the lounge area, feigning listlessness. Dropping out of an occasional card game or leaving the dining room early led friends to voice their concerns to the management. Her complaint of, "I have one foot on the nana and another in the split," proved useful. It also gave her friends a nervous chuckle when she was out of earshot.

Winnie was convincing. Jules and Axel reluctantly approved her plan, allowing 'Operation Chum' to proceed. The doctor examined her. His diagnosis? She was old. Old people fade. He signed off on moving her into the Passing Lane.

To pull this off, they had taken Hector into their little circle, explaining the plan and swearing him to secrecy. Hector moved the Vidbell camera from her old room to the new one with no one the wiser. If she were to be bait for a killer, Axel wanted to make sure they had a full view of the fishbowl.

"I still don't like this," he complained as three phones pinged, showing them the Vidbell worked. "Hector, please keep an eye out for anything out of the ordinary." The big man nodded, clearly aware of the great responsibility.

Winnie produced a fake cough before chiming in, "Don't you worry, with Hector near, nothing bad will happen. Remember, 'Blessed are the meek: for they shall inherit the earth.' Now who would want to inherit a planet with all the global warming and pollution? Not me. This is no time for the faint of heart. We have a killer to catch."

Axel, realizing she got the beatitude right, smiled. He was still nervous but also felt if anyone could pull this off, it would be his feisty grandmother.

Jules pulled Axel aside and whispered, "What are you doing tonight?" When he did not answer right away, she stammered, "I thought maybe we could do the stakeout in my office. I could order us Chinese?"

Axel frowned. "I'd like to, but I have too much going on. Mr. Benton is riding me to finish the preparations for his statue and charity, and I've—"

She cut him off, "Yeah, sure, I get it. I just thought, um, you know." She looked at her feet, not wanting to show her disappointment.

"Maybe tomorrow, huh?" Axel said. Then to finish the conversation, he leaned in close and whispered, "I like Chinese food."

Jules brightened and touched his arm, the disappointment fading. "Me too. Then it's a—" she stopped and thought before finishing the statement, her face turning crimson. "A plan. It's a plan."

Axel, clueless of her faux pas, checked his phone again to make sure Winnie's bed was visible.

"Let Operation Chum commence!" Winnie said happily, as if preparing to blow out birthday candles instead of waiting for a killer to pay a visit.

⌁

The management of the FALM may have welcomed the interviews concerning the stolen medications, but the employees did not. Each one was paraded into the conference room where Detective Gary Kepner sat, ready to ask questions that made everyone except him nervous.

They began innocently enough. "Tell me a little about your family," or "Do you enjoy your work?" Questions easy to answer and enough to get the questioned comfortable speaking with him.

Each visit lasted approximately fifteen to thirty minutes, and the threat of suspicion or suspension thwarted any discussions between employees. Once interviewed, Kepner allowed each employee to leave for the day. The idea to interview at the end of each shift stifled the risk of gossip.

Kepner rubbed his eyes. He was tired, but glad the end of the day was near. Only two more interviews to go. He sipped on the lukewarm coffee and waited as Hector entered the room. The detective asked him to sit across the table, noticing the orderly was nervously tapping his wrist with his index finger. More nervous than the other employees he had spoken with so far. He jotted the observation in his notebook.

"How are you doing today?"

Hector tapped his wrist twice before answering. "Good."

Kepner noticed the tap on bare skin as if attempting to revive a broken watch.

"Would you like some water?"

"No." Hector answered, but not until he had tapped his wrist again.

Kepner noted the odd behavior in his notebook. Sometimes, a tic such as this represented a clue. The person was lying. The only way to find out was to find true answers to see if the tapping continued.

"Is your name Hector Gonzalez?" Kepner asked first.

The orderly again tapped his wrist twice before answering. "Yes."

"Did you drive to work today?" The detective had the license plate numbers of all the employees. Hector took the bus because he did not have a car.

Tap, Tap. "No," Hector answered correctly.

Kepner looked at the employee sheet. Hector had worked here for over five years. "And you've worked here for four years?"

Tap, Tap. "No," answered Hector. Kepner sensed the young man wanted to continue the sentence, but when he did not, the next question followed.

"How many years have you worked here?"

Tap, Tap. "Five," answered Hector.

Kepner had not seen this behavior before. On the police force, he had seen nervous tics but not the tap on the wrist before every answer. He shifted his strategy by asking an open-ended question, requiring more than a one-word answer. "Hector, medication was stolen from the med room." Kepner let the sentence sink in while grabbing a manila folder and waving it in the air. "I have a file on you, and it tells me you have a key for the med room. Can you explain why I shouldn't suspect you as the thief?"

Hector paused before giving his answer. The tapping began again. This time not the two taps but several frustrated taps in rapid fire succession, as if the non-existent watch were being uncooperative. *Tap, Tap, tappity, tap, tap, tap.* "Yes."

Good, here comes the information I'm looking for. Kepner sat patiently, waiting for Hector to speak again but when he didn't, prompted, "Well?"

The detective found asking open-ended questions could lead to answers he wanted. The manila envelope was a prop used to scare his suspects into believing management had more information on them, but held nothing more than blank pages. An old police trick to frighten suspects into talking. Neither worked in Hector's case. He remained silent. Frustrated, Kepner asked point blank, "Did you steal the medication, Hector?"

"No," he answered, leaning in towards the detective. This time there was no tapping. The thirty minutes expired, and the detective still had another employee to interview. He gave Hector the stern warning about discussing this matter while an ongoing investigation took place, then told the orderly he was free to go home.

Hector rose, opened the door and was about to step through when it dawned on Kepner what the employee was doing. He yelled out, "Hector, before you leave…"

Hector turned around while holding the door open with his right foot.

"Do you have the time?" The detective asked.

Hector brought his finger to tap his wrist but caught himself. "No," he said. "I don't wear a watch." He then exited the room.

"Smart," Kepner said, not done with the wrist-tapping Hector Gonzalez. He picked up the last manila folder with the blank sheets inside. The name on it was Benny Palz. Calling the front desk, the receptionist informed him Benny had already left for the day, "Guess I'll hafta wait until tomorrow," he said aloud, interested in speaking with this last employee. He would never get the chance.

Veronica stifled a laugh. "Really? Of all the titles, you picked this one for your new book? Can you even use it in the title? Isn't it copywritten somewhere?" They were sitting on the couch in her apartment before dinner. Each sipped on the Merlot Leif had brought with him.

"I can't use the phrase itself, no," he said, a little hurt by her teasing. "But when you change it to mean something else, it's ok. My publisher assures me I'm fine. No patent office police will stop by my house."

"I'm sorry to laugh, but it sounds kitschy. *When Life Gives You Lemons, Make More than Lemonade?*" She stopped laughing but maintained a smirk as she extended the joke. "When life gives *me* lemons, I look for a drink to put them in."

"Laugh all you want. I found it brilliant," he responded. "It's a metaphor warning people not to stay content, but always strive for more."

"Sounds more like a meme on your social media feed."

"My agent and publisher believe it could outsell *Climb*. If that's the case, you can laugh all you want, cause I'm—"

"Gonna laugh all the way to the bank? Is that the title of your *next* book?" she said, giggling.

"No, but it's not bad. I'll run it by my agent. Self-help books are big business, which means more travel for me. Upside is, I don't have to pay for any of it!"

"You've got all the answers, don't you, mister? Where *do* you get these ideas?"

Leif pondered the question before he gave an answer. "There are two types of people when presented with life's roadblocks. The first throws his hands in the air in frustration. The second, rolls up his sleeves and gets to work. He's the one who benefits."

"Are you quoting your new book?" she asked.

"I was the frustrated guy for a long time. I always blamed others for my misfortune. It wasn't until I met you that I wanted to be the second guy. I imagined you wouldn't want to stay with the first person long."

"So, you changed for me, huh? But what about the first book? Written before we met."

"It wasn't a case of throwing my hands up. I was merely waving to get someone's attention. An attempt to scam a paycheck. I got both. I was more surprised than anyone." He paused as if reflecting on what to say next. He whispered, "I'll never go back to being that guy again."

"I'm proud of you." She reached for his hand and held it. Her phone rang, and she dropped Leif's hand and picked up the call by the second ring. "Oh, hey, Axel," she said, shooting a grimace at Leif. "Wait, what? Jeez, Axel. I'm not sure. When is it again?" The silence brought another face, the one she made when conjuring up an excuse.

"Uh, I have to check my schedule at work. Might have to do a double. But I tell you what, I'd love to attend and if I can, I will, but I can't commit." She added, "If you want to ask someone else, it won't hurt my feelings." She gave Leif a hopeful glance. "Alright, I'll keep you informed. Bye."

"Are you going on a date with my brother?" Leif teased.

"Not remotely funny. He wanted me to be his date for the award he's accepting on Harley Benton's behalf."

Leif laughed. "And you turned him down? What kind of monster are you?"

"We have to talk about this. When do you plan on telling him?"

Leif looked confused. "About the new book?"

"No, silly. About us. You and me."

"Not looking forward to it." It was one thing to challenge Axel to a debate, another to break his heart. He knew he was about to do damage, but hoped to soften the news by telling him on Axel's big night. "Let's go together, and he'll get the picture."

Veronica took another sip of wine, "I'm sure it will bother him, but you need to rip the bandage off and get it over with. The sooner the better."

Leif pondered if sooner *was* better. It was one thing to rip off the bandage. It was the wound underneath he did not care to see.

Axel thought about his conversation with Veronica. She hadn't actually turned him down, but she hadn't agreed to come to the Benton event, either. He didn't want to sit in a roomful of people he barely knew. Although he was quite accomplished giving prepared remarks, he failed miserably at small talk. He needed to hedge his social bet, so he called Gil.

"Are you busy tomorrow night?" he asked.

"Well," Gil answered. "That depends on the time. I made plans to meet some friends out tomorrow night. Why?"

"I'm giving a speech to accept an award for Harley Benton and thought you might want to tag along?" Axel said. "It's a dinner event."

"Darn. I wish you had told me sooner. I've been trying to get together with these folks for the longest time. I'm really sorry. I would have liked to see you perform."

Axel laughed at the word. "'Perform' makes it sound as if I'm a monkey on a leash. It's just a speech, so no big deal. I just thought I it would be nice to have a friendly face in the crowd. Someone I could actually have a conversation with."

"I could cancel." Gil offered.

"Absolutely not," Axel said. It was a nice gesture. Axel was disappointed but didn't want his friend changing plans just because he was uncomfortable playing nice with strangers.

"No, really. It would be no trouble. I like to support my friends."

Axel was heartened by Gil's kindness, but questioned the sincerity. He had generously offered to change plans, yet the tone in Gil's voice said otherwise. Axel likened it to making an offer but hoping he wasn't taken up on it. The offer generous, yet hollow. He let Gil off the hook.

"No," Axel said firmly. "You keep your plans. Veronica said she might show up and I'll get Leif to be my wingman. It'll be fine. But thanks for the offer."

"And of course, Winnie will be there, right?" Gil asked.

Axel paused briefly before answering. "You haven't heard? She's been moved into the passing Lane."

"I'm so sorry, Axel. Is there anything I can do?"

Axel was touched by Gil's concern but didn't want to let anyone else in on their ruse. Too many people knew already and the opportunity for a leak grew as you added more people.

"No, it was inevitable. She's getting to the point where we all go sooner or later." He hated lying, but when the stakes were high, the tactics to achieve the goal were lowered. "There is something you can do. I'm sure she'd appreciate a visit. That would cheer her up."

"Sure, I can do that. Does she like flowers?"

"Does she! Lilies are her favorite."

"Lilies it is, then. I'll see when I can stop in and we'll have a nice chat."

"Just let me know when you can make it so we can be sure she's feeling up to visitors." Axel made a mental note to tell Winnie. "I appreciate it. You're a good friend."

"Thanks. Good luck on the speech."

"Yeah, maybe next time?"

"I don't think so."

This remark caught Axel by surprise. "Why not?"

"Axel," Gil responded. "The next time you speak will most likely be at a funeral. I don't do funerals."

Amused, Axel agreed with him. "I take your point." In fact, Axel couldn't remember seeing Gil at any of the funerals. Brushing the thought aside, he spoke to end the conversation. "Have a good time while I'm nervously speaking to a bunch of people I hardly know."

He heard Gil chuckle, glad to amuse his friend. "I will. Don't worry, you'll do well as usual."

Just before he hung up, Axel asked, "And Gil?"

"Yes?"

"Don't forget the Lilies."

CHAPTER

– 15 –

The evening of the Benton award ceremony found Axel with butterflies in his stomach, even more than when he had to give a eulogy. He had learned to use nerves to gain power and use the power to speak with effectiveness and confidence. He took a trick from the late Yul Brynner. Before he would go on stage, Mr. Brynner used to press his fingers against a wall, pushing with only his fingertips, the pressure making them quiver. Only then would he lift his arms into the air, the energy from the finger press coursing through his arms and giving him the adrenaline essential to building confidence as he strode onto the stage.

Axel now used this trick under his table. Hands held beneath the tablecloth, pressing the underside, and experiencing the surge of energy coursing through his arms and into his chest. A three-by-five card with the bullet points of his remarks sat in his breast pocket as a safeguard. He would not need it tonight. He had practiced the speech with Benton several times and by himself; in the bathroom, on his walks and once in his car, where a police officer had pulled next to him with an expression asking why this person was talking to himself. Axel saw the concerned look on the officer's face, pointed to the radio and pretended he was singing along to the music. The officer nodded in recognition and moved along.

Axel looked around the room filled with politicians and clergy, friends, and fellow parishioners. His nerves sounded an alarm, not because of the speech but because there were important people missing. Veronica and Leif had not yet arrived. They both agreed they would be here, and he hoped they were on their way. At least to catch the acceptance speech for the great Harley Benton.

As dinner ended, Axel found himself too nervous to do anything but pick at the food on his plate. He waited in anticipation as the Master of Ceremonies stood at the podium and began his introduction, "Ladies and gentlemen…" Axel scanned the room once more for his brother and Veronica, pressing his fingers harder beneath the wooden table. "…It is my great pleasure…" *Please, please, walk through the door!* "…to introduce a young man…" Panicking now, Axel had the powerful urge to urinate. *Not now, please.* "…who is helping to facilitate the Benton Foundation. Here to accept the award for our guest of honor…"

He was about to run to the restroom when the door to the hall opened and in walked Veronica, followed by Leif. Axel raised his hand to signal them and stood, relieved they had arrived. No longer nervous, he stepped past the table and began walking to the podium, the urge to urinate having passed.

"…Mr. Axel Ahearne!"

Bounding up the steps to the podium and without pulling his notecard from his pocket, Axel performed another trick.

This one learned when he had begun his public speaking by looking into the audience and belting out the first line of his speech, always memorized, to get the ball rolling.

"Mother Teresa said, 'I alone cannot change the world, but I can cast a stone across the waters to create many ripples.' The man we honor tonight has thrown boulders across the waters of this town and made waves." He began as he cruised through the acceptance speech as though he had been speaking in front of the public all his life. His confidence high, his tone solid, his humility believable with no hint of facetiousness. He thanked his benefactor, Harley Benton, for the opportunity to leave a lasting legacy and humbled he was given the honor of giving tonight's speech. When finished, the audience rewarded him with a standing ovation. Axel stood at the podium, the applause like a symphony, the orchestra playing for an audience of one.

As he returned to the table, people slapped him on the back with congratulations. He was greeted by his brother. "Great job, little brother," Leif said, while Veronica kissed him on the cheek. "Well done," she whispered. "Well done."

"Congratulations Harley Benton!" Axel shouted, the applause rising again.

Surrounded by well-wishers and caught between back slaps and handshakes, Axel could only watch as Leif and Veronica waved to him before turning their backs and heading toward the door. It took him a few moments, but he broke free, chasing after them to see if they would like to go out to celebrate. He pushed open the hall door and stepped out into the cool night air, gazing into the starlit night sky. Jubilant, he leapt down the stairs, scanning for them. As he approached the parking lot, he was about to yell when the words got caught in his throat.

As the pair stood by Leif's car, Axel's shoulders drooped in despair as Veronica, on her tiptoes, planted a soft, lingering kiss on his brother's lips. The urge to urinate came back stronger than ever, but he barely noticed because the bottom of his stomach had fallen out. All the accolades in heaven and earth or tricks of the speaking trade would not be enough to fill the cavernous hole created by their deception.

The Hastener awoke from a nap after eleven PM. There would be no one awake in the building except the on-site nurse stationed at the front entrance. Staying clear of that area, the intruder slid through silent corridors.

The intruder came upon the medication room and, using a key from Hector's ring, found the one to open the door. Once inside, wearing a pair of rubber gloves to avoid fingerprints, the Hastener began filling the hoodie pouch with specific meds to made sure it did not look like a mere grab and go. If this plan were to work, the correct drugs needed to be confiscated. A few drugs people would pay good money for, others to point fingers. Then, the two drugs for promises to keep.

With the pouch filled, the Hastener stepped into the hallway, looking both ways before locking the door again. *Don't want to temp anyone else.* The intruder crept along the hallway until coming upon a resident's door. Mr. Portnoy. The door opened, then closed, the Hastener tiptoeing towards the bed.

Mr. Portnoy suffered from severe rheumatoid arthritis, his fingers curled inward, the knuckles large with inflammation. A blanket covered most of the sleeping man, exposing a knee the size of a grapefruit. A saline drip hung over the man like a small tree, delivering necessary hydration to the roots the man could barely move. The resident must have been in excruciating pain. The intruder had made a promise to free Mr. Portnoy when the chance arose. Today was the day for Mr. Portnoy, a merciful death serving two purposes. Relieve a man with excruciating pain and place the blame on the shoulders of another, soon to join him.

The confiscated vial of morphine filled a hypodermic needle. Severe cases of rheumatoid arthritis caused the immune system to attack the joints. An overdose of the drug would finish what the immune system had begun. The intruder pierced the top of the saline bag with the needle. No need to be careful, leaving a noticeable hole before pushing the plunger. Who cared if they suspected foul play? All part of the plan. The process was repeated until the vial and plunger were both empty.

In the bathroom, the vial was dropped into the wastebasket, leaving additional evidence for the police to find. The needle was tucked back into its case and placed into the hoodie pouch for use later in tonight's agenda. Finally, prayers were said over the man, wishing him Godspeed on this last journey.

The task complete, the Hastener snuck out of the building and once outside began whistling a cheerful tune on the way to finish the plan. It was time to punch a bully in the nose. For good.

The apartment building was dilapidated, with a dirty brown exterior and a sour, musty smell in the entry way. Benny Palz attempted to unlock the front door but found it already unlocked. "Great, someone forgot to lock the front door again. What a bunch of idiots!"

Benny lived alone. He may have shared the building with several occupants, but they were nothing more to him. Surviving on his own all these years, he needed no one. When one of his neighbors greeted him, his response was to grunt and move on. He had no use for any neighbors, especially friendly ones. They gave him his space. Plenty of it.

After work, Benny had stopped off at his favorite watering hole for a few pops, staying longer than planned but not nearly as long as he wanted. Since he had been the only patron at the bar, the bartender closed a little early and kicked Benny out. He did not mind so much when he grabbed takeout at the Burger Haven before it too closed.

He stopped by the mailboxes and opened his. "Trash, trash, trash," he complained as he tossed a flyer on buying lake front property, an oil change postcard and a letter urging him to at once open it for great insurance news. He pulled out a few bills, holding them as if they were infected with anthrax, and tossed them into the trash bucket. "Try to get the money, you blood suckers," he said. One letter he kept was the electric bill. This one he would pay. Had to keep the lights on.

He trudged up the stairwell to his third story apartment, catching his breath on the landing by placing his free hand on one knee. *You would think I'd get used to these stairs by now.* The word "smoking" appeared in his mind as a reminder the habit could be responsible for the wheezing. Benny shook his head, knowing he would never quit, no matter how gross those TV commercials looked, with their actors made up to look like they had no jaw or had a hole in their throat. All fake news.

Once he caught his breath, he reached for his key. All his keys were on a ring attached to a metal wire leading to the recoil hanging on a belt loop. He found the key to his door, but before he put it in the lock, he tested the knob to make sure it was locked, recalling the front door incident. It was.

Unlocking the door and stepping in, he turned on the light, illuminating the small kitchen leading into an equally small sitting room. Off to the right was the bathroom, to the left a bedroom.

He threw his electric bill and the food bag on the table. He reached into his hoodie pouch and pulled out a pack of smokes and withdrew one. He dropped the pack on the table and picked up a lighter. A drag on the cigarette felt good after a long day in the hell hole where he worked. "Idiots," he said to no one but referring to his coworkers. Including the big dumb oaf, Gonzalez. "Gentle Giant, my ass. More like a big pussy." He took another drag and then opened his food bag but before he could reach in, felt a sharp pain in the right side of his neck, instinctively reacting by turning towards it, eyes wide in surprise.

"Who's the pussy now?" Benny heard someone behind him say as he slumped to the floor. *Idiot* was the final thought before he passed out. The last one he would ever have.

Axel sat on the steps of his brother's house, fuming. Purchased with the help of his advance money, the irony not lost on Axel. With his newfound success, the author of *Climb Your Own Tree* had put down roots. The tuxedo he was wearing from the awards dinner crinkled at the knees. He pulled his overcoat around him to keep it from falling off his shoulders. He did not need it for warmth; his anger took care of that problem.

Leif's car approached and pulled into the driveway. As he got out, Axel noticed something on his brother's face he rarely saw. Confusion.

"What are you doing here?" Leif said as he came around the side of the car.

"How long has this been going on!" Axel asked through clenched teeth, in no mood for any explanations from his brother.

"How long has wha—"

"You and Veronica…You know exactly what I'm saying. How long?" Axel demanded.

His brother sighed. "Oh. Only recently. We talked, and we kinda clicked."

"But you knew I liked her!" Axel said, raising his voice and taking a step towards his brother.

"You *liked* her? Are we still in high school?"

"You always take whatever you want," barked Axel, his upper lip in a snarl making him resemble a junk yard dog protecting his turf. "Take. Take. Take. Selfish bastard! God Damn you!"

Axel lunged for Leif, who sidestepped the assault and pushed his brother to the ground.

"Whoa, take it easy. I don't want to hurt you," warned Leif.

Axel scrambled to his feet and charged once more. Once more, Leif sidestepped his brother, again pushing him to the ground. This time, he put a hand against the back of Axel's neck, holding his face to the sidewalk.

"Get off me you, horses' ass!" Axel screamed as he struggled underneath the weight of his brother.

"Not until you calm down. I took nothing. We spoke after your lunch and she asked me out to dinner. From there it kinda took off. I said nothing because I wanted to protect you."

Axel's breathing slowed as he lay against the pavement. "Protect me?" He began but stopped as it registered. "Wait, *she* asked you out?"

"Yes, I swear. Now, can we discuss this in a civilized manner, or do I have to hold you on this sidewalk all night?"

Axel slapped his left hand on the sidewalk, a gesture showing surrender. This ploy was familiar from their childhood. He had to do it every time they got into a squabble. He never saw his brother ever making the sign. *Just once, I would like to see that happen*, he thought before Leif released his hold. Axel stood and brushed the dirt from his pants. "You always get everything," he said, his resignation clear.

"Oh, hell, that's not true. You're the responsible one. Why do you think Winnie gave you the house?"

"Because you'd screw it up." Axel said, regretting the words at once, but could not reach out and grab them once they had left his lips.

"Yeah, in the past, maybe. But I've changed."

"Oh yeah? I've heard *that* before," Axel said, still angry but no longer hostile. "Many times."

Leif sat next to Axel, who noticed another expression he had never seen from his brother. It looked like contentment.

"No, I'm serious. Ever since Veronica has come into my life, everything changed. For the first time in my life, I found something I'd been lacking."

Axel, losing steam, felt the need to ask. "And what was lacking?"

"Purpose," Leif said with conviction, as if finally recognizing the meaning. "I found a purpose." Softening his tone added, "Dude, the heart wants what the heart wants. You don't want to pine after a woman who wants to be with someone else, do you? You've got to see reason in this."

Axel pondered the question before answering, taking a deep breath. He had blamed Leif for taking away his girl but had not considered the possibility she had initiated the romance. She was not someone's possession, like a pet, but a confident woman who knew her own mind. Qualities he had admired and found attractive. How could he argue with the fact if she wanted to be with someone else, she did not want *him?*

"Look, there are lots of women out there who would be proud to be with you. You need to find one. Pain sucks. But it's like those playground monkey bars. To move on, you have to let go—" Leif paused.

"Leif?" asked Axel. "Did you make that up?"

"No. C. S. Lewis," he answered, fumbling for his cell. "Monkey bars," he repeated, tapping on the cell keyboard.

"How do you know this stuff?" Axel was incredulous Leif could repeat a quote, let alone know the author.

"I read. Something you ought to take up…" Leif kept typing. "Hold on, I got an idea and need to write it down. Don't want to lose it. Gimme a sec." As Leif typed about monkey bars, Axel waited impatiently to finish the discussion. There was always something interrupting the dialogue between the two. Leif's penchant for wandering, his need to be the center of attention, Veronica, and now this idea thing. Items that should bring the two together often had the opposite effect.

"OK, I'm back. Where were we?" Leif asked, placing the cell on the sidewalk in case a new idea sprang forth.

Axel put his face in his hands and sighed. He was bone tired. The exhaustion you get when you have had a long, stressful day, and it ends in heartbreak. He was no longer angry, unprepared to continue this fight. In fact, Veronica made the choice so he could not put the blame solely on his brother. If the tables were turned, he might do the same thing.

"Never mind, if you both want to date, I give my blessing. I wish you told me rather than me finding out like this."

"Finding out?"

"I saw her kiss you in the parking lot after the ceremony," he said, head still hanging low. "It hurt. Still does."

"Sorry, brother. I never meant to hurt you. Are we good?"

Axel sighed. Even if Leif had not meant to cause pain and apologized, it did not mean his actions had no impact.

"Tell you what," Leif interjected. "Let's go out to dinner to celebrate. Just the two of us. How's next week?"

"What do we have to celebrate?" Axel asked, believing his confetti wet, the cake moldy, and all the balloons had popped.

"Purpose. The success of my book and new career path. You can pick the restaurant. On me."

Another sigh came to Axels lips, saddened by the events of the evening. A passage from Matthew 19:23 came to mind. *Then Jesus said to His disciples, "Truly I tell you; it is hard for a rich man to enter the kingdom of heaven."*

As he sat on the sidewalk near the house of his brother, he pondered the verse wondering if this was God's plan; give everything to Leif on Earth, yet not let him enter his Kingdom. Axel, although still angry, did not want to consider an eternity without his brother, but glad he himself was not a rich man.

⌐⌐

The hooded intruder stood over the drugged Benny Palz and whispered, "No more bullying for you." Benny's drugged body was moved to the ratty couch and his own hoodie splayed across it. The intruder stepped back into the kitchen, extracting a spoon from a drawer and Benny's lighter off the table with a gloved hand. The lit cigarette from the floor was placed in the ashtray near the small table by the couch. "Don't want to start a fire, now, do we?" The unconscious Palz did not respond.

The candle on the table next to the ashtray was lit, and the spoon placed next to it. Two items were pulled from the hoodie pocket. A rubber tube pilfered from the med room and a clear resealable packet, the contents the texture of sugar. Not the white refined kind, but the dark cane crystals you would find in the brown packets at a diner. The intruder marveled at how easy it was to get the drug. For a small town, it sure had its share of drug addicts and dealers.

Benny was then positioned to lie against the sofa as though taking a nap; arms splayed out, head resting against the top of the cushion, mouth agape.

The rubber hose was wrapped around the drugged man's left arm before emptying the contents of heroin into the spoon and guiding it over the candle to cook the mixture until it liquified. A vein was found to inject the poison into the man's left arm. *Enough to kill ten men, let alone this one piece of shit.* To stay on the safe side, the intruder took off the man's shoes and socks and made a few punctures in between Benny's toes before putting the footwear back on the dying man. Research had shown junkies did this to hide the track marks. It also made it appear as though Benny had been taking this drug for a while. For good measure, the needle left between Benny's fingers, his thumb on the plunger head as if he had just finished the injection.

Once satisfied, the intruder stepped back to admire the handiwork. Not wanting to leave any reason to suspect anything but a drug overdose, Hector's keys were placed in Benny's pocket. The stolen medication from the nursing home dumped onto the counter near the sink, saving one vial for a special hastening. Benny's fingerprints made every bottle, the ultimate indignity to the bully who had given Hector this much trouble. There was only one thing worse than a junkie. And when the authorities found him, they would report to the nursing home they had found the drugs in his apartment, solving the case of the missing meds. Yes, Benny Palz would go down in his puny, wasteful, and shitty life as not only a junkie, but a thief. And if it ever came to it, a murderer.

"Who's the Rat Boy now, asshat?" the intruder mumbled.

The final act would come in the form of an anonymous phone call to the police complaining of an unpleasant odor emanating from underneath Benny's door. Rats stink when they are alive, but even more so when they are dead.

The killer stepped to the door but before opening it, stopped, and turned back to the table with the bag of food Palz had left. Inside were two burgers and a bag of fries. Grabbing the bag, the intruder flipped the lock on the door before exiting. All this hard work would leave anyone hungry.

CHAPTER
- 16 -

Not all the dead stay with you, a burden much too heavy. But some do. Like the pine sap from a conifer tree, once the stickiness leaves, a residue remains. And it is black.

The Hastener awoke, unsettled to find the light already shining in through the bedroom window. A cold sweat had returned, as did the recurring childhood dream. Same bedroom, same pajamas, same robe. This was where the similarities ended. This time as bare feet lay flat against the floor, the gnarled hands with wretched fingernails enveloped them, pulling them through the planks as if made of water.

The grotesque hands slid up legs to grab pajamas, the nails tearing fabric, biting into flesh, drawing blood. They pulled at knees, then the waist and finally, chest. By the time the hands reached the neck, a scream escaped. A crying, pitiful wail. Arms outstretched for a savior who was not coming, before slipping beneath the floorboards, drowning in darkness.

Fully awake now and shaking, the dreamer thought, If this wasn't a sign, what was? Dreams never held much sway, but this one moved the dreamer to the core. The realization forgiveness was necessary. Not for the sin of hastening, believing those were from God's hands. No, the need for repentance and forgiveness came from the others. The priest and Palz. Those were not hastening's, but murder committed out of hubris. Of hate. Asking now produced only silence. Like the absent savior of the latest dream, God was nowhere to be found.

Disregarding the earlier notion of addressing God, the sinner resorted to an old pattern. Dressing and heading out the door, not for work but for church. This was too important to leave to chance. Pulling into the church parking lot, the sinner rushed into the church, needing a priest for God's forgiveness.

In God's silence, the message was crystal clear. In the absence of light, only two things remain: Darkness and terror.

"How long do you think he'll stay angry?" Veronica asked as she tucked her head comfortably against his chest, a hand placed over his heart.

"He's been pre-occupied lately; we haven't spoken much. No worries, I'm confident the cold war thaw is coming soon."

"What makes you say that?" Veronica wrinkled her nose, scratching it with an index finger, his chest hairs tickling her. "I hate this rift between us."

"Axel doesn't stay mad at anyone for long. He's a super Christian and those types forgive readily. He always says, 'Forgiveness is the—'"

"The gift you give yourself." She interrupted him with the line she had heard often. "Yeah, it's a good saying, but I'm not so sure."

"He'll get over it. Besides, I'm his brother. He can't stay mad at us forever."

"He can chill me out as long as he wants. I'm not a part of his family," she said, twirling his chest hairs with her fingers.

"Yet," stated Leif.

Understanding his intended message, she warned, "Don't toy with me, mister. When you hint at something this important, you better be prepared to follow through."

The two had taken their relationship to the next level. Veronica had never known a man like Leif or fallen head over heels in love with anyone else. Until now. Her nursing career was on track and his career was taking off. His bad boy persona morphing from me-first mode to helping others straighten out their own lives pleased her to no end. Their dual success took away pressure of the financial strain most young couples face. If there were other tests to their relationship, they would overcome those too.

Leif laughed. "You Catholic girls may start late, but more than make up for it."

She playfully slapped his chin, and he playfully acted hurt before adding, "Give it time and he'll come around."

"I hope so. But he can be stubborn. He should be prone to forgiveness, but this test might be too hard for him."

"I predict he will. Let's give him a little space. Do you have any girlfriends looking for love? The fastest way to mend a broken heart is to fill it with another love. Love is like glue, baby. You and I are stuck together."

"Man, how cheesy," she said, grimacing. "Maybe someone at the hospital. The idea is sound. Your delivery? Not so much."

"Well, that hurt," he said, in a mock tone of pain. "You should respect my advice. I am an up-and-coming Self-help maven. I've hundreds of followers. Who knows how many more I can get?"

"You keep bragging, Mr. Man, and you'll have one less fan," she said, kissing him on the nose.

"Aw, you couldn't live without me, we're joined at the hip. Isn't it time you gave yourself a gift?"

"Forgive this," she whispered as she straddled him.

"That, my dear, is not my hip," he mumbled through a kiss.

"Forgive *this*," she repeated. The last words either spoke for quite a while.

"Bless me father, for I have sinned. It's been a week since my last…" The sinner stumbled on the word *confession* while looking at the disabled light switch.

"What is it, my child? What troubles you?"

The sinner thought hard about what to say next. Although confident the purpose was right, others may not see it the same. Especially a priest. But there was a way around this conundrum. Research had given the sinner a potential Catch twenty-two.

"Father, may I ask you a question?"

"Of course," was the priest's response.

"If told of a sin you may find grievous, would you report it to the authorities?"

The priest wiggled in his seat. The sinner guessed he was wrestling with the answer. "No, my son. Canon law is clear. The seal of the confessional is sacred between a priest and his confessor. No matter how grievous the sin, the confessor answers only to God. No. A priest cannot violate the seal."

A wave of relief swept in, but the sinner asked another question to make sure hearing it from the priest, himself. "But Father, what would happen if a priest *violated* the seal?"

"Excommunication. And no priest in good standing would ever want that. Ease your mind and please tell me and God your sins in order to forgive you."

"And are you a priest in good standing, Father?" The sinner asked, hammering the last nail in the coffin.

"I am. Very good standing. I love my vocation and respect my vows, never to be broken."

The research had paid off. Priests were banned from exposing confessions to anyone, even the police, under penalty from a higher power. Like a journalist protecting their source or a lawyer their client, the sinner was now under no threat for the confession of sins. Grievous or not.

Satisfied, the sinner began telling the priest about the hastening's, all those released including the priest and Palz, explaining the mission and whatever consequences would follow.

The priest listened until the sinner was through. He was silent a long time prompting a question, "Father? Are you all right?"

The priest sighed before answering, "My child, you are mistaken. This is the work of the devil, not our lord. You may think you are doing these people a great service, but you are wrong and must stop."

"I can't father. As you were called to do God's work, so have I been called."

"God's work? Murder is a mortal sin, not an act of good, as if you helped an old woman cross the street!"

The sinner countered with another justification. "Mark 5:7 says, 'Blessed are the merciful, for they shall be shown mercy.' What I'm doing is merciful."

The priests' voice rose past the whisper stage, "But you cannot! What must I do to convince you? This is morally wrong."

"Nothing, Father. You've told me what I need to know." The sinner said, confidence returning. The confession and conversation lifting the large boulder of guilt. For the first time in a long while, the sinner could breathe comfortably. "Although I respect your authority, there is a higher one I respect even more."

"Please, listen to me!" the priest pleaded before being cut off.

"The only thing I need to hear right now is your penance." The priest had been shaken but the sinner, no longer concerned about the man's emotional state, had only one issue in mind. Absolution.

"I, uh, I've never been confronted with this type of sin before. Please give me a moment." After what seemed like an eternity to the sinner, the priest took a deep breath and dispensed what his duty called for. "You must say the rosary every night for a full year. It is not enough for me to grant absolution; you now need God more than ever." The sinner made the sign of the cross as the priest finished.

"May God absolve you of your sins in the name of the Father, Son and Holy Spirit. Amen. Go in peace and sin no more. But please heed my—"

The sinner exiting the confessional, never heard the priest finish. Walking to the front of the altar, the newly absolved genuflected and made the sign of the cross before striding to the side door, opening it with a loud bang, thankful for the first time to leave a church.

Axel arrived at Benton Manor for his weekly dinner date. Benton had proved to be both a smart mentor and gracious host. Axel enjoyed these meetings, the food, cocktails, and the conversation. He had even come to disregard the urine aroma.

Axel was about to knock on Benton's large door, then decided against it. Every time he tried, Kennedy was there a half second before his knuckles touched the hardwood. As he waited with no Kennedy, impatience prompted him to knock, anyway. Before his clenched fist knocked on the door, it opened and there stood the butler, his back arched, gazing out past Axel.

"Good evening, Mr. Ahearne. Mr. Benton is in the study."

"How do you do that?" asked Axel, shaking his head in bewilderment.

The butler gave Axel a small smirk, "Do what, sir?"

"The door," he began, but decided it unworthy of further discussion. "Never mind. The study?"

"Yes sir. I'll deliver your cocktail post haste," assured Kennedy as he walked towards the pantry, leaving Axel to escort himself through the double doors of the study. Benton sat in his wheelchair close to the fire, an attempt to warm his frail body.

"Ah, lad. Good of you to come. Sit, sit." Benton waved bony fingers toward the armchair Axel used on his visits. "We have much to discuss."

"My pleasure, sir. I enjoy our weekly visits."

"I'd like to discuss other arrangements in our business agreement," Benton began, huddling closer to the fire. "I'd like to add a few codicils."

Axel, nodded. It was Benton's money. How could a few additions prove harmful?

"I'm not getting any younger, nor is my health improving. I am aware the end could come at any time, and I am resigned to prepare for the eventuality...." He paused as Kennedy entered the room, handed Axel his drink, then left, all without a word.

"I've spoken to my attorney and put an addition into my will whereby my estate will donate the same amount each year from this date until the day of my passing." The old man produced a document from his desk and waved it in the air.

Axel's eyes went wide, but he said nothing. "When I'm deceased, I will give a large percent of my wealth to the trust so you can do greater acts of charity at your choosing. And because I have no heirs, I am making you executor of my estate."

"That's very generous, Mr. Benton. I... I'm not sure how to respond?" Axel stammered, incredulous at the old man's offer.

"How about a 'thank you,'" joked the old man. "But there's more. This is merely my offer. A request is forthcoming." Benton coughed again, a small but wet sound emanating from the old man. This time no sourness or handkerchief. "This request is twofold. One, we name the charity the Harley Benton fund, and I will offer the services of my accountant to handle the trust for you."

Axel eyed the old man before answering, "And the second?"

The old man chuckled, "You are a sharp one. I hope you are as compassionate as your grandmother. As I am the last in line of the Benton's with no heirs, I need this legacy. The money in time will become irrelevant to me. The only thing left for me is time and in my case, in short supply, I'm afraid." Benton paused, reflecting on his future irrelevance in this world.

"I have been afraid of very little during my lifetime," he said. "But one thing disturbs me these days. Do you want to venture a guess?"

Axel sipped his drink as he pondered an answer. Death? Too easy an answer, so he spoke of a scenario he had witnessed before. "Would it have to do with being immobile or perhaps falling into a coma?"

"Right again, young man. As a man of action all these years, it bothers me to be in this chair, but it frightens me to be stuck in bed, unable to communicate with the outside world."

Axel was troubled, "But you wouldn't know if you were comatose." From Mr. Strong, Axel had learned this to be false, but used it as an attempt to get out of this task. He underestimated the curiosity of the old man.

"Not necessarily. I've done research on this issue. Yes, some unfortunate people who've been in comas for years, appear to be asleep. In reality, awake, yet immobile. You see my dilemma. It's a terrifying prospect of being stuck alone inside my head. Nothing but darkness."

Axel took another sip, the whiskey causing a comfortable burn as it slid down his throat before he placed the glass on the table. *What is it with these people?* First Winnie and now Benton. Who did they think he was, the Angel of Death? He missed the coaster as he protested. "Now wait a minute—" Benton cut him off as he fumbled to correct his glass to coaster mistake.

"When the time comes where I can no longer be mobile, can no longer fend for myself, I need someone strong, like you, to make sure I don't find myself in this terrifying predicament. In essence, I'll need you to realize what is happening and to assist…"

Axel interrupted, "In helping you pass?"

"Oh, heavens no. That is what a DNR is for. I want you to allow me the privilege of staying in my own home, my own bed."

Axel sat back in his chair, relieved.

"Mr. Ahearne, forgive me," Benton said. "I didn't mean to offend. I'm not asking for you to do anything other than show mercy to an old man. I am afraid of lingering on, stuck in a strange and unwelcoming place with nothing but my thoughts. It would be like living in a prison. At least this home is *my* prison. Surely you can understand, can't you?"

Axel could, but there was a string attached, Axel was sure of it. The fear crept up his body like a rash. A sip of whiskey did not help.

"It may not come to that young man. I could die in my sleep tonight. It's a contingency if no hope for recovery. Sort of like insurance if you will." The old man paused, and a gave a gentle sigh, like air escaping a slow leak from a balloon. "Please," he begged. "I wish to stay here as long as possible. I can trust you to accommodate my wish, can't I?"

Axel put his hand to his forehead as he pondered this development. The scenario Shakespearian in nature. "What about adding to your will? Or do you need to make sure an actual person carries out your wish?"

"You are a smart boy," said the old man and pressed a button on his chair. "You'll do fine. The first part of the plan has been in place for a while."

Axel looked confused as the old man explained, "Why do you think you've been coming to dinner each week?" When Axel did not answer, Benton did it for him. "So as not to arouse suspicion of your presence in the house when it's time. The dutiful ward loses his mentor and now fights to let the man live out whatever time he has left in his own home."

Axel grabbed the glass of whiskey and finished it. *If this was the pre-amble to dinner, how would the rest of the evening turn out?*

∼ɔ

Gary Kepner had been a detective on the police force for only a short while after several years walking a beat. In both roles he prided himself on being professional and thorough.

Most cases in Benton Falls were petty. A teen taking a joy ride, domestic disturbances, and an occasional DUI. He could not recall the last time they were dispatched for a homicide because those types of crimes did not happen in this small town. The case he was working on involved several smash and grabs at local jewelry stores. His theory claimed robberies caused by those addicts hooked on meth or opioids needed money for their habits by fencing said jewelry to pawn shops or undesirables who would take the contraband off their hands for quick cash. Gary planned to stop both habits before they strangled his town.

He was making a list of all the pawn shops in the state to cross reference with the descriptions of the stolen goods when he was tapped on the shoulder by Detective Holmes.

"Need a partner, mine called in sick. C'mon."

Gary looked up from his list at the detective. Nick Holmes was a twenty-five-year veteran of the force and a man of few words. He was adept at solving crimes where others had failed. To his face, everyone called him Detective, but behind his back, they knew him as "Bulldog." No one ever called him Bulldog to his face for fear he was capable of murder himself. And as both perp and the detective on the case, he would make certain this was one that would go unsolved.

"Now!" Bulldog yelled to Gary, who scrambled to his feet, spilling his coffee across the desk. "Shit!" he whispered, as he attempted to wipe the table with his hand.

"Right. Now!" Bulldog bellowed. Gary looked at the mess and decided it could wait. He was not sure he'd be *able* to clean the mess should he ignore the large detective.

They got in the unmarked sedan and drove through town to the seedier side. To Gary, "Across the tracks" meant across literal railroad tracks and wondered if the saying came from old towns shoving the less affluent residents on less desirable land. They were heading for a part of town called Furnaceville, where an old pig iron blast furnace once stood. It had employed a fair number of residents in the early and mid-1900s but was hot and dirty work. No person of means ever considered building a home near the furnace, the ash from its chimney settling on the old homes like a snow fall, requiring constant sweeping or window washing. Most people who lived there found it easier to leave the ash on their property alone. No sense in trying to rid yourself of something only to find it resurface the following day. Today, there was no trace of the soot, the forge having shuttered along with the jobs it once produced.

A wide path led by the side of the old shell of the building where the rail cars would unload coal for the blast furnaces then send the materials smelted there for destinations across the country. Grass covered the path now, the iron rails long gone.

Bulldog pulled into an old apartment complex, the street littered with debris, a dog barking in the distance and several police cruisers with their lights flashing nearby.

"Looks like we're a little late to the party," Gary said as the detectives got out of the car and walked past the police tape. They took three flights of stairs before standing at the front door of one Benny Palz. The door was already open, a yellow police tape across it both men ignored, lifting it, and entering the apartment to find a forensic team combing through the property.

Bulldog grabbed a police officer by the arm. "Whatcha got here?"

The officer extricated his arm, but not too quickly for fear of offending the detective before responding, "Over there. Thirty-year-old male. Deceased. Looks like a drug overdose." Benny lay haphazardly on the couch. The officer pointed as he spoke, "On the table there's drug paraphernalia. Take a look over at the counter."

Gary and Bulldog both turned at the same time to see numerous pill bottles and vials set up like a tiny village. Gary stifled a smile as he thought, With a bit of cocaine sprinkled around, it would look like a toy Christmas village. He reached for a bottle when his hand was slapped away with a pair of rubber gloves one would find at a hospital. Or a police investigation.

"Put these on before you touch anything, rook," scolded Bulldog, shaking his head at Gary's mistake. "Don't contaminate evidence."

Gary slipped the gloves on and examined the bottle village again, Opioids, Potassium Chloride, Succinyl Choline, Morphine. Digitalis. He picked up a bottle and read *Falls Assisted Living and Memory Care* on the label.

He yelled to the cop who had spoken to him. "Hey, did you find any ID?"

"Yeah, he works at the FALM on Barley and Fourth. Here's his badge." The officer handed the white ID badge to Gary, showing Benny's face. He took the ID over to the deceased to match. It did. Gary lifted the short sleeve from Benny's arm locating the injection site. There was a red ring forming around it. Scanning the corpse, he noticed a mark on Palz's neck. Pushing his chin to the right showed another red ring. *Do junkies inject themselves in the neck?* He thought, jotting the find in his notebook. Turning back to the bottles on the sink, he commented, "A regular pharmacy, here."

Detective Gary looked once again at the corpse of Benny Palz. Something did not seem right, but he couldn't put a finger on it.

Bulldog grunted back, "Looks pretty cut and dried to me. Sellers should never taste their own wares."

Scrunching his mouth to one corner, Detective Gary could not help but wonder how cut and dried this case really was. He was determined to find out. In the meantime, he had solved one crime tonight. He couldn't wait to tell Jules that he'd found her medication thief.

CHAPTER
– 17 –

There is no place that states finality like the morgue. The Benton Falls morgue was in the hospital's basement and run by coroner, Dr. Grant Houseman.

"Hey doc," Detective Gary said, as he stepped through the door.

"Gawd, I hate it when people sneak up on me," said the agitated doctor. "You come slinkin' in here and whisperin', like it's one of them talkin' to me." He pointed over his shoulder at the body of Palz lying on the table.

The detective walked over to Palz and lifted the sheet. "Doc, was wondering what you found out about this character?"

Houseman knew Detective Gary Kepner was an officer of the law who took details seriously when it came to his work. The detective was renowned for having solved crimes using the most miniscule of details; an innocent-looking email to a 'friend.' A change in behavior, a newcomer to town. No detail seemed too small to overlook.

"Like what? Guy stuck a needle in his arm, injected poison and Voila. Deceased," the coroner said, trying to act disinterested. "When you see this many cadavers each week, death became commonplace. The causes easy to diagnose."

"Was the volume consistent with a usual addict?"

"Hmm, always hard to tell. It's not only the volume killing the addict. Potency plays a major role."

"Was the potency higher than normal?" The detective pressed.

The coroner had seen quite a few overdoses in his day and knew this question led to a dead end. "Toxicology came back in the normal street range."

"Did toxicology find anything else in his system?" The detective pressed, not giving up.

"Yeah, alcohol, but normal for anyone his age, addict or not." The coroner turned to Palz's corpse.

"No other drugs in his system? No opioids? Heart medication? Potassium?"

"Nope. H and alcohol, only," explained the coroner. Then he turned to face the detective, an eyebrow raised. "Why are you asking about those other drugs?"

"Never mind, doc. My partner says it's a pretty cut and dried case. Thanks for your time."

Watch what you say, the doctor thought, his suspicious nature on alert. "Ok, no worries, gotta insert him back into the cooler now."

The detective stopped at the door and turned back towards the coroner to ask one more question. "Before you do, can I see the track marks?"

The coroner stopped. He took a deep breath before composing himself, "I don't know. Protocol and all," he challenged. "Like you said, It's a cut and dried case?"

The detective cocked his head, imploring, "Please indulge me?"

Reluctantly, Doc Houseman rolled the gurney carrying the corpse of Benny Palz back to the examining area. Under the harsh light, he pulled the sheet exposing the dead man's right arm. Around the site was a ring and the beginnings of a red rash.

"What's this?" asked the detective, pointing to the marks.

"Injection burn," lied the coroner, not wanting to reveal he knew the fact Benny Palz would not have injected himself. The marks caused by a reaction of a different sort. "I see it all the time. Damn shame."

"And this one on his neck? Do addicts inject themselves in the neck?"

Doc Houseman stooped to look, adjusting his glasses. "Hmm," he said in an attempt to come up with a good answer. Standing up he replied. "You'd be surprised where these junkies inject. Look here." He proceeded to pull the sheet away from the corpse's toes and spread them one at a time. In between each was a small telltale red ring.

The answer seemed to placate the detective, and he left the coroner to the cold and the corpses.

Houseman picked up the phone and dialed. "Mr. Benton? We may have a problem," he said, explaining the detective's inquiries. He listened to his instructions and acknowledged his role by agreeing. "I'll make sure no one gets another look." After hanging up, he walked back to his desk, putting his hands flat against the top and let out his longest sigh of the evening.

"Julia? It's Gary Kepner. Have you seen employee Benny Palz at FALM lately?"

"Yes, but he hasn't been to work in a few days. Why?"

"We found him dead in his apartment," responded the detective.

"What?!? Gary, what happened?"

"Heroin overdose. The official call by the coroner. Did you have any idea he was an addict?"

Julia plopped into her chair, stunned at the revelation. "What? No, I had no idea. Are you sure?"

"The coroner is."

She recalled the old doctor who also handled all the deceased from the FALM. "Really?"

"Really. I have a few questions for you."

"Of course." Jules wasn't shocked there was another death. She didn't think it would be an employee.

"Did he recently get fired?"

"No! As I said, I saw him the other day."

"Would you say he was an exemplary employee?"

Jules bit her lip at the question. *Not supposed to speak ill of the dead.* "I wouldn't use that term. He had issues, say, fitting in."

"Any drug issues at work?" The detective pressed.

Jules guessed the detective was fishing. But for what? "I wasn't aware of any. He came in on time, did his work and left. Seldom called in sick."

"Ok, you know that missing medication issue we're investigating?"

There it is, she thought. The fish. "Yes, but what does that have to do with Benny?"

The detective paused. Jules noticed he took a breath before continuing. "We found several bottles of drugs including prescription pain killers on his counter. All marked from the FALM."

"I see," she said. So, Benny *was* the thief.

"Let me ask you another question. Does FALM have a drug testing policy?"

"Of course, We test randomly..." Julia stopped. "Oh. Are you asking to see a history of his drug tests?"

"Nope, I want to see them from everyone in your building."

"Gary, c'mon. I can't make that call. It's well above my pay grade. You'll have to talk with our administrator, Harriet Spellman." A thought occurred to Jules, "Wait, if he's the thief and the addict, why investigate anyone else?"

"Sorry, can't comment on an ongoing investigation."

"Oh." Julia said at the standard police lingo. She felt it was her time to do a little fishing. "Wait a second, do you think it could be a homicide?"

"Julia, you know I can't comment. Could you be so kind to patch me through to the head of your nursing home? I'll request the drug tests."

"And if they won't provide? You'll get a warrant?"

"Last time, Julia." She could tell he was exasperated with her questions. "I cannot comment on an ongoing murder investigation."

"I understand perfectly, detective. Let me patch you right through." Although Jules sensed the frustration of Detective Gary Kepner, she was glad she caught something coming from it. The word 'Murder.'

Harley Benton proved to be a man determined to hold on to the puppet strings despite his age and diminishing health. In his town he would continue to call the shots when needed. At his desk, he pushed papers around to appear busy while Kennedy held the waste basket full of handkerchiefs at arms-length. Like a mother with a full diaper pail, he headed to the laundry room. Once left alone, Benton took a key from his breast pocket and opened a drawer. He pulled a file and opened it, laying it flat on his desk, then made a phone call. Normally, he'd make Kennedy dial, but he wanted no one else to be a part of this call.

"Chief Reardon, please," he said into the receiver. When a cough came on, he pulled a handkerchief from his pocket, just in case.

"Chief, Harley Benton here," he said. "I understand you have a suspect in the FALM theft."

"Yes, sir, but you shouldn't bother yourself with petty crime. We've got it under control."

"Might I remind you I hold a vested interest in what goes on in my town and especially when it concerns the elderly. Not only do I own the FALM, but I *am* one of the elderly myself."

"Sir, I meant no disrespect," said the Chief. Benton noticed a hint of fear in the police chief's voice. *Good.*

"Now, how would it look letting a thief run around a rest home? Next thing, people will be defacing headstones. Or worse." Benton loved theatrics; an act he played to show he still pulled the strings.

"No, of course not, sir, not my intent—"

Benton now had the man on the ropes. Time for the kill shot. "Do I need to remind you who put you into this job?" The implied threat-*And I can take you out as well.* "There is a dead junkie caught with the evidence. We need to close this case as quietly as possible. Don't you think?" The implication? *That's what I think.*

"But there are questions…" The Chief began.

"And who is asking these questions?" Benton's patience grew as thin as a worn-out shirt.

"Ahem." The Chief cleared his throat, "Now Mr. Benton, my detective believes there are clues to show Mr. Palz didn't inject himself. I'm sure you'd want us to be thorough in our investigation and make sure we come to the correct conclusion."

"Wrong. The answer is obvious. The man was a drug addict and overdosed on heroin. End of story." What the old man didn't want was a police investigation in one of his properties.

"But Mr. Benton, we want to do a thorough examination of the body to make sure."

"You can't," Benton began his lie. "The coroner had the body cremated this morning. There is nothing to investigate now, is there?" Benton knew Houseman wouldn't be cremating the body until tomorrow, a fact the chief didn't possess.

When Chief Reardon didn't answer, Benton asked again, this time with whatever force he could muster, "IS THERE?"

"No Sir, I guess not," the Chief said, with a sigh of resignation. Power caused a lot of things to happen, capitulation one of them.

"Good. Close the case." It was impossible the chief misunderstood the implication this time. *Or else.*

"Yes, sir," said the Chief, his voice barely above a deferential whisper.

"And Chief?" Benton said, not done with the officer yet. "Stay near your phone. I'm certain I'll be needing you shortly."

"Yes, sir," said the officer once more, the defeat in his voice replacing the deference.

As Benton hung up the phone, a satisfied smile appeared on his face. He replaced the file in the drawer and locked it before placing the key back into his front breast pocket.

Taping his index fingers over his crossed hands, a notion occurred to him. He hadn't coughed once during the conversation. Power was a medicine which could cure a lot of ills.

Encouraged, Benton flipped through his Rolodex to see what other strings he could pull today. Although the Puppet Master couldn't walk, this fact didn't deter his gnarled fingers from pulling the right strings. His money produced power, the most effective string of all.

The intercom on Julia's phone squawked, jarring the woman out of her thoughts and back to reality. "Julia, can you come to my office please?" It was Harriet. Julia hated getting summoned. It was demeaning. Why couldn't her boss march her ass over to Julia's office? Exasperated, Julia replied, "On my way."

She left her office wondering what this discussion would entail. The resident numbers had increased, there were no recent deaths, and the med thief had been caught. I'm positive he's the thief, she thought as she opened the door to her boss's office. *Not sure he's a murderer, though.*

Harriet sat at her desk, a stern expression on her face as she spoke. "Job well done on your latest numbers. We're on track to reach resident capacity."

Why doesn't this feel like a congratulatory meeting? The words are right, the attitude, not so much. Julia was good at non-verbal cues and Harriet was giving off mixed messages.

"I want to talk about Mr. Palz," said Harriet, with distaste, as if she had a mouth full of sour milk and nowhere to spit it. "Now that the med thief problem has come to a satisfactory conclusion, we now must bolster our hiring practices so a situation such as this never happens again."

Julia didn't buy the overdose conclusion, and she was sure the recently deceased Benny Palz would agree with her. "I agree, but shouldn't this be an HR issue?" Julia worked hard, but she didn't want to take on any additional duties.

Harriet tapped her two index fingers together. "It is. But I'm asking you to vet any new hires with care. You have shown an aptitude towards protecting the integrity of our establishment and I'm certain you could make sure the talent pool stays... *untainted.*"

"You mean, no thieves?"

"I do. We're thankful other than the thievery, the authorities have found no evidence of foul play in these halls."

"Wait, what? Didn't you speak with Detective Kepner? Isn't there an ongoing murder investigation?"

"Yes," Harriet said, placing her palms on the desk. "I did speak to your 'friend,' the detective. And no, there isn't any murder investigation. From now on, this is the message I want you to convey should suspicions continue to arise. All of our deceased residents have left us under natural causes. Any ideas to the contrary must be met with a firm denial. Understood?"

It was *not* understood. Julia's gut told her there was more to the deaths in the FALM than God's plan. She and Axel weren't able to find proof. Yet. Without it, there was only conjecture.

"I don't understand and I don't agree with it. Are you realizing maybe I'm onto something? The possibility of a murderer amongst us as a credible threat?"

"Your job," Harriet said leaning forward, her eyes squinting, "is not to understand, but to agree with the facts and do your job to protect the interests of the FALM. Without it, there is no FALM, and you'd be out looking for another job. We can't have unsubstantiated suspicions of murder floating around here, can we? No one in their right mind would want to place their parents with us under those circumstances. Now do you understand?" The veins on the administrator's neck were now visible, her lips pursed in anger. Julia understood a lot of things. Those physical signs meant it was time to back down.

"Understood," she said, with as much respect as she could muster.

Harriet sat back in her chair, "Good. I'm glad we agree. The police are also on the same page. I spoke to the chief a short while ago and he assures me the investigation of the missing medication is now complete."

Julia's shoulders sank in defeat. How could the police sweep these suspicions under the rug? Was it because they were inept? Overworked? Or was there a more nefarious reason? Jules didn't know what the reason was, but as she stood up and turned towards the door, she said back to her boss. "Complete."

Under her breath as she exited Harriet's office, she mumbled, "Not."

Jules had no intentions of leaving her suspicions to the police or anyone else. She smelled a rat and wanted to find it. The first thing she did back in her office was to place a call to Detective Gary Kepner and give him an earful." You said it was a murder investigation! How does that crime go away?"

"Julia, hold on. So far there isn't a crime, just an investigation. We didn't have enough evidence to link anyone to the death of Benny Palz. According to the coroner, he died of a lethal injection of heroin. An overdose. Plain and simple."

Jules could hear the words but something in the detective's tone made her question his belief in what he had related to her.

"Gary, let's check off the facts," Jules began, digging in her heels. "First, Benny was not a known drug user. He passed every drug test over the course of his tenure at the FALM, so isn't it odd for a heroin junkie?"

"Well," he began, but Jules cut him off.

"Second, He may have been the med thief but if we do not have any heroin in the building, where did he get it?"

"On the street—" She cut him off again.

"And third, Where is the forensic evidence proving he was a junkie? The coroner won't release the report."

The detective tried again, "If you want facts—"

"If you are going to lie to me about the report, save your breath right now. As a friend, I understand you might want to shield me from anything unpleasant. But as a police officer, you swore to uphold the law and you're letting your superiors railroad you into dropping the case, right?"

Kepner gave an audible sigh, one Jules did not interrupt. She let the question sit in the air like cigarette smoke in a bar. Uncomfortable to those non-smokers it encircled.

After a long pause, she asked, "Gary, let me ask you this question. In your professional opinion, do you believe Benny Palz overdosed? Or was murdered?"

"Rings," he said. Another sigh ensued.

"Excuse me?" Jules asked, unsure of what she'd heard.

"Rings," Kepner repeated. "Your hunch is right this time. I am supposed to uphold the law but in this case my hands are tied."

"Rings?" Jules asked again. "What am I supposed to do with this information?"

"Find them. All I can say. And you didn't get the info from me. Find the rings and you'll have the answer to your first question."

"So, you *do* have reservations about the case." Jules had the detective on the ropes and would not let go without more answers.

"I do, but again, we never had this conversation. You wanted answers, and I told you to find them. Look for the rings."

"Ok, I get it. But where do I find these rings?"

"You said the coroner wouldn't release the findings of the Palz autopsy. I can't tell you where to find the rings, you must do that yourself. Then when you find them, it's up to you what to do with the information. But you better hurry. It has to be tonight."

Jules pondered this riddle. Rings? Coroner? Autopsy? it occurred to her maybe the rings weren't at a location, but *on something* at the location.

"The morgue?" she asked. *He's telling me the answer is at the morgue.*

His silence confirmed it.

"So, now we know where to find the rings, how do I get in?"

The detective answered and this time she let him finish. "I can help. But Julia, you have to promise to keep me out of this if any blowback. We need to do the right thing but I also have a family to feed and protect." He paused before adding, "I hope I don't live to regret this."

"Done, and you won't. You help me," she promised. "And I'll help you. That's what friends do."

Her hunches proved correct. She had smelled a rat and now she knew what to do next. The best way to catch a rat was to go where it lived. In this case, the vermin lived in the city morgue.

Later that evening, Jules pulled into the parking lot of Benton Memorial. She drove to the rear of the building and parked the car. She walked to the service entrance as instructed by Detective Kepner. She followed the steps down to a long corridor reminiscent of a scene from a scary movie. She'd done nothing like this before but determined to do what was right. What did they say about courage? Being frightened, but doing it anyway? She walked along the corridor, the light footsteps echoing around her. Jules came to a corner and stopped. Voices echoed to her left. *Kepner.*

"It's a gift," he said. "For giving me forensic lessons the other day."

Jules peeked around the corner. Gary was facing Doc Houseman who had his back to her. Kepner was waving a bottle of whiskey in the air. "We can take a little nip right now if you want?"

Houseman took the bottle and inspected it. "Irish," he said. "I gotta prep that Palz guy for cremation but, hell, for this," he shook the bottle at the detective, "I can do it in the morning."

The doctor took Kepner's arm with one hand, the bottle of Irish whiskey with the other. "In here," he said as he escorted the detective into a side room. Before Kepner stepped in, he glanced at Jules, waving his head towards the morgue's door.

Jules waited for a few seconds more, then sprinted through the hall on her toes, careful not to make much noise. She opened the door to the morgue and stepped in, putting a hand over her nose as the odor of chemicals filled her nostrils. At the refrigerated morgue drawers where the bodies were stored, she ran a finger across the names on the placards until she came to the one she sought.

Opening the drawer and pulling the gurney out, she shivered in the cold as she pulled back the sheet exposing the corpse and causing her to gag. She had seen him a few days ago walking the halls but now he lay still, his complexion a pasty white.

Fighting the urge to run, she carefully lifted his arm with the tips of her thumb and index finger but had to grab his wrist as the rigor mortis fought against her. In the crook of his arm, she saw the injection site. A tiny red mark. A mark she expected. What she did not expect was the red rash flaring out from the injection site and a large red circle surrounding the rash. A *ring*.

She did not stop there. Finding the neck injection site with its harsh red rash and another red ring, she searched further until reaching his feet and lifted the sheet and separating his toes. The urge to vomit reappeared, but she swallowed hard and focused on pulling her camera from her pocket.

She began snapping pictures of all the rings on Benny Palz's corpse and was almost finished when noises came from outside in the corridor. Hastily covering the body, she slid the gurney back into the drawer with an audible click, cringing at the loudness. Jules found a place to hide beside the bank of drawers, fitting herself into the tight crevice as Doc Houseman entered the morgue. "Thanks again!" he shouted behind him.

The old man puttered around his desk, then began shutting off lights, finishing with the last light switch near the exit, leaving Jules cowering in the dark alone with all those dead people. She forced herself to stay put, extricating herself only after she was sure Houseman had been long gone. She had what she came for. Pictures of the rings on Benny's corpse. She did not know what they meant, but she was determined to find out. When she did, she'd share everything with Kepner. And the newspaper. Starting as soon as she left this wretched place. She slipped out the door and walked quickly up the corridor, a shoulder against the concrete wall, shivering all the way to her car.

CHAPTER
— 18 —

A xel sat at his desk, staring at the computer screen. Fear slammed into his gut, forcing him to bend toward the screen as if doing so would change what it showed. Sweat did not trickle down his face, it poured as he struggled to push back the urge to throw up.

He'd been going over his plan for the Benton memorials, mapping out his Profit and Loss sheet when he checked the account for the updated balance after certain checks had cleared.

"That can't be," he said with an incredulity of one presented with an incomprehensible fact. Refreshing the screen, he looked again. Same result, the balance showed zero. *Numbers never lie.*

"There should be over one hundred thousand dollars in this account!" he said, frantically searching the website for a flaw. He found none.

Gone. It's all gone.

The phone rang and its shrill noise elevated his already jangled nerves. "Yes?" he answered, trying to maintain a semblance of calm.

"Mr. Axel?" asked the voice on the telephone. "Kennedy here, it's Mr. Benton. He's asking for you."

The fear gripping Axel by the throat squeezed tighter as sweat began to stain his shirt.

"Mr. Axel? Are you alright?"

Axel responded, "Fine, I'm fine. Is Mr. Benton OK?"

"He's under the weather and asked for you to come straight away, the car should be in your drive."

Axel looked out the window and sure enough, Benton's Rolls Royce sat there, idling. "I'm on my way," he said into the receiver and bounded out the door, the fear providing an overabundance of energy. As he settled into the back of the limo, he wracked his brain to find an answer to the missing funds. It had to be a mistake.

On his way to the mansion, emotions poured over him like the sweat from his brow. The fear kept its firm grip. There was a considerable amount of money missing and no explanation. Embarrassment added to his discomfort. Benton had put his trust in him, and Axel let the man down. Annoyance poked its head into his mind, as if blame could be diverted. Axel did not like to be summoned, and the old man didn't take into consideration he might have other plans. The fact he had none made little difference, but the principle did. Lastly, anxiety caused physical manifestations. His left foot pistoned up and down, his right hand gripped the door's arm rest so firmly, his knuckles turned white. "What am I going to do?" he asked out loud.

"Sir?" asked the driver. "Do you need anything?" The driver's response shook Axel back to reality.

"No, sorry," he mumbled, forcing himself to take a deep breath, stop his foot movement and letting go of the arm rest.

Relax, he thought. Winnie's voice came next. *Buck up, son. Remember, in order to overcome your fears, you have to face them.*

"Good advice," he said, no longer concerned about the driver. "We can fix this. Mr. Benton will help me sort this out."

The car came to a halt in the driveway. Axel leapt from the vehicle and strode to the door where Kennedy met him and pointed towards the staircase. Axel sped up the steps, arriving at the old man's bedroom door. He knocked lightly out of respect and slipped through. The old man lay still in his bed, giving the impression he had gotten there too late. The old man lifted his gnarled hand and motioned for Axel to approach the bed, disavowing him of the notion.

"Mr. B? Are you ok?" Axel asked and took the man's hand in his.

"No. I'm not," came the gravelly response as he pulled his hand away from Axel.

"I'm a tired old man. For years I've been at the top of my game. I believed myself an excellent judge of character, but I must be slipping."

"I'm not sure I follow," said Axel in confusion.

The old man's eyes drooped into a squint; the mouth pinched in what Axel perceived as contempt. Benton's tone confirmed the perception. "Oh, I'm sure you do. I may be old, but I'm no fool." A cough was an exclamation point to the statement. Benton tossed the phlegm filled handkerchief over the side of the bed, the heavy linen dropping to the floor with a splat.

Benton had never treated him like this. Like he treated Kennedy. Alarm bells clanged in Axels head. He had developed a keen sense of danger since Winnie's run in with the intruder, and it was warning him now. He moved the wheelchair out of the way and sat on the bed.

"Boy, move the chair back," Benton snapped. "No one told you to touch it!" Axel flinched at the outburst but did as he was told. "I'm sorry, I didn't mean to—"

The old man cut him off, "I don't care what you meant to do, leave my things be! You've done enough damage!"

Who is this man? Axel thought as he stepped back away from the bed. The old man glared at Axel, his anger evident.

He knows.

"Did we not have a bargain?" The veins on the old man's forehead protruded like earth worms wriggling under his thin skin. His lips pursed together in a menacing frown as he lifted a bony finger towards Axel.

"Mr. Benton, let me explain what happened," Axel began.

Benton squinted his eyes and grinned. Gone was the kind benefactor smile, replaced with an expression Axel cringed at. The word 'ominous' came to mind. Axel put both hands in his front pockets and rocked on his heals, like a young man ready for a lecture.

"I know exactly what happened. You took advantage of an old man's generosity and made off with the money."

Axel stammered, "No, it just disappeared. We need to call the bank. I'm sure they can figure out what happened."

"Oh, quite unnecessary. We both know what happened. Theft, bank fraud, and maybe even an extortion charge might be on the table, yes?"

"What?" Yelled Axel, "No, this is all a mis—" He stopped mid-sentence, the idea forming was incomprehensible. Benton, no longer his benefactor, but his nightmare.

He did this?

"Yes, the wheels are turning. You finally realized, eh?" The old man chortled. "You are a smart boy. But not smart enough."

"But why? Why would you do such a thing?"

"Hasn't it occurred to you yet? Why I would set you up for success only to watch you fall?" Axel felt the old man pulling on levers which could result in a prison sentence.

He lifted his head in recognition. "It's not about me, is it?"

"No, you are merely a pawn in this game."

"Winnie." Axel whispered.

"Very good young man. I want to watch the pain on her face, embarrassed her good little boy has to spend years in prison because he's nothing but a low life thief." Axel could tell the old man enjoyed this game.

"Before your time, your grandfather had rumors swirling about an alleged affair. It never happened, but almost broke up their marriage. That was me. Many health department inspections at the restaurant? Me again. Bank rolling a competitor who eventually put your grandmother out of business?"

"You," said an astonished Axel.

"Correct, boy. Me. But you want to know what the final indignity will be? The cherry on top, so to speak?" Benton let his words sink in before putting a note of finality down, like the corners of his mouth. "You in federal prison."

"What? But why? What has my grandmother ever done to you to make you come up with this evil plot to destroy her and her family?"

"The first part is because I can. I *am* this town and can do whatever I want." The old man looked pleased at his handiwork, relishing his revenge. "I'm told she has entered the Passing Lane, which means time is of the essence. I'd like to give your grandmother a parting gift. You in prison. Did you even wonder why I would make you executor of my estate? Did you believe for a moment I'd let you handle my affairs?" The old man chortled. "Please."

"This is all because she wouldn't date you?"

The old man's eyes closed to a squint once more. "I would have married her and made her the richest woman in town. But she was ungrateful." Axel watched as Benton's anger spilled out. "No one says no to a Benton. NO ONE!" Composing himself, Benton began again.

"Now you have the full, no, almost the full picture. I would also have destroyed your brother, but he's done a rather fine job of doing that himself. Of course, I may have to reconsider after the success of his book. Some men kill people, but far too messy for me. I prefer to kill something else. Reputations. And I'll start with yours and see where that leads."

Rage bubbled up inside Axel. He had trusted this man. Hell, he was trying to erect a statue to honor this… monster. "She warned me about you, but I didn't listen."

"It's too late now, isn't it? Benton said, unfinished with the torture. "It has taken a long time to complete, but I've had my fun pulling the strings along the way. And although I had nothing to do with the actual deaths of your parents, I made sure they never found the person who killed them." A sneer formed on his face as he drove his last vengeful point home. "You know what they say about revenge being a dish served best cold?"

This last statement forced Axel to act. He wouldn't go down without a fight. Taking a deep breath to compose himself, he pulled his hands from his pockets, along with his cell phone, and waved it at the old man.

"A cell phone?" mocked Benton. "Are you going to call your granny to save you? It would have been smarter to bring a gun."

"I know a thing or two about revenge. But it's not cold, it's red hot." Axel said, turning the phone toward the old man. Recognition registered in the man's eyes. Fear.

"You're recording?" he asked, surprised at this change of events. The red light blinked on the small screen.

"I am." answered Axel calmly.

Axel watched with interest as the old man struggled to figure out a way to extricate himself from this predicament. He was not about to let Harley Benton escape as he again recalled his grandmother's words. *Face your fear.* This was no longer about him, but also about his grandmother and brother. "Who needs a gun when I have your confession… and this?" Axel said as he grabbed a pillow from the foot of the bed and approached the old man.

"No, wait. What are you doing!?!!" Benton pulled himself up on his elbows, his hands in the air to ward off his attacker, screeching, "Stop!" He yelled out to his butler before falling back on the bed with a coughing spell even the most inexperienced care giver would recognize as fake. The anger rising as Axel closed in on the old man. "There's been a change of plans," he said ominously.

Benton reached for the chair and attempted to summon Kennedy, but Axel slapped his hand away. "Old man, you picked the wrong adversary." A sneer forced the corners of his mouth downward. No one threatened his Winnie. Some strings cannot be pulled. Or purchased.

"You're ruining my plan!" Benton screeched, the rasp back as he coughed gooey phlegm which dribbled out of his mouth and onto his pajama top.

He reached again for the button, but Axel moved the chair out of his reach with his left hand, holding the pillow with the other. "No! No!" The old man cried as Axel brought the pillow closer. "Please Axel, STOP! I'll give you whatever you want!"

Axel enjoyed the power he now had over the decrepit fiend. He brought the pillow towards the man's face. Then, at the last second, placed it behind the old man's head and fluffed it before stepping away. "There, comfy now?" He stood back with a grin of a gardener admiring his blossoming handiwork.

Movement came from the doorway as Kennedy, standing silently, watched on.

"Kennedy, thank God you're here!" the old man rasped, out of breath. "He... he tried to kill me!" Kennedy looked at the old man and then towards Axel, who was surprised at the butler. It was the first time Kennedy had looked directly in the eyes of the young man.

"What are you waiting for, call the police? NOW!" ordered Benton.

Kennedy walked over and stood next to Axel, an insincere smile forming. "But sir," he exclaimed, "You must be mistaken. Mr. Axel was merely fluffing your pillow for you, not trying to harm you. Mr. Axel, you're not a person who goes around killing anyone, are you?"

Dumbfounded at his new ally, Axel could only shake his head.

"Kennedy, I demand you call the police this instance! I order you! The Chief is expecting your call." The old man, now more agitated than ever, thrashed about in his bed, the phlegm bobbled slowly onto his pajama top. The butler did not move to extract it.

"Not going to happen, Harley," stated Kennedy with conviction. Another first. The butler calling his employer anything but sir, his tone filled with malice. Gone was the subservient butler, replaced by a man firmly in control.

"Then get me Gertrude, because you are fired!" Benton yelled. Spidery veins bulged from his forehead.

Kennedy stood firm. "I'm afraid I can't. I sent her home. Gave her a well-deserved day off. She thanks you, by the way."

"Why you ungrateful son of a…" Benton never finished the sentence. His eyes glazed over as he fell back onto the bed. The right half of his face drooped and saliva leaked from the corner of his mouth. His left hand raised and lowered like the warning arm on a railroad crossing.

"Is he having a stroke?" Axel asked, rushing over to the bedside.

"It appears so, Mr. Axel," said Kennedy as he too stepped closer.

"We need to call an ambulance, now!"

Kennedy rested a soft hand onto Axel's shoulder, pulling him back from the bed. Yet another first. Contact.

"No," said the butler. "Ponder this for a moment. If we call 911 now and he recovers, life as you know it is over. We wait and he fades? Damage done and we're all safe." As an afterthought, he added, "The cell phone bit was a nice move, did you get any of it recorded?"

Axel considered the butler's meaning. *If you can't kill a monster, what's the next best thing? Cage him.* "Not sure," Axel replied. "I had it in my pocket. It was a bluff." Axel used the back of his hand to wipe sweat from his brow.

"Smart," commented Kennedy. Turning to Benton, he asked, "Comfy, Harley? We'll let this little scene play out, shall we?"

"Grrsssly," growled Benton.

"I can't believe he set me up," Axel exclaimed, incredulous at the allegation. "I've been nothing but kind to him."

"You are a kind man, Mr. Axel, but he isn't. I've worked under this tyrant my entire adult life and he's treated both Gertrude and I as slaves when he needed us and invisible when he didn't. Years of working for the man, you realize what he's capable of by listening. Invisibility has its advantages."

Benton interjected, "Kuraxlxel."

"A man like him can't stand not getting what he wants. He loved your grandmother too much to harm her physically. To punish you in turn, punishes your grandmother. To hurt her like she had hurt him." Kennedy paused a moment, "If not for me, you'd be going to prison for embezzlement."

"Wait, you were aware of the plot?"

"I was. Again, I'm very good at two things. Invisibility and listening."

Realization crossed Axel's face. Then it turned to anger. "So, you were going to let me go to jail?"

The butler lifted both palms to calm Axel. "Of course not," he reassured. "I had a plan to save you."

"Ssrxxk" Benton responded, still trying to join in the discussion.

"Hush, you," The butler said to his former boss as he walked over to the bed as if taking a leisurely stroll on a warm day. "I need one more item to complete the plan before we call 911." He stuck his hand in the old man's pajama pocket and pulled out a key before whispering in his ear, "How's it feel to be invisible? Do you like it? Do you?" and then with a sneer reserved for the recently liberated, spat, "Get used to it."

"Flofbal," was the old man's reply.

"Exactly," said the butler, depositing the key into his own pocket. He turned towards the door before summoning Axel to follow him. Axel looked over his shoulder, the hatred consuming him. His shame rising for being duped.

"Come now, young sir," Kennedy ordered. The old man's garbled voice followed them as Kennedy shut the door behind them, leading Axel to Benton's office. "Let me tell you how we've come to this point. I had been a faithful servant to Mr. Benton my entire life and being invisible was not the only tool I used to gather information. Information is power, and I needed to gather enough to get myself extracted from this intolerable situation."

Axel looked puzzled, "Don't you like working here?"

Kennedy shook his head. "No, I do not. But one has to do whatever it takes to survive. Another tool I used to survive was deception. But let me start from the beginning. Powerful men use their power to get what they want. Mr. Benton wanted complete loyalty, so he found someone who would, no, the correct word here is, *need* to be loyal."

"I don't understand," Axel replied, confused.

"It is complicated. I was in a bit of trouble when Benton found me. I almost had a run in with the authorities, but Mr. Benton took care of the issue on one condition."

"You go to work for him," Axel said. "He extorted you?"

"Yes, and I hated every minute. But I vowed to gather as much information on him so he would release me from this indentured servitude. And I did. There are certain places around his study where it's possible to listen in on his conversations. I also created a space to peer into the room to watch his actions.

There is much you do not know about the man upstairs. His attempt to destroy you and your family merely one of them."

"Besides invisibility and listening skills, you also had to practice patience. To strike at the perfect time. You're like a superhero."

The butler bowed his head at the compliment. "No, I'm not. But I had to wait until the time was right. I needed to make sure I could right a wrong." The butler pulled the key from his pocket. "With you, and this key, I have been put into a position to do so."

"I'm not sure I follow."

"You will," said Kennedy, walking into Benton's office as the former butler strolled to the old man's desk as if it was his. With the key, he opened the drawers on either side and began searching. He found what he was looking for, holding them for up Axel. "Ah, here we are."

Kennedy handed two ledgers to Axel. "You are the accountant, show me the money trail." Axel went over the ledgers and found where Benton hid the money and an easy fix to bring it back. Numbers never lied, illuminating the truth to set Axel free.

"Tell me, what did you do that was so bad?" A relieved Axel asked.

The ex-butler pulled out another file, offering it to Axel.

"I was a different man back then. Young, foolish, weak. I'm afraid if I tell you, you'll hold it against me." The butler looked at his feet. "But righting a wrong comes first regardless of the consequences."

"Kennedy. Whatever it is, it can't too bad." Noticing the shame, Axel felt sorry for the man.

"Oh, it can. I remember the night your parents died. An awful thing. They never found the driver of the other car; a hit and run. Never found the car either." Kennedy's head remained lowered. "It was an accident turned into a crime."

Axel was no longer confused, realizing who the driver was. "You," was all he could muster, the strength leaking out of him like a loosely tied balloon. He fell into his regular chair, the leather enveloping him like a glove.

"Like I said. Young, foolish, weak… and scared," Kennedy said to the floor.

"He helped you cover it up?"

"Yes, and I regret it every day of my life. Powerful people crave more power. It was how he kept me in this prison." Kennedy took the file from Axel and walked over to the fireplace.

"I have two favors to ask of you," the butler said as he placed the file into the fire, the flames licking at the edges before engulfing it. "The first one is to ask your forgiveness." He walked back to the desk and began taking files of other Benton victims and treating them in the same manner.

Benton had abused this man for over twenty-five years. Axel did not want to carry any more resentment or guilt; he'd had enough of it to last two lifetimes. "It may take time, you understand." The butler gave him a sorrowful look. "But I'll try." *Forgiveness is the gift we give ourselves.* "And number two?"

"Well, as the master is incapacitated, it looks like I'm going to need another job."

This was a tall order for Axel to process. But after comprehending the crushing weight of guilt himself, he decided Kennedy also needed relief. As he sat with his parents' killer, he realized there was more to do. Eyes moving towards the ceiling, said, "We have one last duty to complete before we can discuss the future."

Butler Kennedy, now Mr. Kennedy, nodded in agreement. He pulled another document from Benton's desk, forcing a large grin. "Actually, we have two duties, Master Axel.

Axel was confused. "Master? You mean mister, don't you?"

Kennedy handed the document to Axel. As he read, he understood Kennedy had not made a mistake. In his hands he held Benton's last will and testament naming Axel executor of the estate, effectively making him the new master. Turning to the last page, Axel dropped his shoulders. "It's no good. He didn't sign it."

Kennedy took the document and looked it over as a teacher checking for spelling errors. Laying it down, he picked up Benton's pen. "Of course, he did," said the ex- butler as he forged the signature. Lifting it to show Axel, he pointed at the paper. "And he dated it last week."

"Kennedy—" Axel began his protest, but the ex-butler held up one finger to silence him.

"Master Axel consider how much good you can do for the people of this town who've suffered under this tyrant. You could start with your grandmother."

Axel, uneasy about the forged will, wondered if they could pull it off. Kennedy must have sensed his uneasiness.

"Master Kennedy, have you ever seen this document before?"

Axel looked at his wrist, recalling the lesson he'd taught Hector. *Tick Tock.*

"No," he lied.

"Good. Any more questions?"

"Yes, I do. About your plan to save me," Axel asked, his head cocked in curiosity. "What would you have done had Benton not had a stroke?"

Kennedy raised an eyebrow while looking Axel in the eye. "Fortunately, that's one question we'll never have to answer."

Axel saw the butler in a whole new light. He was cunning and intelligent. And he was loyal. The kind of man Axel would need to help manage the fortune he would soon inherit.

Glad to escape an unsavory answer implicating him in a crime, Leif's message of deception sprang to mind.

Oh the lies we tell ourselves.

CHAPTER
— 19 —

After Axel and the paramedics had left, Kennedy dug through Benton's desk, finding more evidence of blackmail. "Not surprising," he said aloud, freeing the victims as each file found its way into the fireplace.

What did surprise him came next. Hidden underneath a fake drawer bottom was a leather-bound ledger. Upon closer inspection, Kennedy realized this was no ordinary ledger. In it was a list of names with payments attached. A list of very prominent names. It seems the puppet master had used the green colored strings to pull whenever he wished. Axel would be very interested in seeing this book and would know what to do next. Kennedy had a few ideas of his own.

Sitting at Benton's desk as the new temporary master, Kennedy called the attorney to inform him of Benton's condition and asked the lawyer what came next. As expected, the lawyer confirmed Axel's position as executor of the estate due to Benton's incapacitation. Evidently, Benton had waited to rescind the order before exposing Axel's alleged crimes. Kennedy promised the attorney he'd drop off the forged will, certain it would be validated as the last will and testament of Harley Benton. Years of practice had paid off for the ex-butler.

Benton's charity would benefit from a part of the incapacitated man's fortune, allowing Kennedy to have the last word over his ex-boss and a pleasant surprise to offer Axel, hoping this could make it easier for the young man to forgive him. Long gone was any idea of a street named after the last Benton. A statue also no longer in consideration. Now the money set aside for two purposes. One to give away money to those Benton Falls residents most in need. The second? Well, Kennedy agreed this to be as satisfying as helping the poor.

Kennedy would convince Axel to speak to the town leaders on an idea to keep the benefactor of the town's memory alive for years to come. If they balked, he had a rather convincing closer in the leather-bound ledger in his possession. After the harm Harley Benton had caused, Kennedy felt no remorse in a little extortion.

The plan was to turn the house and grounds over to the city of Benton Falls as a living museum. People visiting would take tours of the mansion, and the tour money raised would help pay for the property upkeep. He chuckled at what his ex-boss would think of *that* notion.

Commoners traipsing through his home, touching his belongings and trampling his well-coiffed lawns. And what of Harley Benton? Kennedy had an idea for him, too. Axel had promised the old man he would see to it Benton could live out his life in Benton Manor. But Kennedy had not promised any such thing. *If the old man wasn't going to hell yet, this would surely act as one on earth.*

⁓

Although Harriet hated interviewing the new residents, it was a necessary evil. One she would quickly dispense of once the resident entered her office. Get them in, push them out. Take their money.

How things change. She smiled in jubilation as the new resident sat in front of her. For once she would not have to listen to the ramblings of an elderly newbie. No talk about a past life, spouse, children. On how much they'd miss their previous lives but encouraged by this new adventure. Blah, blah, blah. No, today she would do all the talking. For she had a very special new resident who could no longer boss her around. "We'll put you into the Passing Lane because no one is sure how long you'll be with us here at the FALM. Don't you worry, we'll make you nice and comfy."

"Grfaxle," said Harley Benton, out of the good corner of his mouth. The not so good corner allowed spittle to slide down his drooped face, hanging like an icicle off a tin roof during a warm trend. It hung there but you could not be sure for how long.

"You'll no doubt be pleased with how well we care for our residents." Not attempting to hide the contempt in her voice. "Your executor. Mr. Ahearne, has already signed you in with a very generous donation and might I say in advance, thank you, for an even larger one after you, um... leave us?"

The old man sat silently, slumped in his chair.

"Nothing to add?" Harriet asked, almost giddy at the prospect the man who once pulled all the strings could no longer move those fingers to wipe his mouth. The puppeteer turned puppet.

She walked to the door and opened it, finding Hector waiting on the bench. "Hector," she said, "Be a dear and show Mr. Benton to his new room, will you?"

As Hector pushed the old man out of view, Harriet waved a hand. "Hope you have a pleasant stay here," she called after them. "A nice long, quiet stay," she said to herself as she closed her door. She sat behind her desk, a contented smile visible. For the first time since meeting Harley Benton, she no longer felt the need to get up and wash her hands.

～⊃

He knew it was late, but he could not wait. She would be happy he had finally come for a visit because when he told her the news, she would be ecstatic. Or at least he hoped she would. He prepared what to say as he drove to the FALM. *First, an apology for not coming sooner. Then share the good news.*

Leif never was one for keeping his emotions inside, and it played well that he was telling Winnie first, even before he had asked Veronica. Did not matter. She was going to say yes anyway. Veronica wanted to get together this evening, but Leif declined with a made-up story. He had an errand to run and once finished, he would meet her back at home. He did not mind the little white lie; it was for her own good.

Leif parked the car and sprinted up the steps to the FALM and pushed open both doors, the pulsing adrenaline driving him forward. He stopped at her door and calmed himself before sliding open the door and smiling, called out, "Winnie? Are you up for a visitor?" As he looked in, the smile faded as he saw she already had one.

Winnie lay in bed. Standing beside her was a figure in a black hoodie.

⟿

"He did what?" Jules could not fathom what she had heard. They had decided after such a whirlwind day, each deserved a break and were having a late supper in Jules' office. Axel explained the whole sordid Benton plan. He left out the part about the hit-and-run driver who killed his parents. No need to add to the drama of the day while he sorted out his emotions on *that* topic. after all, Kennedy had saved him from prison.

"The worst part of this total mess was this. Benton controlled everything from the police department to the Mayor's office. There's this secret ledger Kennedy found explaining it a—"

Axel never finished the sentence as Jules jumped into his arms, surprising him. "I don't know what I'd do without you," she exclaimed. Realizing her action, she extricated herself with an explanation. "I mean, we've become such good friends." Axel had a goofy grin on his face.

Both cellphones pinged at the same time. "Vidbell again." Axel said, the frustration clear. "Every time she sneezes, the darn thing goes off." He swiped the alarm away.

"I have the same trouble," offered Jules. "Even though it's on people motion only, it goes off at the slightest movement," she lamented. "But a small price to pay to keep Winnie safe."

"Jules, I have something to ask you." Axel watched as she took a small bite of salad. After wiping her mouth, she looked straight into his eyes. "Go ahead," she prompted.

"Now that I'm the executor of the Benton Estate, Kennedy and I have plans. And I wanted to ask you if…"

Both alarms chimed in again. Both resisted the urge to look, swiping to silence once again.

"What I mean to say is," Axel stammered. "I'd like you to play a larger role, one to better serve your ambitions…" The vidbell alarm went off once more. This time they both looked at their screens.

"What on earth is she doing?" Axel said, exasperated. "she should be fast asleep by now. Wait, What the? … Is she holding her nose?" Then added, "Who's in there with her? What is…"

"She *is* holding her nose," Jules said, her head cocked to the side in confusion. "Like something stinks. There, she did it again, this time right at the camera. The last time she held her nose, she smelled…"

Realization struck them both at the same time. "Chlorine!" yelled Axel. Jules pushed him into the hallway. They began to run.

Axel reached Winnie's room first, bursting through the heavy wooden door, his shoulder taking the brunt of the hit while Jules slid in behind him. He saw Leif on one side of Winnie's bed. Gil was on the other. There was a faint aroma of chlorine in the air.

"A little late to be visiting, isn't it?" Axel said, noticing the vase of flowers on the table. "You didn't forget the lilies," he commented, as his mind tried to compartmentalize the contrasting information. To make sense of it all.

Leif had not looked at him since busting in. In fact, he was staring at Gil.

"Stay put, Axel," Leif said, a hand raised in his direction, his gaze fixed across the bed. Addressing Gil, he said, "Put it down."

Axel's eyes trained on Gil, noticing a syringe in Gil's left hand, a scalpel resting in his right. The needle was long and thin. Placing the pointed needle precariously close to Winnie's arm made it as deadly as if holding a scimitar against her neck. Confusion continued to cloud Axel's mind. "Gil, what are you doing?"

The answer came from the bed. "He means to kill me," Winnie replied calmly.

Gil corrected her, "Hasten, dear. Not kill, hasten. Don't you know murder is a mortal sin?"

Axel now saw his fellow Angel was sweating, the beads forming across his brow, his complexion a waxy gray. "It's my job," Gil began his explanation. "God's work." His voice eerily calm. With his scalpel hand he spun Winnie's wrist so the underside faced the ceiling without cutting her. She grimaced under his grip.

Axel stepped closer to the end of the bed, "Gil, think about what you're doing. That's my grandmother!"

"I have thought about it," said Gil. "Long and hard. Everyone else has one, and for years I had nothing. But one day I found it. And all seemed right with the world for once."

"Found what?" Axel asked, stalling for time. "What did you find?"

"Purpose," said Winnie. "He means he found his purpose." Gil shook his head in agreement.

"Gil, there is no good purpose in killing the elderly," Axel said, stepping closer around the bed. "It's plain murder. You have to realize this don't you?"

"Again, not murder, not killing. That would be against the commandments and you know it. But you're wrong. The good purpose is God's work. I hasten the sick and infirm to meet their lord and savior. Been doing this since we began the Visiting Angels." He counted off a few victims, "Mr. Franz, Mrs. Jones, Even Hobie. All to ease their suffering for an eternity in paradise. Now wouldn't you call that purpose? Wouldn't it be considered good?"

Axel grimaced at a bitter recollection, *the lies we tell ourselves...*

Leif chimed in. "Father Blake, was he part of the purpose?"

The accusation caught Gil off guard. His face closed in, as if he would cry.

Leif pressed on. "No, it was retribution, wasn't it, Gil? He molested you, too. Didn't he?"

"You two escaped the old pervert," Gil spat. "You quit altar boys and left me with no defense."

"I escaped nothing," Leif admitted. "He molested me, too. But I didn't kill him for it."

"And Palz, he was the fall guy, wasn't he?" Axel asked. All the pieces falling in place. If they could keep Gil talking, Winnie might get out of this safely.

"Benny Palz was a rotten human being. Mean, abusive. A bully. He deserved to die and made the perfect scape goat," Gil answered. Turning back to Leif asked, "If you knew the priest was a pervert, why did you leave me alone with him?" Tears of shame now streamed down his face.

"They didn't leave you. *I* made them quit. Leif told me there was something not right with the priest. He was protecting his brother," Winnie said. "I'm sorry I didn't speak up. I had no idea he abused you, too."

"You're saying I should blame *you* for all of this?" Gil said bitterly. As his anger rose, so did his volume. "You left me there. Alone with the monster. I'd call that complicity."

"Me, I'd call it crazy," said Leif as he stepped closer to the bed, his arm still outstretched in a non-verbal hold pattern.

"You would," said Gil. "You're a non-believer, an atheist. A *heathen*. And if you take one more step…" He flashed the scalpel but did not finish the statement, instead sliding the needle into Winnie's arm and pushing the plunger. She made a hissing sound as she pulled air through her teeth.

Both brothers moved at once. Axel rounded the bed to grab Gil, but Leif took a shorter route. He leapt onto the side of the bed and launched himself over it, hovering over Gil like a bird of prey before smashing into him and taking them both to the ground. The collision knocked Axel against the wall and out of harm's way. As Axel scrambled to his feet, he saw Jules run out the door in search of medical help.

Turning back to the fracas, he grabbed Gil in a chokehold. The murderer's hands reaching up to grab his arms in a desperate struggle to free himself. "Winnie, are you OK?" Axel gasped as he struggled to keep his grip.

She looked at him with glazed eyes, her breathing shallow. Whatever Gil put in the syringe was having its desired effect. She closed her eyes but opened them again. Cycling between the powerful urge to sleep and the stronger one to live. She closed her eyes again, and the damaged arm slumped to the side of the bed. She opened them one last time before passing out, raising her right hand. In it was the syringe. She had pulled it out, a droplet hung from the needle like a rain drop on the tip of a leaf. "I got it." she said. Silence fell with her hand, dropping the syringe to the floor.

"Leif!" Axel yelled, still struggling with Gil. "A little help here?" He was swinging Gil around like a rag doll but his grip was loosening, because Gil's hands were slick with blood. "I can't hold him! Help me!"

But Leif lay still on the floor. Axel noticed the scalpel lying beside him. And the pool of blood spreading from underneath his brother's arm.

Axel and Jules sat by Winnie's hospital bed watching as the intravenous saline drip did its magic. The doctor had told them the syringe had contained Succinylcholine; a medicine used to calm muscles during surgery. Because of the quick action of Nurse May in identifying the drug and using intubation and a blood transfusion to thwart the effects, Winnie was still among the living and now resting comfortably.

She opened her eyes. "So, no Irish funeral?" Her voice raspy from the intubation.

Axel gave a pained look to Jules, who in return bowed her head.

"No, Winnie, not for you. You'll have to wait a while longer." Axel said without making eye contact.

"Damn, was looking forward to having a picnic with your parents."

Her grandson produced a soft smile at the comment, but the expression did not last.

"What happened?" the old woman asked.

"Gil had a deranged outlook on things. He believed he was doing God's work by killing those suffering." Jules explained.

"Right, and you called it," said the old woman. "You saw it before anyone else."

"Just in time, too. If it weren't for Jules, we'd have lost you," Axel added.

"Thank you dear. I always say a woman's heroism is never done."

Axel shook his head, a small laugh escaping. Again, the moment turned sour.

"What was with the chlorine smell? It was noticeable the night I got knocked over and again when he came into my room."

"Gil would hide in the pool area waiting for everyone to leave before he could do his business. Hector found his hiding spot," Jules offered. "He kept the hoodie in a storage room, and it picked up the odor. Smart move to give us a sign by holding your nose."

"Only signal that made sense at the time. Blessed are the…" Winnie stopped in mid-sentence as a notion occurred to her. "Wait, where's Leif? Is he coming by later?" she asked, her eyebrows raised. "I want to thank him."

Axel gave a sad look to Jules and addressed the question. "No. He's not coming back."

Winnie blinked a few times before the tears fell in realization. "What happened?"

"I tried, Winnie, I really tried but…"

She reached out and took Axel's hand in hers. "You didn't catch him, did you?" There was no accusation, no blame. Only fact.

The tears fell, running down the gaps on either side of his nose.

"No, I didn't. I tried, but I didn't."

"Axel," she said through her own tears. "Perhaps, he wasn't catchable." She wiped her eyes and sat up as best she could. "There is one thing you must do now."

Axel looked up and into her eyes as she spoke. "You must give him the last word." This was not a request.

He got it right away, picking up her hand in his. "Blessed are those who mourn, for they shall be comforted."

Veronica sat on the toilet and stared at the stick sitting on the bathroom sink as if reading the same confusing passage over again in a book. It had only been a few minutes since she had slipped it between her thighs and urinated. This Catholic girl was late. Much too late. *For being unmarried.*

As time crawled, she recalled the reasons for the test purchase; missed period, sensitive breasts, and the nausea. Ugh, the nausea. She hated vomiting the most. It should only happen when sick or hungover. If this was how a pregnancy began, it gave her a second reason to hope the stick would display the negative sign.

"How stupid," she said to the stick as if it could respond. "Of all things to happen. As a nurse, I should have known better." She and Leif had been lovers for a short while, making sure he was careful not to ejaculate inside her except during her period. Then all bets were off. "The rhythm method sucks," she said, on one hand angry her Catholic upbringing forbade conventional birth control. On the other hand frustrated at her own hypocrisy, well aware that sex before marriage was a sin.

She heard the dainty ring of her cell phone in the other room. *Let it go to voicemail,* she decided, there was a more pressing issue.

"C'mon! Do something," she yelled at the stick. "The suspense is killing me!" Regardless of her pleadings, it remained silent. And colorless. Veronica looked at the directions on the box. It advised to be patient, the results taking as long as ten minutes for a minus or plus sign. One telling her they could go back to their simple life together. Another changing their lives forever. The cell chimed in again. Again, she ignored it.

She tapped her right foot as if pressing a car accelerator in an attempt to force an answer from the stick, but it remained blank. Thoughts of her perfect wedding evaporated, replaced with images of dirty diapers and little to no sleep. Glad her parents were not alive to witness the sin of their unmarried, potentially knocked up daughter. She glanced again at the stick. The sign appeared as a blue minus sign. "Thank Go..." she began, before seeing another blue line run straight through the negative sign forming a cross.

"Shit!" She cried as she realized today would begin the rest of her life not as a single woman, now responsible for another human being. "Shit! Shit! SHIT!"

It was not supposed to go this way. She and Leif were destined to walk down the aisle, build a home together, and *then* have children. Looked like they would have to adjust the dream.

"Buck up," she said as she wiped the tears away, before patting her stomach. "Isn't it time to go tell Daddy?" She sniffled, recognizing the sound of the cell phone once more.

Agitated, she stormed out of the bathroom and looked for her phone. She picked up the offending machine and saw it was Axel. "I'm a little busy right now," she said, harsher than intended, before hearing what he had to say. "Wha-at!" she yelled, the second syllable cut off as she listened, no longer angry but in disbelief. The news of her pregnancy now took a backseat to another adjustment turning a manageable dream into an unimaginable nightmare.

CHAPTER
— 20 —

lthough Axel did not catch Leif in this lifetime. it did not mean the opposite wasn't true. In the search for absolution, it was Leif, who in death, caught Axel.

Summoned to Attorney Ossont's office, he was informed Leif had made a last Will and Testament prior to his death.

"Why now?" Axel had asked.

"Your brother told me it was the law of averages," answered the attorney. "He said he'd climbed a lot of trees in his life, and the chance for a fall got better each day. He wanted to be prepared."

And prepared he was. Leif had left his estate to Veronica and Axel including the rights to his first and second book, the residual sales the building block to his company. Axel advised the attorney to send the royalty checks to Veronica. He did not need them but certain they would come in handy for her.

Leif had finally made plans. He never needed them before having no assets to leave behind until now. His first book was selling exceptionally well adding new converts daily. This forced a scramble to release his second book soon. While building a new company, Leif needed assurances if something happened to him, the right people and not the government, would benefit from his good fortune. Life had given Leif lemons. He was making more than lemonade.

Axel stepped into the Attorneys bathroom to collect himself. Guilt weighed on him like a soaked overcoat; heavy, wet, and cold. He couldn't catch his brother and withheld medical attention to Benton. It was as effective as putting his hands around the man's throat and choking the life out of him.

Axel had sinned because of pride and self-importance. Sins he would have to pay for. He tried to lift his head, but the sorrow and pain caused him to keep his eyes toward the sink for fear of what he might see. Until a thought encouraged him. *Absolution comes from the strangest places. Begin with yourself.*

"Enough," he resolved, knowing what Leif would say. After his brother, there would be no more eulogies. Instead, there would be the need for real penance, tasks to help people instead of sending them off with a few crafted words. He would have to find people to help and Leif would show him the way.

He tried again to look up, and it took a monumental effort but finally locking eyes with the person in the mirror. What he saw was not an accountant, brother, or Catholic but a flawed human. A sinner craving redemption. One who needed self-forgiveness before receiving any from elsewhere. "I forgive you," he said to the likeness in the mirror.

Splashing water on his face felt cleansing, calling to mind a baptism. The erasure of original sin. This time he spoke the words with conviction. "I forgive you." Axel realized he could do nothing about his original sin, but had power over those he'd committed since.

What needed to be done now became clear. Redemption starts with forgiveness and ends with unselfish acts of charity. Leif had shown him the door to redemption and the charity behind it. Axel vowed he would not only open the door. He would kick it in.

The church smelled of incense from an Easter week celebration the night before. Light streamed in from the stained glass illuminating each one the Stations of the Cross as they gazed upon the pews. Axel walked toward the podium on the altar, his stride causing echoes in the empty church. Leif did not have a casket, nor did he need one, his wish to be cremated granted. The urn sat in the sacristy waiting to be placed on a pedestal near the podium, a reminder from dust we came, to dust we shall return.

Axel stepped onto the altar, genuflected in front of the cross behind it and stepped into the sacristy, glad Father Tom had yet to arrive. He opened the urn holding the ashes of his brother. Next, he pulled a resealable plastic sandwich bag and a spoon from his pocket and scooped Leif's ashes from the urn into the baggie, careful not to spill any of his brother's remains. Once half full, he sealed the bag and put it in his breast pocket, tossing the spoon into the waste basket near the closet and replacing the top to the urn. The division of ashes was not the most practical option, as if carrying half of his brother with him, but Veronica wanted to keep the urn for herself, so he agreed. Half of Leif was better than none. Besides, she would not look to see if any of the ashes had disappeared. He smiled, hearing the words of Winnie ringing in his ears, "Life is to be experienced, not hoarded like a squirrel collecting nuts." Leif's ashes would be the last thing he collected. There would be no more hoarding going forward.

Axel quickly stuffed the baggie into the inside pocket of his coat when he heard the door to the sacristy open and Father Tom entered, the look of concern on his face. "Again, I'm very sorry for your loss," the priest said, comforting Axel.

"Thank you again for being there for Winnie. We're both convinced the prodigal son has returned to his parents." *I certainly hope so.*

Father Tom added, "Your faith was always stronger than his. I'm sure our prayers sent him home to God, where he belongs."

"I can only hope God can protect me from him when it's my turn to go."

They both silently chuckled and then stood in an awkward silence until Axel nodded to the priest. Axel walked out to the altar, genuflected, and headed to the front pew where Veronica sat in silence. He whispered a few words to her as he placed an envelope into her hands before turning back towards the altar. He genuflected once again and took his spot behind the podium, waiting for his turn to speak. Father Tom came out onto the altar and began the mass for the dead.

Veronica sat in the front row dressed in black. She could hardly fathom what had happened. She played with the choir book nervously as the crowd began filling the church, their quiet shuffling and whispers reverberating off the walls. Her tears stood ready to come pouring out but held them back. If she wanted to have a good cry, she would do it later in the comfort of her own home. Without the prying eyes of the mourners behind her.

Last week, the couple was happy and in love, thoughts of a long life filling her head. A wedding to plan, making her impression on their house to make it a home, *their* home. And then a baby or two. How it was supposed to work. Veronica guessed when they say, "God has other plans for you," what they really mean is, "death has other plans for you." She was not under any impression God had anything to do with this. God did not make them fall in love. Nor did God take him away. The most important Non-God event happened while the Almighty must have been dozing. She rubbed her belly softly.

Placing the choir book back in its holder, she sat on her hands to stop the fidgeting. *I miss him so much*, she thought, her heart pained to the point it would burst from her chest. A nervous giggle ensued, recalling the monster from the Alien movies. Love lost and the alien had the same thing in common. They both broke open your heart leaving nothing but a bloody mess.

She turned from side to side to see if anyone had seen her smile. The last thing she wanted was to appear disrespectful. Nervous laughter had a way of being taken in the wrong context and the mere appearance of disrespecting the man she had loved and lost brought the tears forefront once again. And once again, she pushed them back.

Nausea overcame her. She put a handkerchief to her mouth and coughed. The smell of incense proved too powerful for even the staunchest Catholics, let alone a pregnant one. To distract herself, she pulled the rosary beads from her black clutch, made the sign of the cross with the crucifix, and began to pray. *I believe in God, the Father Almighty, Creator of Heaven and earth...*

She paused, bowing her head. How could she in good conscience mutter these words when she was not certain she believed them? She heard Leif's voice comment in her head, forcing her to cover her weak smile, *Hey, atheism is my gig, not yours.* And then the punchline. *But if you're going to come over to the dark side, then I was right. Catholic girls do start much too late.*

She did not know what to think anymore. Heartaches woke her each morning since Leif's death. A never ending, aching pain reminding her of what she had lost. Not only her fiancé, but her future; the father of her unborn. Questions occupied these few days with the final one coming from Leif: *How could a merciful God allow this to happen?*

No answer would come this day and it would be a long time before the aching dissolved into a dull twitch, appearing when she least expected, a subtle alarm reminding her of the frailty of life. For now, it was time to pray for the soul of her beloved and send him to the next life in style. *If there is one.*

She was mid prayer when she noticed Axel walk across the altar, genuflect in front of the cross and move towards her. Their eyes met. Their sorrow shared.

Axel waved to someone behind her. She turned to see a large man sitting in the next pew.

"Veronica, this is my friend Hector. He'll escort you back to my place after the mass."

"Nice to meet you, Miss Veronica," Hector said extending his hand. "I'm so sorry for your loss." Veronica took it and smiled weakly.

He then handed her an envelope and whispered, "Open only after you get back to my place." She felt a hard object inside before slipping the envelope into her clutch.

Leif had left them both to pick up the pieces. She hoped they could do it together because with all the pain and suffering of Leif's untimely passing, there was one bright light to take away from all of this. If this was God's plan, then he had a very sick sense of humor. *As soon as mass is over and we get back to the house, I'll tell him,* she thought as Axel began to speak.

Little did she know it would be awhile before she would inform Axel he was about to be an uncle. A long while.

All was quiet in the church, the soft inner ear buzz of silence the only thing audible. Axel was acutely aware the parishioners watched his every move. He let out a little cough and put his hand over his heart to feel the inside pocket of his suit coat for the baggie, the same way one might pat a wallet or a cell phone to make sure it was still there. He also patted the plane ticket next to the ashes. When convinced everything was accounted for, he began to speak.

"I am Axel. I am 29 and have outlived the great Leif Ahearne. It seems heartless to say. I never imagined I would. I'm shocked. I'm hurt. I'm confused. He always seemed so invincible to me. Nothing could hurt Leif. Yet here we all are. Can you hear him having his first discussion with St. Peter at the gates of heaven?

St. Peter: "Next"

Leif: "I'm not even supposed to be here. I don't care what the big book of yours says. I've got a new book to promote, for Chris sake.

St. Peter: "Careful now, you're one step closer to this gate or one step away from the other direction."

Leif: "But I wasn't supposed to go like this."

St. Pete: "I know, they all say the same thing, but The Book is always correct. You are in the right place at the right time."

Leif: "Wait a sec. You couldn't have done better than getting stabbed? I climbed treacherous mountains. You couldn't have had me fall three thousand feet? Smash into a valley? A parachute that doesn't open a few miles above land, screaming wildly all the way? Or how about getting gored by a bull in Pamplona? But nooo, A scalpel? Is this how you want people to remember me? Something so arcane as a scalpel????"

Axel let the smattering of laughter die before continuing.

"Leif was an adventurer. The world was his playground. Sure, he fell. But he had the courage to climb, a trait most of us don't have. He wrote books showing others a glimpse of the larger world around them. His life was one of learning then doing. Taking risks. And in doing so, he found his purpose.

The takeaway for me at least is, with the little time you have on this earth, the only thing that matters is how you use what time you have. To find your own purpose. So, go out, use your time wisely. Take some risks. Test your own limits. Climb your own tree. Sure, you may fall. But you might also soar."

And then Axel did something he had never done at the conclusion of any eulogy. He went off script.

"Normally, this would be the end where I step down, you reflect on the words, the priest or minister prepares for their next duty. But I cannot."

He looked over at Father Tom who nodded for him to proceed. *"Because I have to announce this as my final eulogy. This is where one chapter of my life ends, and another begins. Leif taught us life is to be lived. We have a finite number of seconds and every one of them precious. I have lived a cautious life. The avoidance of* adventure rather than the embrace of it and that stops today." After a pause to gauge the crowd reaction before continuing.

"My grandmother was right when she told me Leif's fall from trees. But in order to fall, you have to climb first. The core message from his novel, and I wouldn't listen." Another pause.

"I am listening now. I have to find my own tree to climb. Let someone else lift this mantle, to speak for those who no longer can. Because in the whole scheme of life, the best we can hope for is when it's our time to leave this world, someone steps up to the podium to be our exclamation point; For a brief moment, even in death, we get in the last word. I leave you with this question: When it comes to last words, what will yours be?"

The eulogist let the last sentence hang in the air before stepping off the podium and walking down the aisle. The eyes of every parishioner followed him as he strode to the exit.

Those in attendance would talk about this eulogy for some time to come. Some not in attendance would later boast they were.

As Axel opened the large church doors, he paused for a moment breathing in the cool spring air, still conscious of those stares. He danced down the steps, the warm sun splashing in his face. He took a left onto the sidewalk and headed toward his car. "You're right, Leif. We all die someday," Axel said, patting the ashes in his breast pocket. "But not me, and certainly not today!"

With the wave of his hand, Hector escorted Veronica into the parlor of Axel's house and she called for him, "Axel? Are you here yet?" She was answered only by her echo. They walked into the kitchen and found dishes and plates of food covering the table, cellophane covering each, a force field to ward off flies. At the sink stood a middle-aged man with a dish towel in his hands. Frightened, her shoulders flinched to her jawline, head snapping in his direction.

"I'm Ken- Pardon, Mr. Kennedy," the man said, introducing himself. "Sorry if I frightened you. I'm a friend of Axel's. And you must be Miss Veronica? I'm so very sorry for your loss."

Veronica caught her breath. This elderly gentleman seemed harmless enough. She thanked him before introducing Hector, glad he had accompanied her. "Can I help you? I didn't see you at the church," she asked.

"Miss Veronica, it is I who am here to assist you. Axel informed me you'd be here, and I was to take good care of you. I'm sure we'll become good friends now that we'll be working together."

Veronica looked at Mr. Kennedy, her head tilted to the side in confusion. "Working together?"

"Why yes. On the new Winnie Foundation and the Benton Museum. Mr. Axel has generously asked me to take his spot as Chairman of the Board. And I accepted. It's such a worthwhile endeavor."

"I see," she said, although she did not.

"You mustn't worry yourself about anything today. You have greater things on your mind. May I get you something to eat or drink?"

Veronica wondered where Axel found these polite men. "Nothing for me, thanks. I need to sit for a moment." She left the men in the kitchen, stepping back into the parlor to rest into Axel's recliner.

"Allow me to bring you a glass of water," Kennedy called after her and took a glass from the cabinet, filled it from the tap before bringing it over to her. Veronica took it from him with a "Thank you."

"Please let me know if I can get anything for you. I'll be in the kitchen while you read." Kennedy stepped back into the kitchen.

"Read?" she said to the walls as she rested in Axel's chair before remembering the letter he had given her at the church. Slicing it open, a key fell out, the hard object breaking the silence as it tinkled onto the hardwood floor. She lifted the letter out as if diseased and began to read.

Dear Veronica,

Please forgive this form of communication, but I could not bear a goodbye in person. I wasn't wrong in my eulogy today. I've left to find my own tree to climb and am not sure when I'll return.

Leif was fond of saying, "Stop hoarding, start doing." And I finally realized what he meant. I've been stubborn in my own beliefs missing opportunities to experience life the way I should. And you should do the same. I've decided instead of giving the dead the last word, it's better to help the living find their own voice.

This is the reason I've left you the key to my house so you can begin anew rather than go back to Leif's house. I know it would hold you prisoner with all the memories you've made there, but you are no prisoner. Like myself, you are free; Leif saw to that.

This is your house now. Make the most of the lemons you've been given. It's a gift.

P.S. Don't you just love Kennedy?

Love,

Axel

Veronica wiped a tear from her eye as she folded the letter and placed it back into her clutch. The doorbell rang announcing the arrival of the first guests. As she was about to rise, Kennedy came through the room, a hand up to stop her. He headed to the front door to let the guests into her new home, their arrival the first of many to pay their final respects to one brother no longer able to share it with her, the other unreachable for comfort.

Harley Benton had ruled Benton Falls for years. The puppet master had pulled all the right strings while he was able. Once apparent he could do so no longer. the puppetry collapsed into a pile of bones.

With no one to coerce, cajole or blackmail them, the leaders in the community stopped doing Benton's bidding and began doing what they were paid to do. No matter how hard each guilty one tried, none of those good intentions mattered. Benny Palz was cremated, but with 'ring' pictures Jules took from the morgue and Kennedy's newfound ledger, Detective Kepner built a strong case against the corrupt.

Doc Houseman had to retire his medical license rather than be exposed in a malpractice scandal. He retired permanently in warmer Key West to forget about the cold of the morgue and the dead bodies it held.

Because of his exposure of corruption, Detective Gary Kepner became the next Chief of Police and cleaned house. He began with the former chief, now sitting in a jail cell for obstruction of justice concerning Palz's murder. Nick 'Bulldog' Holmes became the undersheriff. Every law enforcer needs back up.

The Mayor fought the allegations from Benton's ledger but to no avail. Although he was not convicted of any crime, the negative publicity proved too difficult a hurdle. His access to a second term was blocked.

And Benton sat alone in his own room at the FALM, the Puppet Master's strings severed for good. Although too frail to see prosecution, the Passing Lane served as a fitting jail cell the remaining Angels, or anyone else, avoided visiting.

Free from Palz's bullying, Hector put his parents on the legal path to citizenship with the help of Kennedy and Veronica. He repaid them by volunteering to help with their charitable efforts. He looked forward to becoming 'Uncle Hector.'

Gil Pooler was found not guilty of the many murders he committed by reason of insanity and is housed in the psychiatric ward fifty miles west of Benton Falls. He prays for forgiveness every day and when allowed outside, can be seen talking to cardinals.

After the firing of Harriet Spellman, Jules was appointed the new administrator of the FALM. Both the medication thefts and the suspicious deaths of the residents had ceased.

Axel, who would not be around to see the aftermath unfold, was too busy climbing his own tree.

EPILOGUE

rom where does absolution come? A priest, deaf or not? A God who never talks back? Or from within?

Axel wrestled with these concepts after Leif's death. The answer had taken time to reach but, but he had accepted it. *Forgiveness is the gift you give yourself.*

He concluded the best place to give himself this gift was a purpose. To do something worthy of absolution. It helped to tamp down but never rid himself of the guilt. A purpose to make him worthy of his own forgiveness.

His own absolution arrived in the form of helping those in need. People like him, each seeking their own purpose. It occurred to him, he could help both the rudderless *and* his brother at the same time. Like those in the audience he was about to address. Those with plenty of time to make their own mark. The premature departure of his brother did not mean his legacy died with him.

From the wings of the stage, Axel looked out at a full house. It didn't matter he was not the principal attraction; he was here to continue what Leif had begun. He patted the baggie with Leif's remains as he prepared to go on stage.

The nerve endings fired, filling his arms and legs with a thousand bee stings, but practice taught him how to manage the issue, so it wasn't debilitating. First, belt out the first line to get the adrenaline pumping. Next, he would scan the audience in the front row and look for a smile. At least, in theory, he would have one friend.

The final trick came from Mr. Yul Brynner. By placing his fingers against a wall, he eliminated the bee stings, replaced by tension spreading through his hands to his arms. The tension did not sting. On the contrary. It felt like power.

"Thirty seconds, Mr. Ahearne," the stage manager notified him as Axel pressed, counting as he did. Before he had a chance to push away, Jules stepped behind him and spun him around, kissing him passionately on the lips. "Who needs tricks to prepare when you have me?" she whispered.

A surprised Axel stood wide eyed and motionless, all thoughts of his preparation dissipating with the kiss. "What are you doing here? Shouldn't you be running the FALM?"

Jules grabbed his hand and said, "I'm turning down the job. I have a new one. *You* are my purpose. If I waited for you, I'd be eligible for entry in the FALM!"

"If you're here, who's in charge there?"

"Winnie, of course. We both know she's the best person for the job."

"Ten seconds," said the stage manager, lifting his hand in preparation to drop it at zero, Axel's cue to step onto the stage. He stood gazing at Jules, the goofy grin returning. As she pushed him toward the stage she whispered in his ear, "Go get 'em tiger! I'll be here when you get done."

Axel stumbled out on stage, remembering to switch on his microphone. At center stage, he waved to the audience before he bellowed his practiced first line, "Good evening, Indianapolis, I'm Axel Ahearne and you may know my brother, Leif!"

The audience greeted him with a thunderous applause as if he had scored the winning touchdown in a football game. He scanned the front row and all he saw were smiles. They had come to hear him talk about new beginnings, about doing your own thing and the purpose accompanying such an undertaking. About resurrection. Topics he was well versed and prepared to deliver. And with Leif's second book coming out, he would have plenty of material for the long haul.

"Let's start from the ending," Axel prompted. "My brother Leif ended his life the same way it began. Asking a pivotal question. Not why? But why not? Never tied to a particular job or career, he was constantly on the move searching for what was right for him. I was under the mistaken impression it was due to laziness, selfish behavior, or plain old stubbornness."

He let the sentence sink into an audience who revered Leif Ahearne. To them, he was a hero. A visionary. Axel brought out Leif's flaws to skirt the issue of idolatry.

"But I found out I was the lazy and stubborn one. For years I took the path traveled by many while he followed the way of the few. I played it safe. Saved for a rainy day while Leif walked each day in sunshine, free from the shackles of a boring, uncomplicated, and uneventful life.

"It is said there is safety in numbers for a reason. Most of us will follow like lemmings and jump off the cliff time and time again, waiting for a few scant years where we can retire from the drudgery of being the follower.

Leif never carried that burden because he took action and created something most of us only dream about. But now you are awakening from the dream by sitting here tonight! Give yourself a round of applause!"

Axel stood erect, hands on hips as he gazed out into the audience. Leif was right in a way. Maybe self-help was the new religion. Or at the very least, God's way of expressing the concept of free will, helping those who help themselves.

He had pumped them up, and it was now time for the one liner bringing everyone to their feet. He waited for the applause to subside before continuing. "It took me a while to come around, to step out of my stubborn shoes, to step into the unknown. And it has been the best decision of my life! So," he paused once more. "Who's ready to *climb their own tree?*"

The applause was only amplified by the stomping feet of the audience, the combined weight shaking the building. Leif began a revolution and Axel's job was to carry on this mission, leaving the business of eulogizing to others. Instead of giving the dead the last word, why not give the living hope instead? To breathe life into the lifeless, offer advice to the rudderless and purpose to the uninspired. This task was now Axel's purpose, his own tree base. Leif may have planted it, but it was now Axel's to climb.

As the applause surrounded him, Axel felt proud. His Sumday had finally arrived. And even though Axel Ahearne had failed to do as Winnie asked, to catch Leif when he fell, he was now doing the next best thing. To keep his brother's name alive and to make sure, at least as long as he himself was on this earth, the guarantee Leif Ahearne would *never* have a last word.

ACKNOWLEDGEMENTS

I'd like to thank Eileene Dillman, Russ Holihan, Dutch Ireland and Jim Puckey for their honest and valuable feedback. Every writer should have beta readers as insightful and forthcoming as all of you.

My editor Kim Conrey for her artful suggestions, nudging me to produce the best possible story.

And Kimberly Martin from Jera Publishing. Helping authors is an unselfish act and you do so admirably.

BIOGRAPHY - BRIAN DELANEY

Brian is a former Advertising Executive with years of marketing and creative messaging experience and is member of the Atlanta Writers Club. He writes because he likes to make stuff up.

Brian lives in Alpharetta, Georgia with his wife Cynthia and near children Kelly, Kirstie and Samson and their families. Together they enjoy traveling and frequently visiting their grandchildren. Brian also enjoys camping, kayaking, yard work, and playing his guitar. This is Brian's first novel.